at Seafall
Cottage

ALSO BY LILY GRAHAM

The Summer Escape
A Cornish Christmas

Summer at Seafall Cottage

LILY GRAHAM

bookouture

Published by Bookouture
An imprint of StoryFire Ltd.
23 Sussex Road, Ickenham, UB10 8PN
United Kingdom
www.bookouture.com

ISBN: 978-1-78681-997-0
ISBN: 978-1-786811-153-0
eBook ISBN: 978-1-78681-152-3

For Rui

PART ONE

Present day, Cornwall

CHAPTER ONE

The past has a way of calling out. Memories are living things that whisper beneath the floors and run their fingers along walls. They wait and they hope that someday you'll come and find them.

That day, the past called for me alright.

Though I almost didn't hear it. That's the part that makes me catch my breath, and makes me wonder how different things might have been. What if I'd never found Seafall Cottage?

Would I have just driven back that day? Picked up the broken pieces and tried somehow to put it all back together again? Tried to ignore the bits that I simply couldn't?

It's strange how sometimes the smallest thing can have the power to change everything. For me, a small bit of loose rock in my path was all it took to change my life. Though I didn't realise it then. How could I? I was too busy walking. Too busy not seeing beyond the all-consuming anger and pain to notice anything, except very distantly, like a dull toothache. I was freezing cold in the dead of winter in rural Cornwall, still wearing the ugly, highlighter-pink cardigan my mother had given me for Christmas two weeks later, when my foot stumbled on the uneven earth. I straightened and looked up, and in that moment the old place with its half-forgotten secrets let down its guard – and that's when I saw it.

Beyond the vast expanse of wild countryside, and the rocky outcrop that hugged the coastline, my eyes alighted on an unusual house, tucked high up into the cliffs, yet seemingly ready to fall into the hungry sea below.

I'm not sure if it was some unknowable pull from the place itself or simply curiosity that drove me forward, wanting to see it up close, but for the first time in days I wasn't thinking about what had happened, why I'd run away to Cornwall, the failure of my marriage, about anything really, and perhaps that was enough to drive me forward, wanting to see more of the house I'd spied.

I set off, feet slipping up the steep path that time had forged into the rock face, the seagrass silver-green and rustling as I moved.

My mobile began to ring, and I switched it to silent. I didn't need to check to know it was Mark, one of several calls he'd made since yesterday.

I swallowed, attempting to get the words Mark had hurled at me out of my brain, trying not to think about what had happened, but it was hopeless…

The door echoed shut as I hurried down the drive, loaded down with the mishmash of gym bags that I'd hastily crammed with clothes, not wanting to delay my exit from our house any further with something as meaningless as luggage.

A second bang followed and Mark hurtled down the drive after me, tearing a bag from my hands, the strap scraping my shoulder and causing me to wince in pain. His eyes were cold. 'Don't be ridiculous, Victoria – you can't leave.'

I shot him a look of disbelief as I ripped open the car door, flinging the rest of my stuff inside. It landed with a hollow thud against the passenger window.

'I think you'll find that I can do whatever the hell I want!'

'*Victoria – please,*' he said, grabbing my arm. '*Let's just talk about this.*'

I wrenched myself out of his grip. '*Maybe you should have thought about talking about things before you invited someone else into our bed?*'

He ran a hand through his brown hair, and it stuck up wildly. '*Jesus, I did try, that's all we've done this past year – we haven't stopped talking. It's not like this is out of nowhere. And you're acting as if you found her here or something – I wouldn't have done that—*'

'*Oh yes, you're such a bloody gentleman, thank you so much for telling me instead of having me find you two together. What do you want – a gold star?*'

'*For Christ's sake!*' He wiped a hand over his face in anger. '*Because you're so fucking perfect? You haven't been home in WEEKS. You're never here! What the hell did you expect?*'

'*What did I expect? Um, perhaps that you wouldn't cheat on me just because I had to WORK!*' I screamed, my fists balled at my side.

He closed his eyes. '*That's just it – everything comes second to your work.*'

I sighed. '*I'm tired of fighting about this, Mark.*'

His eyes widened. '*Yeah, funny that you're sick of fighting about something that doesn't affect you—*'

'*What?*' I snapped, my mouth twisting. '*You don't think this affects me?*'

He was standing on the cold pavement in his bare feet. Behind us, the little Christmas wreath threaded with fairy lights that I'd bought in a rush of holiday spirit – still up though we were well into the new year – seemed to mock me. I stared at his toes, curling on the sleet-covered pavement, and tried to ignore the way they seemed to be turning blue. I couldn't.

'*It's cold, just go inside—*'

'No, you can't leave like this—'

'Please put on some shoes.'

He ignored me. 'Where are you going? Just tell me.'

'Does it matter?'

His mouth fell open. 'Of course it matters. Christ!'

'Why? You're leaving me anyway,' I pointed out.

He blinked. 'That's not true – I just need time to think, to decide.'

I made for the car door. 'I'll help. There, it's decided.'

'No, it's not. Bloody hell, you're acting as if you had nothing to do with this—'

'Yes, it's all my fault! And you – what? Slipped and fell on top of someone else?' I shouted, climbing into the car and locking the door, sick of hearing his excuses. Not looking at him through the haze of tears as I put the car into reverse.

'It is *your fault!' he snarled, palms beating the window, fingers scrabbling to open the locked door, while I set a course for anywhere but there.*

It turned out to be Cornwall that I fled to. Lately all my roads seemed to lead down here: for work, family – and now an escape from my marriage.

Last night, I'd got as far as the sign for Cloudsea, the little village full of whitewashed stone cottages that ribboned around a small stretch along the Atlantic, home to my brother and his wife. I thought I'd find solace there, but I couldn't do it, couldn't face them. It had all seemed so simple while I was driving, but as I neared, I couldn't face the inevitable dissection of my marriage or their pitying looks, however kindly meant.

I felt like a jar that had been scraped out till there was nothing left inside, and all I wanted right then was a warm bed and no human interaction. I stopped my car and searched on my mobile for a hotel that was still open. I found the Black Horse Inn, forty minutes away in the opposite direction, and hit navigate.

It was a gothic-looking building down an empty coastal road, and when I pulled open the heavy oak front door some time later I noticed dimly that the decor looked similarly ghoulish. The only nod to the current century was a neon sign that read '*Open 24 hours*'.

'Looks like you've been through the wringer,' said a gravelly voice from behind a black marbled counter. The craggy face belonging to the voice was illuminated by a faint light from the wall behind, where a large, ornate brass plate gleamed.

She was a thin woman with short magenta hair. In her claw-like hand she was clutching a packet of cigarettes, and she had the wrinkled sort of mouth that looked like it was often set to purse.

Catching sight of myself in the brass plate behind her head, I couldn't help thinking that she had reason to purse her lips. I was wearing Mark's faded AC/DC T-shirt, along with the hideous, shockingly pink cardigan, and my long, black curly hair was a wet, ratty mess from when I'd got caught in the rain. Whatever make-up I'd had on was now in a pool down my face and neck, and my dark eyes had deep circles beneath them, like bruises. I looked like an angsty teenager instead of a woman in her early thirties.

'You should see the other guy,' I said, with a lopsided smile.

Her eyes widened. 'If I give you a room I'm not going to have any trouble, am I?'

'No, I just got lost,' I lied. 'And stuck in the rain.' I decided not to mention the last six hours in which my life and marriage had turned to ashes.

'Where were you heading?'

'Cloudsea,' I said, picturing the lovely village full of white-washed cottages ribboning the Atlantic, home to my brother and his wife, with a pang.

Her demeanour changed. 'That's miles from Tregollan.' It almost sounded a little like sympathy.

'Tregollan?'

She looked at me in disbelief. 'That's where you are – didn't you know?'

I shook my head. I'd just focused on turning left or right as the talking map instructed; I hadn't paid much attention to which town I'd stumbled into. I eyed the cigarettes on the desk, and for a second had to stop myself from asking if I could bum one.

'Well, 'tisn't like Cloudsea here. 'Tis wild and beautiful though,' she admitted.

'Yeah...' All I'd seen was night and fog and a very dark road.

'Well, welcome anyway. I'm Gilly, and this is the Black Horse Inn. I'm sure everything will seem better in the morning,' she said with a smile that was surprising in its gentleness, softening the lines along her mouth.

Things didn't seem better in the morning. But she was right about one thing: from what I'd seen since I'd set off for a walk to try and clear my head an hour before, it was beautiful here. For the first time in hours I wasn't thinking about my imploding marriage – just the hidden cottage I'd spied amongst the cliffs.

It took half an hour to get to the clifftop, by which time my arms and legs were covered in razor-like scratches from the sharp-pronged bushes, all of which seemed bent on enacting some personal vendetta against my flesh. When I got there I stopped in surprise. There was no house in sight, just the cliff wall itself.

I hugged my cardigan to my frozen skin, my breath coming out in a fog, and despite the long walk, which by rights should have warmed my blood, I stamped my feet from the cold. Mentally, I retraced my steps. Had I made a wrong turn somewhere? It had seemed a fairly straight path from below, so at some point I should have found the house somewhere around here.

I carried on walking, wondering if I'd simply wasted my time, when suddenly the cliffs began to change and I came across a high stone wall that seemed made from the rock face itself. I spied an unexpected, concealed entrance, which led to an iron gate that was covered in rust and ivy and invitation. It hung slightly off its hinges, revealing a garden almost out of view. I pushed it open, and with some effort, making a sound like a distant sigh, it obliged.

On the threshold, I paused, hesitant. What if someone saw me and demanded to know why I was here? What would, or could, I say?

All too soon though, I found that my fear was ungrounded. It was unlikely that anyone had lived here for many years. At least I hoped so, as living here would only qualify as 'living' in the loosest possible terms.

Before my eyes stretched the ghostly shape of a garden, covered in long-dead plants and strangled by weeds. It was a forlorn piece of earth, littered with mountains of abandoned beer bottles, a mould-infested sofa, a collection of mildewed pizza boxes, a rusted car with missing tyres and several decades' worth of seagull droppings.

I heard them before I saw them, perched on top of the house's slate roof, just visible from where I was standing, their cries a mix of warning and welcome. As I made my way down the terraced garden, their pebble-black eyes followed my every move as the house came into view. It was made of a faded sepia stone that time had aged like pale cognac. One wall was threaded with a creeping rose that seemed unusual for this time of year, yet despite the wintry chill, welcomed the visitor like a first blush.

The front door was missing, making the empty space seem all the more eerie. Etched into the stone above the doorless entry-way was the house's name: Seafall Cottage.

Apt, I couldn't help thinking, as the old place looked about ready to fall into the ocean below.

I crept inside, half afraid of what I might find. As my eyes adjusted to the darkness, I saw that at every point, the cottage seemed to invite nature in along with the overwhelming scent of brine and damp.

An overturned range was all that was left of the kitchen, and the living room fared no better, with vines attaching themselves to the walls like veins, binding an old window seat in their embrace, the fabric turned green with lichen.

Wine bottles and cigarette buts littered the wooden floors, which had warped and split apart at the seams, yet all of it was simply background to the view. Dominating most of an entire wall was a massive circular window made up of a series of petal-shaped panes of glass, most of which were missing. It offered a breath-stealing view of the blue-green ocean below, lending an air of magic despite the ruin, as if it were a kind of enchanted sea garden. Despite its state of disrepair, it was beautiful.

I couldn't help but wonder why it had been abandoned. I guessed that it had been used as a sort of local hangout for parties, perhaps serving as a camp for the town's teenage population or for more nefarious purposes. But what I couldn't fathom was why. I thought of the roses, the cottage's pretty name – someone had put care into this place, why had it been left like this?

As I explored the rest of the house, I found a pantry with empty shelves, a heavy glass jar filled with decaying fruit. In a smaller room was a broken sleeping cot, its frame sagging in the middle, the mattress grey and spotted with mould.

The stairs that led from the living room were spiralled like a turret shell, and as I looked up, I could see sea glass patterning each curving balustrade. My way was blocked by several pieces of heavy furniture that had been left on the steps.

When I turned back, I saw a door set into the front wall of the house. It had an old brass knob, sticky with age, and I had to batter it open with a shoulder.

My old mentor, my history professor from university, Stan Fenridge, had once told me, 'If you're going to make the past your present, be prepared for a lifetime of dust...' It was a motto of sorts. Dust, and sometimes bruised shoulders, were an occupational hazard of the biographer's trade.

I'd been telling other people's life stories now for over a decade; it's what had brought me down to Cornwall for most of the past year, as I worked on a new biography of Daphne du Maurier. I'd been transcribing some never-before-seen letters from an old family friend of hers down in Fowey, and piecing together her story, particularly about how so much of it was influenced by this remarkable county, its history, enchantment and mythology. Perhaps it had begun to influence me too – though, truth be told, I'd always been a bit too curious for my own good.

After my third attempt, the door sprung wide, and I stumbled out onto a veranda a metre wide, spanning the length of the house. The railing was broken, offering a barrier-free drop to the open sky and the churning blue-green waves below. I stood, gasping, my knees shaking with fear as I peered down.

A sudden movement to my left caught my eye. I wasn't alone. I turned my head towards the side of the house and saw an old man staring straight back at me. I blinked in shock. In the seconds that my eyes were closed, he was gone. A sudden fear gripped me. Had he run off to go and call someone?

With mincing steps, keeping to the wall, I made my way towards the side of the house, where the veranda joined level ground – and where the man had been standing moments before. There, I found an entryway to a walled kitchen garden just off the house. As I watched, I saw him go through a canopy of foliage with a wheelbarrow.

'Wait, please. I can explain!' I called. Though I didn't see how I could explain that I'd simply decided to trespass. But he was moving at high speed, ignoring my calls, the wheels creaking in time to his brisk pace.

'It's not how it looks!' I shouted. That was a lie. It looked like trespassing, which it was.

The old man didn't slow down, just made for the faint amber light coming from the small garden shed at the end of the path.

I stood rooted for a second in an agony of indecision – go after him or make a run for it? Something told me that an idiot wearing an electric-pink cardigan in the middle of nowhere wouldn't be that hard to track down, should he decide to report me. So I made my way to the shed, hoping he'd give me a chance to discuss it before he called someone. The door was open as I launched into an explanation, but there was no one there.

I spun on my heel in surprise. The shed was cold and dark, and when I left, I saw the wheelbarrow lying on its side, an empty beer bottle rolling out onto the frosted grass.

I sighed.

Of course, he'd been a trespasser as well. I'd startled him too.

I set the wheelbarrow right, only to frown. He'd left something else behind. I bent down, finding an old tan leather book, bound by a long, thin ribbon of aquamarine-hued suede. I picked it up, and then started; the old man was standing an arm's length away. His eyes were pinned on me, on the book in my hands.

I couldn't make out his face in the gloomy light. He was wearing a knitted cap and an old tweed jacket, the kind with leather patching the elbows.

'Y-you forgot this…' I said, holding it out, edging closer to him. He shook his head. As I neared I saw that his eyes were sharp, and very blue. I couldn't tell how old he was. He was the sort who could have been seventy or a hundred and you wouldn't be all that surprised either way.

He stared at me for a long time, making no move to take the book. Finally, one shoulder came up in a sort of dismissal. ''Tisn't mine,' he muttered, his voice hard, like gravel.

'Oh,' I said, lowering my arm, preparing to put the book back where I'd found it.

'May as well keep it,' he said. 'Not like they're coming back for it.' He nodded towards Seafall Cottage. We both looked. No, that seemed unlikely.

'What is it?' I asked, looking at the leather book in my grasp and wondering that I was having such a strange conversation with an old man in this wintry garden. But he didn't answer, and I looked up to find that he'd left as silently as he'd arrived.

It was only later, after I'd trekked back to the Black Horse Inn, following a warm bath with a glass of whisky for company, that I picked up the book, unwound the suede binding, and found that it was a diary.

It was filled with tight, black writing in a slanted hand. There was no helpful inscription in the front cover, no name written on the front page. But that wasn't what made me sit up straight, something like a smile ghosting across my face for the first time in days, nor was it that the diary belonged to that oddly haunting house. It was the fact that it was all written in code.

CHAPTER TWO

I read somewhere that the receptors in the brain respond to emotional pain in the same way they do physical pain. I wasn't sure how reliable the article was, but allegedly it makes little difference whether we've been hit by a hammer or jilted by a lover. In fact, the article suggested that if you take a painkiller during a traumatic period, you might end up feeling better.

It was hard to believe that an ibuprofen might help, but I took one anyway, washing it down with whisky for good measure. What was the standard prescription for when your husband told you he was in love with someone else?

Morphine, I supposed.

It was so cold that my breath came out in a fog. Heating in this dead-end inn seemed to be something of a myth. I felt old and tired; my face wan, eyes swollen and red-rimmed. The inn's bland instant coffee did nothing to fight the fatigue from the needle-like bedsprings that had found purchase in the small of my back the night before, no matter how much I tried to twist away in the night.

As I climbed into bed for my second night at the Black Horse Inn, I pulled the duvet around my shoulders in an effort to keep warm and the diary fell onto the floor. I picked it up and rifled through the pages, noting the tight black writing, the frequent use of numbers that made up the coded text, and wondering again what it was doing at that house and why someone had decided to write it this way. It was hard to tell if the writer was male or female, but I suspected the latter. The penmanship was elegant – though back then that wasn't uncommon in either sex. My thoughts turned to the curious old man. He'd said it wasn't like *they* were coming back. Like he knew who *they* were. I rubbed my eyes, and with it, rubbed away the thought. It was just a turn of phrase, nothing more; a tired brain looking for a distraction. The code was a puzzle – and I've never really been able to resist them.

I shook my head. It was typical that this would fall into my hands now that I had wound up my latest biography, after four straight years of zero holidays or time off, of endless travel for work, which had involved over thirty-two trips last year alone for book tours, all of which had gone a long way towards the disintegration of my marriage. I was meant to be looking forward to a much-needed break. I'd had lengthy discussions with my editor at Rain River Books, and we'd agreed that a sabbatical was a good idea – there was never a good time to do this sort of thing, but I had insisted. I'd spent years working twelve- to fifteen-hour days, getting up every morning at 5 a.m., even on weekends. Especially on weekends. I was tired. I loved my job more than anything in the world, but what I loved most was the research, the discovery, the writing. But the curse of doing that well meant that I got to do it even less, my time spent talking about my work rather than doing it. We'd carved out six months of freedom, six wondrous months of idle stillness as delicious as thick Cornish clotted cream with strawberry jam.

I was supposed to be lying in bed past nine, rediscovering the joys of wearing pyjamas past noon, of wearing flat shoes and relegating heels to date nights only, not worrying if I put on weight because I wouldn't be in a press shot for some time.

The next six months were meant to be time for me to re-charge, recover my creative energy and focus on my marriage to Mark.

They say life happens when you're making other plans, I just wished that the bastard who'd said that wasn't always right.

Another missed call from Mark.

I took a breath, my chest tightening painfully, and called him back. He answered on the first ring. 'Where the hell are you?' he snapped.

I stayed silent while his voice got higher, more agitated. 'I've been out of my bloody mind, Victoria! Jesus Christ! WHAT. THE. FUCK. Were you thinking? It's been almost two days!'

I closed my eyes, pictured him pacing the linoleum, bare-foot, in his old pyjamas, the ones with the grey, vertical stripes. I pulled a loose thread from the duvet cover; watched as it puck-ered and rent the otherwise smooth surface.

'That you had an affair with your personal trainer, which you lied about for weeks, and that you only told me about while we were having—' I couldn't finish. He'd told me that he was hav-ing an affair while we were having sex. I still felt shamed, like I'd never feel clean again.

There was a sharp intake of breath. He was silent for a long time. Despite everything, maybe I was still hoping he'd tell me that he wanted to fix it, that he loved me. But there was no ab-solution. Not from this.

'Oh, Smudge,' he said softly, pleading. The word, the old nickname, like a dagger through my shattered heart. 'Please, just tell me where you are.'

'Don't call me that,' I said, trying not to cry.

I heard him swallow. It didn't make me feel any better when he said, 'Okay.' Like he'd do whatever I asked. Anything except take it back. 'I still care about you,' he said.

The tears came then, stinging the raw skin where the past tears had already burnt. I was beginning to make that sound again, like something wild. Nine years of marriage reduced to 'care'? I didn't have it in me to bite off a sarcastic retort. 'Mark, you were the one who asked to be apart... That's what this *is*. And I'm in Cornwall,' I said, and hung up.

I decided against finishing the bottle of whisky, choosing instead to find the landlady, Gilly, to complain about the lack of heating.

I unzipped the first kitbag I found, slipped on a pair of Converse trainers, pulled on a Batman jumper, followed by my thick, old coachman's coat and went downstairs.

My classless 'biographer's coat' was a charity find, chosen more for its warmth than its style, and was a source of despair for my mother, someone mildly stuck in the eighties, who still believed that power came in suits.

I wrapped my scarf around the lower half of my face, thrust my gloveless hands into my pockets and headed towards the bar. I found Gilly wiping down the counter with a well-worn rag, deep in conversation with a red-haired man who, despite the early hour, was nursing a beer. Sitting next to him was an old woman with a blue-rinse helmet of hair, huddled under a heavy brown shawl, her expression bleak as she contemplated her morning meal of baked beans on toast.

I took a seat opposite. Gilly nodded her spiky magenta head in my direction and then carried on her conversation with the woman about a spring festival at the nearby daffodil farm that had been cancelled.

'It's been the longest winter in history,' said the woman to me. 'I feel like I've forgotten what it's like to be warm.'

I nodded. 'Me too. Though I think the heating seems to be off in my room.'

The red-haired man grunted in response. Gilly shot him a look. 'Told yer,' she said.

He sighed loudly. 'Blast it all! These pipes are the Devil's work this winter. I'll go have a look,' he said, draining his glass.

Gilly shook her head. 'Like I haven't asked yer to go and check the heating since sun-up?'

I heard him mutter darkly as he went up the stairs.

'Sorry,' said Gilly, with a pained look in his direction. 'I coulda got yer some blankets until Henry arrived, if you'd let us know earlier.' She nodded in the direction the red-haired man had just left. 'Local handyman,' she explained. 'Useless as anything, but he's all we've got.'

'You mentioned a daffodil farm. Is that near here?' I asked. I hadn't seen it yesterday.

'Not far, about a fifteen-minute drive. It's near the cliff road along the coast. An absolute picture in the spring months, I can tell you.'

The woman next to me nodded, and her bleak expression seemed to melt momentarily. ''Tis a real sight in the spring, I don't mind telling yer, golden flowers for miles…'

Gilly looked at me. 'Can I get yer something to drink or eat?'

'Tea would be great, and some toast with jam,' I said, not willing to risk the instant coffee again.

While she was busy, I thought about the abandoned cottage I'd found. It couldn't be too far from the farm, as that was the only coastal path around here.

'Have you lived here long?' I asked.

'All my life,' she said, handing me a teapot, cup and saucer.

I nodded. 'Perhaps, then, you could tell me about a house I found. It's close to the farm, I think?'

'A house by the farm? There are no houses down there…
Though the new owners have converted some of the old barns
for holiday lets,' she said with a disapproving sniff, obviously
not keen on the competition.

The old woman next to me, who was now eating her baked
beans on toast, muttered, 'Couldn't you have even heated them
up, Gill?'

Gilly ignored this. 'Betsy, it's just the farmhouse up there
these days, right?'

Betsy nodded but didn't volunteer any speech while she
chewed, her expression grim.

I shook my head. 'But I saw one – a couple miles from
here, sort of unusual, tucked away really, and set in the cliffs
themselves. I was walking yesterday and I saw it – sort of by
accident.'

'A house in the cliffs?' said Gilly, as if I were mad.

'I think it's called Seafall Cottage,' I said, tensing as I said
the name aloud, as if I were exposing something delicate to the
light, though I had no idea why I should feel that way.

'*Seafall* Cottage?' She shook her head slowly, then her gimlet
eyes went large and she turned to Betsy, smacking her hand on
the wooden counter. I jumped back slightly. 'She can't mean
Cursed Cottage!'

The older woman's mouth grew tight. 'You want to stay away
from that place,' she said, giving me a similar look to the one
that she'd given her cold beans.

'The Cursed Cottage?' I said in disbelief, wondering vaguely
if she was pulling my leg, perhaps any minute now I'd hear the
opening strains to *Psycho*.

Gilly nodded quite seriously though. 'Oh yes. I don' much
put stock in curses and things like that…' She rolled her eyes.
'Especially here.'

I took that to mean Cornwall and its propensity for myth and fable.

'But that place' – she gave a shudder – 'makes it hard *not* to believe. Gives me the creeps.'

Betsy nodded. 'Aye, it does. Was horrible what happened there.'

'What happened?' I asked.

Gilly gave me a meaningful sort of look, her black eyes boring into mine. 'It's hard to say, exactly… was all kept quiet, like. Even me nan wouldn't talk about it, and she worked at the big house as a girl, yer know, during the summers. The only thing I know for sure is that it happened during the Great War, and that it had to do with the Aspreys, of course. They say that it's why they all sold up and left.'

'The Aspreys?'

'Oh aye,' said Betsy. 'They used to own the farm and all the land around it, back when it was a grand estate.' She pulled her shawl close around her body. 'Most of it's been developed over the years into the village of Tregollan now.'

'Why did they leave? What rumours?' I asked.

'That old John Asprey kept someone locked up there – someone mad.'

My mouth fell open in surprise.

Betsy nodded. 'People think whoever it was still haunts the place now.'

'That's because it *is* haunted…' said Gilly.

Betsy shrugged. 'I didn't really put much stock in the rumours myself, until what happened a few years back.'

'What happened?' I asked.

'A girl from the village disappeared there in the eighties, local teenager by the name of Mary Evans. She'd gone to meet some of her friends up there – they used to sneak inside and have a bit of a party. Except when it came time to leave, no one could find her.'

'She just disappeared into thin air, they didn't find her body or anything,' said Gilly.

Betsy gave her a look, and I wondered if they'd had this conversation before, because she said, with a look of exasperation, 'We don't know for sure what happened, really. Mary was in a bit of trouble, some of her friends admitted as much later, so it's possible that she just ran away. One of her classmates said she thought she saw her a few years ago, working in Shropshire.'

'Shropshire?' scoffed Gilly. 'And what trouble could *Mary Evans* have really been in?' She looked at me. 'She wasn't the sharpest tool in the shed, if you get my meaning...'

'She could have been pregnant,' said Betsy. 'You know how harsh Ted Evans was – he would have killed her, if he'd known.' Then, for my benefit, she added, 'The girl's father, Ted, was the strict type, fire and brimstone and all that. All the Evans children were terrified of him.'

Gilly shrugged. 'Yeah, but to run away? Most people around here think that the police just invented that story as a cover-up for what really happened, just so that they could finally sell the place. No one wants to buy a haunted house. Not that it worked. No one would touch it. Would yer believe they're *still* trying to sell it – like anyone'd buy it.'

'It's for sale?' I asked in surprise.

'Must be more than thirty years now. No one here will go near it, of course, don't blame them. I heard even old Waters has given up on the place at last. Going to demolish it and sell off the land. Though why he took this long to give up is anyone's guess.'

'Waters?'

'Graham Waters. Local lawyer up in town – he got stuck with the deed. No estate agent round here would touch it.'

'Really? Because of some old rumours?'

Gilly gave me a look, like pity mixed with something else. 'You're not from around here, are you?'

CHAPTER THREE

The village of Tregollan had a natural harbour and a small high street that served its population of some two hundred residents. It was the kind of tiny, seaside place where everyone knew each other's names and nobody minded their own business.

The whitewashed cottages and terraced homes perched along the water's edge had doors and shutters in shades of cherry, mint, salmon and sea foam. There were leftover Christmas wreaths and plants that grew sideways from the sea wind, and here and there the odd rose bloomed in defiance to the icy chill.

As I walked, I breathed in the briny scent of the water, and listened to the cry of sea birds that circled above, snuggling my chin into my thick tweed scarf.

There was a general store with a half-price special on Christmas goods, a library that only seemed to open twice a week, a coffee shop, a post office, an antique store and a solicitor's office – the one Gilly and Betsy had referred to, back at the inn. It had a small sign that read '*Waters Solicitors*' in elegant copperplate. I stopped and peered through the window, trying to see if anyone was there.

'Closed for the afternoon. They've taken Graham to Truro for treatment,' said a woman's voice from behind, clearly assuming that I knew the people from the office. 'Don't know why they don't just use the closed sign.'

I turned. A woman in her fifties with short, ash-blonde hair, wearing a gilet and rubber boots, was staring at me. She had warm brown eyes and soil beneath her fingernails.

'Was it urgent?' she asked. 'I have Adam's mobile.'

'Oh, no… I just wanted to ask them about a property they manage.'

I expected her to say something along the lines of 'Try tomorrow.' Instead, she surprised me by asking, 'Is it Rose Cottage? I heard that the Waymans' tree split that wall. Told Angie just the other day that the new owners were likely to kick up a fuss.'

I frowned. 'No, um – it's not about that. I don't live here.'

The woman laughed. 'Sorry, sticking my nose where it doesn't belong. Professional hazard, you know.'

'How's that?'

'I help manage the Harbour Cafe, there,' she said, pointing at a small shop with a blue and white awning just off the high street next to the harbour. 'Any news worth knowing round here seems to break there first.'

I smiled. 'I can imagine.'

'I'm Sue,' she said, holding out a hand, and then wincing when she spied her fingernails. 'The state of these – sorry! I'm just back from the allotment. The water was turned off, so I haven't had a chance to scrub up properly.'

'I'm Victoria,' I said. 'An allotment! That's wonderful. My brother got the green fingers in our family, but I must admit every time I see his polytunnel I feel a bit envious. I'd love to have a garden of my own some day, but until recently I haven't had the time to give it a try.'

'You should! I never could keep a thing alive, to tell you the truth, but then a few years ago my friend, Abbie – she owns the cafe – got a space at a nearby allotment and asked me to share it with her, and I thought why not. Now I'm hooked. Can't wait for spring. We use a lot of the produce at the cafe – best butternut risotto in Cornwall, if I do say so myself.'

Thinking of the inn's cold beans and instant coffee, I said hopefully, 'Is that available today?'

She grinned. 'Of course! We could whip you up some right now if you want.'

'Well, you've sold me,' I said. 'I'm starving. This is a great sales technique, by the way. Do you always round up the tourists this way?'

'I should! Come on then, step right up, best risotto in town!' she said, beckoning for me to follow, like she was a circus ringmaster.

I laughed. It was the lightest I'd felt in days. The blue door to the cafe opened with the sound of a tinkling bell and I felt a wave of warmth enfold me. A few minutes later I was watching the boats in the harbour and sipping on a cappuccino so good it was like a little taste of Italy itself. Sue had laughed at my visible pleasure when I'd taken the first sip, and I'd had to explain about the tasteless instant coffee at the inn.

Hands freshly scrubbed, she asked, 'So, will that be one butternut risotto then?'

I gave her a crooked smile. 'Yes, please.' The scent coming from the kitchen was indeed mouth-watering. When was the last time I'd eaten a proper meal, I wondered.

She winked. 'Excellent choice.' And she went off to hand in the order, and then busied herself behind the counter, restacking the cups.

When Sue arrived with my risotto, I said, 'You said that you heard all the news here… Do you know if it's true that the lawyers in town are going to go ahead and demolish a cottage near the daffodil farm?'

She looked at me in surprise. 'The abandoned house there, do you mean?'

'Yes.'

She nodded. 'Happening the end of the month.'

My eyes widened. 'So soon?'

I felt a twinge of sadness. I couldn't help feeling that it wasn't the end that the place deserved.

She gave me a puzzled look. 'That place has been abandoned for decades! It's because of Adam that it's finally happening now. Still, I suppose it is a bit sad, you could see it was really beautiful once – went there when I was a child.'

I nodded. It was nice to know that I wasn't the only one who'd seen its potential.

'The lawyer – is that Adam?' I asked.

'Graham Water's nephew. He's been looking after the office these past few weeks. Looks like they're getting ready to close it down, what with Graham being so sick. Maybe that's why they've finally made a decision about the cottage. I sort of hoped that they would have found a buyer – despite everything.'

I nodded. 'I've heard that people around here think it's haunted,' I said, thinking of Gilly and Betsy and how they'd called it 'Cursed Cottage'.

She shook her head. 'Hardly haunted. People round here will believe anything. Though it's had its share of scandal. The only thing wrong with that cottage is that it's falling apart. It's just a sad old place really, especially with what happened to the daffodil farm. Did you know it used to be called Idyllwild? Such a pretty name.'

I shook my head. 'What happened?'

'The family that owned it lost it in the First World War. There were so many rumours about what really happened, though my aunt – she grew up on the old estate – said that it was some family scandal that led to it. Afterwards, no one wanted to buy the estate or that cottage, so it was just left. Though, about twenty years ago now, a couple came from abroad and started it up again.'

While Sue left to bring me my plate of butternut risotto, I opened my backpack and looked at the diary I'd found at the cottage, turning the pages full of spidery black handwriting and noting the jumble of letters and symbols. As I turned the pages, a small, folded-up piece of paper fell out onto the counter. I opened it, and found to my surprise that it was part of a letter. I didn't know who wrote it or to whom, but the words washed over me and caused tears to prick my eyes. I felt each word as if I had written it myself.

I feel lost. I don't know what to do with myself, how to carry on with my life. I'm finding myself trying to fill the hours. Everyone is just going about their business as usual. How can I when the world has turned off its axis?

How do I go about my day without you in it? How do I cut out all the years in between? Everyone wants me to forget you, but I can't. How can I forget my best friend? How did this happen to us?

Yours,

T

I folded the letter, put it back in the diary and closed my eyes, taken back to a night filled with lantern light, in the warm June air, beneath a canopy of stars – to what had been the most beautiful night of my life.

'I met my best friend two years ago. I didn't realise that's who she'd become. At first, all I saw was this beautiful

*girl, with this incredibly sexy back...' There were titters
of laughter across the room and a few people raised their
glasses of champagne. My mother grabbed my arm in a
vice-like grip in a rare show of emotion.*

*'She has these soulful eyes and I was smitten from the start
– talk about a lightning bolt. That's the thing about falling
in love. In the stories it's all about that moment, you know?
Girl meets boy. The very important butterflies. All that
jazz – well, we definitely had that, but what I never expected was that here was the one person I wanted to speak
to when I'd had a horrible day and nothing seemed right,
who always knew the exact right thing to say. Here was the
person who could make me laugh so hard – she makes a
grown man cry that he's going to pee his pants.' There were
more titters of laughter.*

*'I didn't know any of this when I first met her. That she'd
have this effect on me. That one day I'd be standing in a
room full of the people I love and marrying my best friend
in the world.'*

'You okay?' asked Sue, as I wiped my eyes.

'Yeah, course – just allergies,' I lied, pushing around the butternut risotto with my fork, my appetite gone.

Later, when I got back to the inn, I poured myself a whisky and
took out the letter again. I felt lost too, and like 'T', whoever
that was, that I'd also given up someone who had once been my
best friend. I couldn't get the letter out of my mind.

I had a shower and wrapped myself in two pairs of pyjamas
and a thick jumper. Afterwards, I paged through the diary, won-

dering if it had been written by the author of the letter, and if its contents were the reason the journal had been written in code. I glanced at my phone, thinking. It was after eleven, but as Stan was a night owl, I didn't think he'd mind. Perhaps my old mentor would know something about cipher text – there was a good chance he'd come across a coded diary in the past.

I sent him a message, as well as a snap of some sample text from the diary.

'I'm in town for a bit. Found a journal. Probably pre-WWI, no one we know, but it's written in code. Any ideas?'

Half an hour later, just as I was nodding off – helped by a large glass of whisky – he sent a response.

'Hello to you too, Smudge. Thanks for sending me Enigma – nice way to ruin an old man's retirement. Why not come for brunch tomorrow?'

I grinned. The Enigma machines had been used by the Nazis to send coded messages during the Second World War. The Bletchley codebreakers had spent years trying to break it. I just hoped it wouldn't take as long for me to unlock the secrets of this diary.

The next day, I embarked upon the long drive to Stan's remote lakeside cabin in rural western Cornwall, the heaters on full.

Stan had always been a bit of a recluse, preferring the company of books to people, but for all his attempts to block out the human race, and his ongoing attempts at retirement, they were a puzzle he couldn't resist. It was something we had in common, and I suspected one of the reasons he had befriended me early on in my career.

I followed the winding path to the lake and pulled up next to a small wooden cabin built on stilts over the water, reminding me of something out of mountainous Canada. Especially when I found Stan sitting on a camping chair on his veranda, fishing. His beard had turned white since I'd seen him last, and he had traded his old patchy suits for country tweed.

'I've set yours up. With any luck we'll have salmon for lunch,' he said, getting up and giving me a whiskery kiss. He had on a green fishing cap and looked more relaxed than the last time I'd seen him, despite his near-white beard. I took a seat next to him in a camping chair and grinned. It was good to see him.

'There's salmon here?'

'Well, no... I doubt it,' he said, eyeing the lake. 'Pike, though.'

I wrinkled my nose, and he shrugged. 'Fennel makes all the difference, trust me.'

'I'll reserve my judgement.'

He grinned. 'So, did you bring it?'

'What?'

He shot me a look. 'Don't play coy. Hand over the goods.'

I grinned as I opened my backpack and handed over the diary, along with a bottle of whisky – both of which were met with enthusiastic approval.

He opened the diary and whistled, turning the pages. 'The handwriting – feminine, would you say?'

I nodded. 'I think so... but it's hard to know for sure. With the code it's difficult to tell.'

He peered at the piece of pale blue leather suede, winding it with his finger. 'I looked at those pages you sent me – ran it into a program on my computer, some cheap app I downloaded a while back, but I couldn't find anything. Probably a waste of money. Who do we know in cryptography?'

I shrugged. 'I can ask around.'

He nodded. 'Have you shown Mark? All those war diaries – maybe he'd have some idea?'

Mark was a biographer too. It's how we'd met.

My face must have shown something, because Stan's grey eyes showed concern. 'What is it?'

'Oh, nothing,' I lied. 'He's away, so maybe when he's back...'

Stan looked at me for some time. He didn't say anything, but then, he didn't have to. There had been nights in the past when I had had to call his couch home, something that had occurred with increasing regularity over the past few years as Mark's career began to stall during the economic downturn. Over time, he'd begun to feel that my success was a mark against his own. What was worse was that he never really came out and said it. If I tried, he looked at me like I was full of it. He'd once ruined a dinner party by making several rather demeaning insinuations that he did all the work in the house while I flitted about being 'an artiste', which in turn had the effect of making me feel both ridiculous and guilty for my full workload and travel schedule. I'd made the mistake, once the guests had left, of asking if he felt a little envious. I wanted us to work through it, perhaps collaborate on something together, or think of a topic that might interest a wider audience. I thought it could be fun. But his reply had stung.

'Jealous? Of you? Honey, I may not sell as many books as the great Victoria Langley, but at least I'm not peddling celebrity biographies. *Any* hack could do that.'

He'd apologised later, said he didn't mean it – he was tired, stressed out from having his last book cancelled. But it still stung, and I couldn't help wondering how we'd gone from being each other's biggest supporters to the ones who could hurt each other the most.

'Whisky?' said Stan.

'Sounds great.'

He popped inside to fetch some tumblers, then pivoted on his heel in the entryway. 'You know, I'm not great at names – I only found out recently that Kerry could be a man or a woman's name, like Ashley. But Tilly has to be a girl's name, unless it's a nickname, don't you think?'

I looked at him in surprise. 'Why do you ask?'

'The name, there on the suede string,' he said, pointing at the diary he'd left on his chair.

I picked up the ribbon. There it was, right at the end and embroidered in the same shade, making it almost impossible to see. I traced over the name: Tilly.

How had I missed it?

CHAPTER FOUR

I went back to the cottage, as I knew I would. I wanted to see it again. I wanted to see it hidden amongst the cliffs, the roses that bloomed despite no one being there to care for them, the round, almost otherworldly window that overlooked the ocean, the spiral staircase patterned with sea glass. This beautiful, eerie place seemed to reach out to me with its neglected beauty, as if it was calling my name in its sleep.

I wanted to find out who Tilly was. Perhaps find the first part of her letter. For I was sure now that she was the one who had written it. This person who had put into words so painfully what I felt now – lost and alone.

I was due in Fowey in a few hours to meet up with a woman called Moira Bates. She'd helped me enormously while I had been writing my latest biography of Daphne du Maurier, offering up never-before-seen letters from the well-known author, written throughout their friendship.

Now that I had finished the book, I should have been looking forward to spending the next few days in Fowey, in a hotel with real central heating, in a room that overlooked the winding, blue estuary, visiting my favourite cafe, the Pinky Murphy, taking time off to recharge, discussing what had been such a special project to me over the past few years with someone who had become a dear friend, but all I could think of was the cottage. I didn't think I could leave without seeing it again – it might be the last chance I ever had if Sue from the Harbour Cafe was right and they demolished it by the end of the month. When I'd most likely be back in London, trying somehow to put my life back together without Mark in it. Every time I thought of it, of Mark, my old life in London, I felt a sense of dread.

When I'd finally gotten round to visiting my brother Stuart, his wife Ivy and new baby Holly in Cloudsea the day after I saw Stan, and told them what had happened to my marriage, they'd suggested that I stay with them for a while. 'You don't have to rush back there – especially now that you're on sabbatical. Why not take some time for yourself down here? We've got a spare bed, stay with us,' said Stuart.

Ivy had agreed. 'We could have such fun, I know Holly would love to see more of her favourite auntie!'

It was a sweet offer, and I was tempted – especially as I'd soak up some quality time with my little niece – but I wasn't sure that I wanted to be a third, broken wheel, infecting their happy home with the gloom from my failed marriage.

What I really wanted was to spend more time down here. There was something about Tregollan, about the cottage and the diary I'd found that wouldn't let me go. I wasn't sure if I wanted it to.

It was quicker to get to the cottage the second time around. I seemed to see more, too. Like the stone steps that led right down the cliffs themselves to a small cove, making for a precarious yet striking footpath. I felt a sense of peace descend as I walked amongst the seagrass, listening to the roar of the ocean below.

I walked around the concealed entrance and stopped in surprise. A tall man with dark blond hair in a slim-fitting navy suit was nailing a noticeboard into the ground.

'Hello?' I called.

He started, and then swore softly when the hammer he'd been holding landed on his foot. He turned to me, his eyes startlingly blue and wide.

'Sorry!' I said.

He laughed. 'Ah, no – it's my fault. Shouldn't have listened to all the rumours.' He shook his head, giving me a sheepish smile that revealed his white, even teeth. He had a deep voice and an American accent, and he was rather, distractingly, handsome.

'For a sec there, I thought you were a ghost,' he said, standing up and holding out a hand. He was very tall, with a slim, athletic build. 'I'm Adam Waters, the lawyer handling the estate. Can I help?'

So this was Adam, I thought.

'Victoria Langley,' I said, shaking his hand. 'It's true then?' I asked, looking at the noticeboard and feeling a sense of inexplicable loss.

He nodded. 'Yeah, 'fraid so. Saw it properly for the first time today – incredible place. I can't understand why it was left like this… I mean, you can see it must have been really something back in its day.'

'I know,' I agreed. 'And you don't know why no one's taken it?'

He shook his head. 'My uncle told me it's been on the books for years – no takers, apparently they all think it's haunted. But now, with one thing and another, we're having to tie up loose ends, like this.'

'What do you mean?'

'My uncle's closing down the business – he's been ill for a while now – so I've come down to help get everything finalised, settle accounts, that sort of thing. A couple of weeks ago I came across this place in the files. I couldn't believe it. My uncle said that they've been trying to sell it since the seventies.

I even went to a few estate agents myself to see if maybe we could get some interest, but, well, no one will touch it. One of them called it "Cursed Cottage",' he scoffed. 'I've never heard anything so rid—' He stopped himself, realising that I might be one of them, and looked a little embarrassed.

I put him out of his misery. 'Don't worry – I'm not from around here. And I agree, it *is* odd, even for Cornwall.'

From what I knew, people in this part of the world liked their myths and legends, but they were practical too. I suppose over the years the rumours had just grown until they had a life of their own. I thought of Sue at the Harbour Cafe. 'Not everyone thinks it's haunted here.'

He shrugged. 'Just most.'

I couldn't argue with that. 'Has the land been sold?'

'Not yet, but a local business owner – owns one of the farms – has said she's interested.' His face split into a grin. 'She's not from round here either. If she buys it, she said she'll probably open up a tea garden...'

My mind started to churn. 'But she hasn't bought it yet? It's still available?'

He looked at me oddly. 'Why? You aren't interested, are you?' It was half jest, half not. I dangled there in the silence, looking back at him, waiting to hear my dismissal, only to hear myself say, as if from a distance, 'I suppose I am, actually.'

CHAPTER FIVE

It should have taken months to buy a house, not days. There should have been a footpath worth of paperwork steeped in sepia-toned ink that led all the way back to 1905, when it was originally built.

There should have been grand obstacles that I had to work my way around, from hundred-year-old tenancy agreements to disputed council bills and massive structural faults.

But there wasn't.

I should have had all manner of financial obstacles to consider, but with the success of my last biography I had a sizeable royalty cheque that meant that I could just manage it, along with most of the repairs. As the first serious buyer in half a century I'd gotten a rather good deal.

Still, I was convinced that something would stop me. And then I found myself holding out my hand for the heavy brass key that opened a door that was no longer there, barely a week later. I'm not someone who believes in fate, not really. But even I had to consider that perhaps this was meant to be.

Mark had been surprised when I phoned to tell him my news. By surprised, I mean completely shocked and furious.

'Have you lost your mind?' he asked, after I explained that I was buying a house in Cornwall. I left out the part that it was abandoned or that I wasn't completely sure if it was haunted or not. It was hard to explain how I'd fallen in love with a house that

was in near ruins and that the locals believed to be cursed, but I
had. It was love and it was all consuming and unconditional.

'This is so typical of you to do something like this. We haven't
even decided what to do about *us* yet. Christ, you can't just go
and buy a house!'

'I can actually.' I didn't mean to sound defensive; I was simply stating the truth. The way we'd set up our finances when we
got married meant that we were largely independent – something his lawyers had insisted upon, as back then he was the
successful one.

'And when it comes to us, well, I think it is decided, don't you?
Surely it was decided when you told me you were in love with
someone else?' It was hard to keep the bitter note out of my voice.

'I said I thought I might be.'

I exhaled for some time. 'Oh yes, silly me.'

'Smudge, look, the truth is that I'm not sure about Jess—'

I closed my eyes. I didn't need this – not now. 'Mark, we're
not good for each other.'

'That's not true. We used to be—'

'We used to be a lot of things.'

Silence followed.

'Still, Smudge, I'm saying this out of love, you can't just throw
your money away on some house.' His tone went brusque.
'They're sharks, my love. They've obviously sensed that you're
vulnerable and have come after you with this place—'

'It's not like that. I want this.'

'You can't be serious. Look, I can come down there, get our lawyers on to this – there must be a way to get you out of this mess.'

The only mess, as far as I could see, was the one we'd made of
our marriage. 'That's just the thing, I don't want to get out of it.
I think actually we need to start settling things.'

'What things?'

'Selling our house. Filing for divorce.'

'Smudge, let's not rush this. You're hurting right now.'

'Yes, but even so. Sometimes you've got to do what's right, even when it hurts like hell.'

Adam, the lawyer, looked at me from across the desk in his uncle's office in Tregollan. The expression in his blue eyes seemed oddly concerned. 'Are you sure you want to go through with this?' he asked, echoing Mark's words.

'I'm not sure that you're meant to be talking your clients out of doing business with you,' I said with a grin.

He gave me a sheepish smile of his own. 'I suppose not – but I thought after a few days you might change your mind?'

Buyer's remorse for abandoned, hundred-year-old properties would be the normal, sane response, I supposed. But I didn't want to change my mind. I felt nervous and excited in equal measure. It was the most alive I'd felt in weeks, and the thought that I could perhaps transform Seafall Cottage into what it once was, breathe new life into it, well, it was what was keeping me going. Right now I needed it as much as it needed me.

'It's in pretty bad shape though,' Adam continued. 'It'll need a lot of work. It's not like you can actually live there. Not for a long while.'

'Why not?'

His eyes went wide. He stared at me as if he was waiting for me to say, 'Just kidding!' When it didn't happen he blinked rapidly, like he was trying to locate the necessary part of his brain to explain something obvious in a way that wasn't too offensive. Then he gave up. 'It's *derelict*. The damp, the roof – most of that needs to be replaced. I mean, there's no electricity, and it's absolutely freezing…'

I shrugged. 'I'll figure something out.'

He shot me a look of disbelief. 'Like what?'

'Maybe I'll pitch a tent.' I stood up, put the paperwork in my bag and made ready to leave.

Adam stood up as well. 'Seriously?'

I looked up, touched by his concern and a little amused. 'Maybe. I don't know. Thanks though.'

All I knew was that I wasn't going to live in London any more. I'm not sure when exactly I'd decided that – some time between signing the paperwork and deciding to buy the house – but I'd come to realise that this was where I was going to stay.

I made to leave, but Adam followed me out the door. 'You can't sleep in a tent,' he protested.

I looked at him. 'Why not? I've done it before.'

'Yeah, but the house will take *months* before it's anywhere near even remotely liveable.'

'Are you worried that I'll freeze to death and prove all the rumours about those vicious ghosts true?'

He grinned. 'Well, maybe not ghosts, I suppose, but it wouldn't look good if we finally sold the property, only to have the new owner die a few days later.'

I laughed. '*O-kay*, so it's just about the firm's reputation then?'

'Yep. Bad for business, you see.'

'Aren't you closing it down?' I pointed out.

'Ah yes, excellent point – never mind then,' he said with a wink.

I laughed.

He gave me a searching look. 'But seriously, where are you going to stay?'

'I haven't quite decided yet. I suppose I'll look at a rental of some kind for the time being.'

Adam's eyes lit up. 'Well, if you've got a spare half hour I might have an idea. It's a bit unconventional...' His gaze trailed over the Brothers Grimm T-shirt I was wearing beneath my coat. 'But then, something tells me that might be alright with you.'

The sun was glinting off the water, the air fizzing with that just-popped champagne colour, when Adam led me to a parcel of houseboats huddled companionably along the river in the small village of Tremenara, ten minutes away from his office.

The wind brought the scent of water, of seaweed, wet wood and churned earth.

We walked past an array of floating homes, each different from the last, from big ones the size of small townhouses, modern and sleek, to small ones that ran the gamut between sweet and shabby. Some had little gardens on their roofs with pots of wintry shrubs and herbs and were strung with amber lights. On a navy barge, a salty river dog with springy fur eyed us with solemn black eyes. Adam came to a stop before a small bottle-green narrowboat with the name *Somersby* painted onto its side in gold lettering.

'I got it a few months ago, when the previous owner decided to become a landlubber.'

I laughed, 'Landlubber? You sound as if you disapprove — do you mean to tell me you also live on a houseboat?'

He grinned. 'Yeah, mine's that one down there,' he said, pointing to a blue and white houseboat about twenty metres from *Somersby*, called *Plain Sailing*. 'I've been there for the past six months or so, since I came down to help my uncle out. I saw it for sale one day and decided it would be a great way to get some space. My uncle's two-bedroom cottage in Tregollan is quaint but tiny. Plus, this way I get to fulfil a boyhood dream.'

'So you liked living on a houseboat so much that you bought another one?'

He shrugged. 'Yeah, kind of. I like projects, to be honest, and this one has been great to work on. I'm not a hundred per cent finished with the paintwork, and the kitchen's really outdated, but it beats a tent. At least there's heating, electricity, a toilet…'

I looked at him in surprise. 'There's central heating? On a houseboat?'

He narrowed his eyes. 'Typical landlubber – of course there is.'

I grinned. 'Can I see it?'

'Sure.'

Adam jumped on board and I climbed on after him.

'It's a narrowboat,' he explained. 'Made for traversing canals and rivers. They come in all sizes, but this one's pretty decent, mid-level I suppose, at fifty-seven feet.'

Inside, there was a living room with a porthole that looked out onto the river. It had a wood burner in the centre and there was space enough for a sofa and a small bookcase.

'It's a multi-fuel stove,' Adam explained. 'I just put it in. Makes a real difference in the winter, heats up this place really fast.'

Just off the living room was a tiny kitchen with a rather sorry-looking stove, which only had one gas ring remaining.

'I'm putting a new stove in – don't worry. That thing was old when Thatcher was prime minister,' he joked.

Below the stove an orange paisley-print curtain pulled aside to reveal storage for pots and utensils alongside a sink and fridge.

'The cabin is pretty good – there's space for a double bed,' he added, showing me to the back of the boat – or aft, as I later learned it was called. It was a tight squeeze with the bed, and there was a small shelf that ran along the wooden wall, but there was space for a wardrobe at least. There was another porthole in there.

'You use these at night,' he said, lifting up a small round cushion that filled the circular space perfectly, like a special padded curtain.

I looked at him, amazed. 'I love that!'

'Yeah, they're great,' he smiled. His eyes crinkled at the corners. It was the sort of smile that certain men had, the sort of smile that, if it could talk, would come out as a drawl. It was languid and easy and hard to resist.

'So just off here's the bathroom,' he repeated.

'Okay,' I said blushing, realising that I'd been staring while he'd been talking. 'It's like a small flat,' I said in surprise. 'And there's plugs!' Somehow I'd thought that there would be wires crisscrossing everywhere. I hadn't expected this neat little water home.

'Yeah, I know what you mean. I was surprised the first time I came on one too. The electricity comes with the mooring – although you can also get power with the engine, which runs on diesel,' he explained.

I looked around. The wood panelling was sleek and polished. Aside from needing a few minor improvements to the decor, it was rather special; there was certainly something appealing about the idea of life on the waterways.

'What's it like living on the water?'

'There's nothing like it – at first it's an adjustment, but there's a real freedom to it.'

'I can imagine,' I said, thinking how incredible it must be to have an estuary for a garden.

He ran a hand through his dark blond hair, and gave me that same lazy smile. 'So, like I said, if you're interested, I thought this might work until the cottage is ready? It's about a ten-minute drive to the cottage from here, so you wouldn't be too far away while you're fixing it up. Just an idea…'

I looked out the window in the kitchen and spotted a little team of ducks swimming alongside. I couldn't help but smile. 'I'm interested.'

CHAPTER SIX

I couldn't avoid London forever. Now that I'd made the decision to move to Cornwall, I had to face our home, not to mention the state of our marriage, even if Mark wouldn't.

I wasn't good at limbo, and that's what this was. Mark seemed happy enough to leave me dangling until he was ready to decide what he wanted. He might need time to see if what he was feeling for some other woman was real or not, but that didn't mean I had to be a part of it. I could choose for the both of us, and what I chose was not this.

Grimly, I set down my things in the hallway of our London house. The last time I'd been here I was barrelling out the door, barely able to see past the haze of tears and the fog of hurt and rage.

The house felt cold, the air stale and grey, even when I switched on the lights.

The photographs from our wedding were still on the entrance table. The paintings that I'd lovingly chosen in the nine years of our marriage were still on the walls. The navy sofa in the middle of the room still had its little splodge from the burnt candlewax when we'd decided to try something different in our lovemaking.

It was all still there. But empty, somehow, as if the soul had gone out of it.

Though it was only eleven in the morning, I poured myself a glass of whisky and started packing up what I'd be taking with me for my new life, Tracy Chapman on loudspeaker for company. She sang about fast cars and broken promises. There was something soothing about Tracy on days like this. Like you could hear in her sad, beautiful voice that she'd been here too.

I'd just poured my second glass of whisky when I heard raised voices in the hall.

I stood in the landing and looked down on Mark and a young woman in the hall below. He seemed to be apologising to her, while also attempting to steer her out the door as quickly as possible. Only she was resisting.

He must have seen my car before they came in. This had obviously resulted in some panicking, on his part at least. She seemed hell-bent on coming inside. Perhaps she was also curious about the other woman in his life. With a calm I didn't feel, I said, 'Hi.'

Mark jumped.

'Hi,' said Mark, looking up, his hazel eyes wide. He ran an awkward hand through his dark hair.

I looked at the woman my husband had told me he may be in love with. She was young, perhaps in her mid-twenties, and had that thin, lithe type of body that managed to be incredibly petite and curvaceous at the same time.

Her hair was silvery blonde and she wore make-up like it was art, her face an exquisite canvas. She was everything I was not. Despite the years I had on her, she seemed every bit the grown-up in comparison to me in my faded T-shirt and battered Converse trainers.

'Jess was just leaving,' said Mark.

She shot him a look, then gave me an awkward smile. 'My mother loves your books, she's a big fan, just wanted to tell you that.'

'Jesus, Jess!' said Mark, eyes wide.

She blinked. 'Maybe that came out wrong, I didn't mean—'

I snorted. 'No, I'm sure you meant to imply that at thirty-two I'm the same age as your mother, which would make you a child, which… Actually, I have no problem believing it.'

'I'm not a child,' Jess scoffed. She closed her eyes and took a breath. 'Whatever, I don't need this shit today.' She looked at Mark. 'I'll call you later?'

'Yeah, yeah, sure,' he said. He flinched when she kissed him goodbye, shooting me a startled, apologetic look. It was almost funny – in the way some things can make you laugh when you're about to cry.

I came down the stairs, and when the door closed behind her, said, 'Kind of fancy for a personal trainer.'

He sighed. 'I didn't know you'd be here.'

'I'm sure.'

He looked like he was gearing himself up for a fight, but I didn't have the energy, not now, not after seeing my husband with her. Could you have a midlife crisis before you'd reached midlife?

'How old is she anyway?'

'Victoria,' he said, his tone almost cautionary, like I was heading down a one-way street to disaster.

'*That* young,' I said tartly.

He stared at me. I rolled my eyes but the fight had truly gone out of me. 'Okay, I'll stop.' I held up my glass. 'Want one?'

'Please.'

As I poured, I said, 'I should have called.'

'No – it's your house too, you don't have to do that.'

I handed him the glass.

'Jesus, I'm an idiot,' he said.

'No arguments here,' I said, pouring myself a glass and knocking it back. My failed marriage was playing havoc on my liver.

'No, seriously,' he said.

'Seriously,' I agreed.

He grinned. 'That's what I mean. She's not like that. She doesn't make me laugh like you do. She's great, but—'

'No, don't do that. Don't launch into some shitty comparison. I don't want to hear it.'

'Well, it's the truth. I mean, look at you – you aren't even wearing any make-up.'

I frowned. 'I *am* actually, just not very much.'

He laughed. 'Well, see, and you're still gorgeous.'

'Stop that. Your fucking *girlfriend* just walked out the door two seconds ago, and now you're – what – flirting with your wife?'

He didn't answer.

'Look, I think it's time we spoke about a divorce – I phoned our lawyer, he said he can start drawing up the paperwork soon.'

'Are you serious? C'mon, Smudge, when we spoke on the phone I was ready to talk about selling the house but not —'

'I've already called the estate agent.'

'What?' he exploded. 'You can't just go ahead and do that without me.'

'Mark, we spoke about this days ago. It's not like I'm going to move back in, not after everything that's happened. And, despite what you say, this relationship with Jess is clearly going strong.'

'But you don't have to move out—'

'I know I don't have to, Mark, but I don't want to live here any more. I mean, if you want to do it another way we can talk about that.'

He looked at me hopefully, 'Like counselling or something? I heard about a couple who started going out on these dates—'

I sighed. 'No, Mark, I mean if you want to buy out my portion of the house instead of selling it, we could do that.' I looked at him and snorted. 'Christ, dating?'

'I thought it sounded sweet.'

'Yeah, maybe it would have been, if, you know, you weren't screwing a twenty-five-year-old at the same time.'

'She's twenty-eight.'

I almost laughed. 'Alright.'

'Okay, look, tell you what – I'll compromise,' he said. I raised a brow and he continued, 'We'll sell the house. After that we'll talk about a divorce.'

I shook my head. 'No, Mark. I'd like us to start talking about it now.'

He didn't agree to that, but he did pack a bag and tell me that he'd give me some space while I was in London.

'I'll stay at a hotel while you're down here – give you some time.'

'Sure,' I said, knowing that he was more than likely going to his girlfriend's house, he just didn't want to announce it to me, especially after pleading with me to delay our divorce.

After he left, I phoned my brother's wife, Ivy.

'She has white hair,' I said in lieu of a hello.

'What?'

'*Her.*'

'*Oh*,' she said, pouring about as much venom into that 'oh' as possible. Loyal to a fault was Ivy. Before she became my sister-in-law, she was my friend, something I've reminded my brother about often enough since he stole her from me.

'Oh, and she's a size six.'

'So she's old and frail?' She sounded confused.

I laughed. 'No, I mean she has that silvery-white hair that only really young people can wear and not look as if they've aged a thousand years.'

'Sounds dreadful.'

I laughed. 'Actually, she's breathtaking.'

Silence greeted this. Then she rallied. 'No one is as gorgeous as you.'

'You only think that because I look like my brother but with long hair.'

She snorted. 'No, you don't! You're a babe, Smudge. You know every time you visit, that old Frenchie, Tomas, from the village walks into walls afterwards, completely dazed by you...'

I giggled. 'Tomas does that because he's about a hundred years old and he's going blind.'

'Please, he's only eighty-something and every time he comes round it's like, "'Ello, here is ze pot of bouillabaisse I have made for no reason, eez Smudge coming for dinner?"' she said, putting on a terrible French accent.

I laughed. 'You're an idiot.'

'So did he agree to talk about a divorce?'

'Not exactly, though he has agreed to sell the house. It's a start, I suppose.'

'A fresh start.' She agreed.

After the call, I carried on packing. Most of what I was boxing up would be going into storage, as there would be no room for it on a fifty-seven-foot houseboat. But there were some things that I could arrange to get moved now, like the rattan rocking chair, shaped like an egg, in my study, and the bed from the spare room – I couldn't face using ours in my new life. I ran the washing machine and packed up most of my clothes, books and research, as well as a few things from the kitchen and living room.

In my study, I arranged all my notebooks, papers and letters, and began to fill my backpack, taking out Tilly's diary from the cottage as I did so.

I took a seat at the desk and opened it. It was a ritual that I couldn't seem to stop myself from doing, even though the coded words meant nothing. Every night, I did the same, just before I went to sleep, trying to see if there was any way I could fathom the code.

I couldn't stop thinking about it, about who Tilly was, who she may have been.

I took a sip of coffee and leafed through, my eyes scanning the columns of tight black writing, jumbled letters mixed in occasionally with the numbers three and nine.

Today, though, as I scanned I saw a word, written in plain script, one that I recognised with a frown. I sat up straight, staring at this word, which seemed to jump straight out at me. For it was something more. It was a name of a family, one that I recognised. If Gilly from the Black Horse Inn was to be believed, this family had locked up a mad person in the house I'd just bought. I flicked through the pages now, ever faster, swallowing as I found it came up again and again, every few pages, along with an X and the numbers 3:1.

Asprey.

CHAPTER SEVEN

The stacks of the London Library have always been my area of refuge. As a young girl, I'd make a game of finding books that famous writers had read, sometimes finding one of their notes in the margins. Agatha Christie, Bram Stoker, Charles Dickens... I collected them all. It gave me a thrill to know that I was reading the very books they had once read, that I was standing between the very shelves they had once browsed. Touching the things they touched.

When other girls wished for designer bags, or shoes, I wished for a lifetime membership to the library. It's what I spent my first royalty cheque on. I figured that, if I never had that much money again, at least I'd have something to show for it.

Online, I'd discovered a small reference to John Asprey on a botany site; a small column mentioned him as the first cultivator of a particular type of daffodil, the 'Idyllwild Jonquil'. Apparently he'd been responsible for developing one of the hardiest varieties, still grown today. I'd come to the London Library in search of one of the sources the site had referenced: a rather large tome on flower farming in Victorian times. It was cold in the stacks, and I shivered as I searched.

Finally, I came across a mention of the Aspreys and their farm. It wasn't much really, just a general history of the cultivation and history of daffodils in Britain and abroad, and the type that John Asprey grew with the head gardener, Michael Waters.

It was said that he sank most of the family's wealth into the production and lost a fair amount. It appeared to be linked to their demise.

There was a picture of the family in faded black and white. The image was grainy and I had to pull the book closer to look at it. A man stood outside, next to two young girls. The youngest had long ringlets and was wearing a pinafore. Her expression was rather solemn. She had thick black eyebrows and dark eyes, which were exactly like the man's. The other girl had pale hair and a pretty, if haughty, countenance.

The caption read, '*Lord John Asprey pictured at Idyllwild Farm with his daughters, Rose (12) and Matilda (10) in 1906. Asprey was the co-creator of the hardy Idyllwild Jonquil daffodil, along with his head gardener, Michael Waters*'.

Next to the family stood a tall man. It was hard to make out his features though, as the image was so grainy. It wasn't much to go on, and didn't really speak about who the family had been or why they'd left Idyllwild.

Rose was a beauty, but the younger sister kept drawing my eye. Her face wasn't quite as pretty, but was somehow more striking. Perhaps it was the vivid brows or the dark eyes. Perhaps it was something else, my subconscious trying to tell me something. I looked at the photograph again. Matilda Asprey.

I blinked. Matilda. Or Tilly, for short? I looked at the diary on my desk, and my eyes widened.

Was this the young girl who had written the letter, which seemed to be an echo of my own feelings more than a hundred years later?

I met her serious, solemn gaze. Was this her diary? And if it was – what was it doing in a house that some thought her father had used to lock up a madman?

CHAPTER EIGHT

The sky was the colour of faded denim when I arrived in Tremenara, at the small marina along the estuary, where my new waterside home was to be found. Something inside me lifted as I drove in.

I could make out the tall masts of sailing boats as I parked my car near to the stretch of houseboats that dotted the water. From here, I could see the swirl of gold lettering on the little green narrowboat, *Somersby*. I couldn't believe that this would be my home for the foreseeable future, until Seafall Cottage was ready for me.

I heard the cry of circling seagulls overhead as I started taking my bags out of the car. The air was fresh and cold, rich with the loamy scent of riverwater.

'Need a hand?' said a voice from behind. I turned around in surprise to see Sue from the Harbour Cafe in Tregollan – the one who'd sold me the impressive butternut risotto the other day.

'Sue, hi!' I said. 'What are you doing here?'

'I live here,' she said with a grin. 'That's ours.' She pointed to a large blue barge that was moored ahead, called *The Endeavour*.

'Adam told me he'd gotten a new recruit for our little water community, couldn't believe it when I found out it was you.'

When I gave her a puzzled look, she said, 'I told you, we hear all the news first down at the cafe. Sorry, small towns. New blood is always a big topic of conversation.' And she held out her arms to show me just how much.

I laughed. 'I don't mind.' And truth be told, I didn't. I'd imagined that living this far away from everyone I knew would be incredibly isolating – the closest family I had was Stuart and Ivy down in Cloudsea, and even that was nearly an hour away – so finding a friendly face was an unexpected and rather welcome surprise.

'C'mon, I'll help you take these aboard.'

'Thanks,' I said, as she reached inside the boot and started hauling things onto the pavement.

'The allotment that I told you about is just down that road,' she said, pointing to a small dirt road that led away from the parking area. 'Like I said, I'm there most mornings if you want to come past and have a cuppa, see the new seedlings.'

'Thanks,' I said, touched at the invitation.

There wasn't much to bring aboard: some clothes, a few cushions, linens and kitchen implements.

'Oh, this is lovely,' she said, her nut-brown eyes taking in the polished wood and cosy living room.

'Thanks.'

I'd arranged for the removal van to meet me a little later. They would be bringing the egg-shaped chair from my study, two boxes and the bed. I didn't have a TV, but then that didn't seem like much of a sacrifice at this point. I had my laptop if I really wanted to watch something. I'd also brought my most treasured books for my little shelf. Books – always my answer to the question 'What one thing would you bring to a desert island?'

'Well, must dash,' said Sue, after she set down the bags on the counter. 'If you're free tonight around seven, come for some mulled wine and meet Dave, my husband? We like to extend the Christmas spirit well past January…'

I laughed. 'Okay, great,' I said. 'Thanks.'

After she left, I looked around my new home. I could see that Adam had had it cleaned and there was now a new stove and a small fridge. There was also a friendly white geranium in a yellow pot in the kitchen as a house-warming gift, along with a little note that said, '*Sue said you liked things that grew. Adam.*' I felt touched. He'd been busy the two days I'd spent in London.

After the removal men arrived with the bed and my chair, there wasn't that much to do, apart from making up the bed and unpacking a few boxes. It was hard to believe that I would be living here from now on. It was so quiet. All I could hear was the gentle lap of the water and the occasional cry from a seabird above.

I hadn't seen any of the other houseboat owners yet, apart from Sue. They were probably at work, but I figured that at nights, weekends and in summer it would be a lively place.

I made myself a cup of tea and enjoyed it while watching the ducks out of the kitchen window as they swam past. I was surprised when they came so close to the glass – they were obviously well used to living amongst humans. I fetched some bread and went out onto the deck to throw it to them, laughing at how they seemed to compete for my attention. There was one who seemed hell-bent on squawking in indignation that he was left out, even when a bit of crumb landed squarely on his head.

'You'll have friends for life now,' said a voice, floating up to me from along the water's edge. I turned and saw an older woman smiling at me from the gangway.

She had very long grey hair and was dressed a bit like a modern-day hippie, with multi-coloured palazzo pants in shades of purple and red. She wore silver jewellery and had smiling green eyes. 'So you're the renter?'

I laughed, wondering if the news had spread to every part of the marina. 'I suppose there's not many of them around here,' I said, thinking that most people probably owned their water homes.

'Most of the time,' she agreed. 'But you'll see, you won't want to be a landlubber again after this.'

I grinned. 'Maybe, though I'm still partial to a bit of earth,' I said, thinking of the cottage. 'I'm Victoria, by the way.'

'Angie,' she said. 'Do you like reading?'

'Reading?'

'Books and things?'

'Oh.' I laughed, as I hadn't expected the question. 'Yeah, I do,' I said, wondering why she was asking.

'Great! Well, I run The Floating Bookstore. It's down there.' She pointed to a rather conspicuous houseboat that looked as if it had been tie-dyed in various shades of sunset. 'Come visit us after you've settled in. I'm moored here from spring to summer, and we're open Tuesday to Saturday. I make a mean chocolate cake as well.'

'You run a bookshop on a houseboat? That's so bloody cool.'

She grinned and nodded. 'Adam said I'd like you.'

At night, the marina seemed to come alive, fairy lights twinkling to life and sparkling across the water. Soft music floated in the wind as I boarded the *The Endeavour*, the barge belonging to Sue and her husband, Dave, a short, balding man with red cheeks, an easy smile and an apron with a cartoon drawing of chiselled abs on the front.

'You must be Victoria,' he said, ladling mulled wine into a glass and handing it to me. The air was cold as it blew off the water, though thick with the scent of oranges and cinnamon. I cradled the wine gratefully and took a sip that warmed my bones.

Perhaps it warmed them a little too much, as when I left I walked straight into Adam on the gangway. He was wearing a suit, but his tie was loose and his dark blond hair was tousled. 'Meeting the neighbours already?' he asked, giving me that lazy smile that crinkled the corners of his eyes. It was a little distracting.

'Dave's mulled wine,' I explained.

'Ah, that should come with a warning, especially in January,' he said.

'Now you tell me.'

He laughed. 'So is everything alright on the boat?'

'Yeah, it's great.' I said. 'Thanks for everything – love the plant.'

'It's all good,' he said, giving me a wink before he left. I watched him walk away, taking in his tall frame in the dark suit and stylish shoes for far longer than was necessary. When I got back on my boat I poured myself a glass of cold water, trying to dilute the effects of the wine, and looked at myself in the small bathroom mirror, inspecting my messy, loose curls and the Wonder Woman T-shirt I was wearing. 'Get a grip,' I laughed. 'We do not need a crush right now.'

The night had brought with it the scent of dinners being made and the gentle sounds of conversations being had. I could hear soft music from the boys in the houseboat next to mine, who Angie had said were in an indie rock band. Despite Sue and Dave's hospitality, I tried to ignore the sudden loneliness I felt.

CHAPTER NINE

The brass key opened a door that no longer existed, and in the dawn light the cottage looked even more eerie and abandoned than I remembered.

I clicked on the flashlight, casting its beam from the kitchen to the sea room, and got to work. I dragged the old, worn settee outside, along with the beer bottles and various scraps from years of transient visitors, making a pile that rivalled the mountain of pizza boxes outside.

I'd stocked up on trash bags and cleaning implements, bringing in buckets, brooms, and garden shears, oddly grateful for the work and the distraction it afforded.

There was so much to do, but cleaning seemed a good place to start – before I attempted to cut away the vegetation that twisted across the walls of the living room. I wore an old checked shirt, my most battered Converse trainers and an old cap, not relishing the idea of getting spiders in my hair later on.

There's something about physical labour that helps to chase away any lingering internal demons. I dragged things outside while I listened to the Rolling Stones on my iPod, and ignored what I knew would be aching, tired muscles come the morning.

By midday though, I'd barely scratched the surface. I pulled out the old, worn mattress in the little room just off the kitchen and got to work on attempting to remove some of the furniture cluttering up the stairs.

A heavy mahogany armoire took up most of the space. Piled on top of it were solid wooden chairs and what looked like a steamer chest. I took the chairs down and got to work on shimmying the chest down the stairs, pulling on a brass handle on the side, balancing one end on a knee and another on the corner of the staircase. But before I knew it, gravity took over. I jumped aside as it fell and landed with a deafening clatter, taking a sizeable portion of the wooden steps with it and raising up a cloud of dust in the process. I coughed, grateful that it hadn't landed on my foot. I brought my sleeve up in front of my mouth and nose and waved a hand in front of me to clear the air.

In the fall, the chest had fallen open, spilling its contents all down the staircase. There were scraps of fabric, spools of thread, shears, botanical prints with names in Latin, spare bits of paper and a clutch of letters tied up with sea-green thread.

I bent down to gather them up and took a seat on the bottom step. The letters were held together with the same ribbon that had bound Tilly's diary.

I felt my pulse begin to quicken as I untied the bundle and found a collection of around twenty letters in thick, creamy envelopes. I pooled them onto my lap, wiping the dust on my fingers onto my shirt, and turned each one over. They were all addressed to the same person: Michael Waters.

I slipped the first letter out of its envelope, my heart beating fast, but then a sound from outside made me look up in surprise. The old man from before was staring at me through the window. I stood up quickly.

As soon as he saw me get up, he was off again.

'Wait!' I cried. This time though, he was the trespasser. I didn't relish the idea of having to tell him that. I couldn't help wondering if he lived on the property. Maybe in that empty shed?

I jiggled the door open that led to the veranda outside and the long fall to the churning ocean below. My knocking knees remembered their fear all too well as the wind whipped my hair back from my face. I took a shuddering breath, making sure I didn't look down while keeping close to the wall until I was on firm ground and in the kitchen garden again.

'Are you there?' I called. 'Don't worry, you're not in trouble or anything... I just think we should talk. I'm not sure if you know about me? Well, I just bought the cottage...'

I walked around the small, walled garden. This time, though, there was no light on in the shed. I wondered how he'd got the light in there the first time when there was no electricity. Battery? I entered the shed but it was cold and empty, apart from a few garden implements that looked almost new.

Back in the garden, I found a packet of seeds on the floor, next to a set of small seedling trays. I picked the packet up and read the label. Lobelia. Pretty, I thought, looking at the old-fashioned illustration on the front of a delicate blue flower.

In the days since I'd been here last, a few shoots had come up in time for spring. I'd assumed the garden was the usual sort of kitchen garden, but noting the early blooms, perhaps not.

Unusual, I couldn't help thinking. Had he planted these?

I looked everywhere, but couldn't find him. I put the seed packet in my pocket and went back inside the house.

When I got inside, the letters were gone.

My skin prickled. Had the old man taken them?

A mad search ensued. I looked behind the chest, in amongst all the fallen debris – nothing. I stood up and frowned. Why would he have taken them? I hated to think that I might need to call someone. I couldn't have him stealing things, could I?

I sighed. I would make a decision on that some other time. For now, I was bone-tired and looking forward to a hot shower back on the boat. I rubbed my neck, and caught sight of something on the mantelpiece across from me. The mantelpiece that had been empty following my thorough clearing away of the collection of dead insects and fallen twigs. Yet right there in the middle, propped up on the marble, was a single envelope. My heart skipped a little as I neared it. Like all the others, it was addressed to Michael Waters.

CHAPTER TEN

The letter sat unopened on my small coffee table for most of the night. Each time it caught my eye, I wondered if I should just put it away.

My neighbour, Angie, was partly to blame. When I'd got home, she'd popped over with a 'welcome to the marina' gift of a bottle of wine. As it was a bottle of really great wine, I felt that it would only be right to invite her over for a glass.

'You know, it's really strange to be here – it's been years since I've been on this boat,' she said, stepping aboard and following me into the living room.

'You've been here before?'

She nodded. 'Years ago. It's really changed.' She started to laugh when she saw the kitchen. 'Except for that! My LORD, that curtain!'

'Yeah, it's a bit retro,' I said, feeling ever so slightly offended. I mean, it *was* hideous, but still...

Her shoulders were shaking. 'I'm so sorry – I shouldn't laugh. Only it's my fault. I mean, I picked it.'

I looked at her in surprise.

She gave me a guilty sort of look. 'The, er, owner of the house-boat before Adam, well, he and I had a bit of a summer romance in the seventies... This was the first houseboat I ever lived on.'

I looked at her in surprise and wonder. The seventies, on a houseboat – it sounded brilliant. 'Really?'

'Yeah, it was a million years ago now. I would have thought he'd change it, but he was always a bit set in his ways, old Stevie.'
'You two still friends?' I asked.
'Yeah. Well, it's been years now, he'd moved on long before I came back... Was really strange to see the old houseboat still here. It's nice to know there's someone on board now.'
'You know, maybe I should keep that curtain after all...'
She nodded. 'Yeah, still looks pretty good, actually.'
I suppressed a grin. Angie's long grey hair hung to her waist, she had on a tie-dyed T-shirt that said '*Born This Way*' and a pair of mustard-coloured bellbottoms.
The geranium that Adam had given me was looking a little droopy, so I took it through to the kitchen and gave it some water.
'Pop him by the window,' was Angie's advice.
'Him?' I asked.
'Looks like a him to me.'
I gave the geranium a thoughtful look. 'Maybe you're right,' I laughed. 'I so want to be the type of person who has a garden, who grows beautiful things, but I can't even seem to keep this one alive. And it – he – was a gift.'
'Give him a name – it might help. My mother used to name everything – the trees had personal names, as did some of the flowers. I used to think she was mad, but I had a fern that was dying so I gave it a try, named it Frances, and would you know, the next day she perked right up? I think she'll outlive me now.'
I laughed. 'Really?'
'Yup.'
I looked at the geranium; he looked ever so slightly like a fussy little man. 'Gerald,' I decided.
She grinned. 'Good name.'

I cleared my research off the table, popped it into my backpack, and poured us some wine.

Angie took a seat at the sofa and scanned the small bookcase opposite. 'Quite eclectic taste you've got there,' she said with approval. I'd brought only my most cherished books with me – with so little space I'd had to be a bit cut-throat. There were children's paperbacks, well-worn and loved, as well as all the Brontës, mixed in with a few Agatha Christie novels and Doctor Who serials. I'd also brought a few of my own biographies. It was a habit I'd gotten into since my first book was published; I used the bottom shelf for the things I had created myself. It wasn't vanity, exactly, but on those days when I'm feeling low, I can look at them and think, I made those. Lately, I'd been having more days where I needed that reminder.

'Victoria Langley?' she said, peering closer, which wasn't hard to do, as the room was tiny.

I hadn't factored on company in my little water home, so I felt a little embarrassed. I hadn't introduced myself properly beyond first names.

She picked up my last one, about Janet Suzman, the anti-apartheid and women's rights activist. 'Oh, this was good. She's got a really great style of writing. You know, I've heard she was working on something in the county – Daphne du Maurier.'

I closed my eyes when she picked it up and flipped it over. My photograph was on the back. She looked at it and gasped. 'It's you? Oh my goodness! And here's me prattling away like an idiot.'

I was beetroot red. 'I'm sorry – I should have said. Well, at least I know you like them,' I joked.

She started to laugh. 'Aye, thank heavens! That would have been dead embarrassing.'

'No, not at all. Like I said, it's my own fault for not introducing myself properly.'

She laughed. 'That's true. So what are you doing here? I thought you lived in London?'

I explained that I had been doing research for my latest book, and she was thrilled to hear that she was right – it was on a new biography of the author of *Rebecca*. 'I always thought Daphne du Maurier was incredibly interesting. Well done you to put so much effort into your research. I never realised that it required you to actually relocate.'

'Ah – not always,' I said, reluctant to go into too much detail or to explain why I was really here in Cornwall now – the failure of my marriage. 'It depends on the level of research involved.'

She had very solemn eyes and they seemed to see so much. She'd glanced at my wedding band but hadn't said anything. Had she guessed? I wondered why I was still wearing it.

To fill the silence, and perhaps to stop myself from telling her about Mark, I found myself talking about Seafall Cottage.

'You'll think I'm mad, and maybe I am, but the truth is, I think I decided to move here the day I came across Seafall Cottage.'

She looked at me in surprise.

'I was out walking when I saw it. It's this half-forgotten cottage in the rock cliffs not far from here. I didn't see it at first, and then when I did, I got curious.'

Her eyes were large. 'I can imagine.'

'It's tucked away high above the rocks, and looks like it's ready to fall into the sea.'

She looked at me, and then blinked as if she was realising something. Her face cleared. 'Is – is it near the cove?'

'Yes – you know of it?'

She nodded. 'Yeah, I mean, we all do, you know, growing up round here. Some of the old folks still call it "Cursed Cottage" because of what happened there.'

I nodded. 'Yeah, I'd heard that, about the owners, the Aspreys. Apparently there was a rumour that they kept someone locked up there. But it's hard to believe that. Not when you're there,' I said, thinking of the roses, the beautiful view, the garden. It had been someone's home, I was sure of that, at least.

Angie took a sip of wine, frowning. 'The Aspreys?' she said, looking at me in surprise. She shook her head. 'They never owned that cottage.'

'What? But what about the estate – Idyllwild? I mean, they had to have.' I faltered. 'That's why I was able to buy it – because the Aspreys abandoned it.'

She whistled, eyes huge. 'You bought it?'

I nodded. 'Yes, I just couldn't bear to see it demolished.'

She blinked. 'So you decided to *buy it*.'

'Sounds mad, I know.'

'So that's how you met Adam,' she said, as if piecing together a puzzle. 'And moved here…'

I nodded.

She frowned. 'But didn't Adam explain anything about it?'

'Well, yes, of course he did. He told me he'd also heard about the rumours. But he's new here too.'

'But still… Why did he let you think the Aspreys owned it?'

I looked at her in surprise. 'What do you mean?'

'Well, didn't you wonder why Adam's family had the deed? Why they could sell it in the first place?'

My mouth gaped open slightly. 'Because it was abandoned…' I said, but I was beginning to see what she meant. What I'd overlooked. It hadn't really been abandoned. If it had, it would have been handed over to the council and purchasing it would have been a lengthy process, the way I'd first imagined.

'That cottage has always belonged to the Waters family,' Angie explained.

'Adam's family?'

Angie nodded.

'But why do people think it belonged to the Aspreys? Is it just because it was on their land?'

Angie took a sip, considering the question. 'I think it's more than that, really. It's because John Asprey built it for them.'

'He built it for the Waters? Why would he do that?'

'That's the thing – no one really knows. From what I heard, he wasn't the type who was prone to that sort of thing either.'

'What do you mean?'

'He was a hard man, so they say. Tough, business-minded. It wouldn't have been in his interest to do something like that.'

'Why do it then?'

'I'm not sure.'

I couldn't help wondering why Adam hadn't told me that the house had belonged to his family. Perhaps he thought I knew. Perhaps it was one of the reasons why he'd offered me this place.

'But if it belonged to them all this time, and they've lived here all along, why was it left to go to ruin like that?'

Angie's eyes darkened. 'Ah, well… now that's where the Aspreys *do* fit in. I don't know the full story, but I think it had to do with all the rumours that John Asprey used that cottage to keep someone away from other people. The Waters didn't want to touch it afterwards, I suppose. People said they used to hear all sorts of noises from that cottage. We all grew up hearing the stories, you understand? They said that if you passed the cliff road you could hear someone screaming. I've never heard it myself.'

I told her that I'd heard similar rumours from Gilly at the Black Horse Inn.

She nodded. 'Many believe it, but I think it's just hogwash. I went there once, years ago now, when I was still a teenager. It was a local party, there was a bonfire in the back garden. I went inside and saw this beautiful round window—'

'It's still there,' I said.

'I'm glad. I remember thinking that it was quite special, and that it was such a shame the house had been left like that. I'm glad you've bought it, especially if you're going to fix it up.'

I nodded. 'That's the plan.'

It was refreshing to hear her approval. I had wondered if she might think I was mad for having bought a place most locals thought was cursed. It was difficult to explain how I'd come to love it as intensely as I did – despite the rumours that surrounded it, or perhaps a little because of them. Maybe Seafall Cottage and I would prove them all wrong. I didn't know why, but my instincts told me that, yes, this was a house that had known sorrow, but it had also known love, real love, too. I felt it every time I was there, like it whispered out from the walls. But I didn't know how to say that aloud without sounding like I was crazy.

So we spoke of my plans to restore it, and she said that she'd love to come see it one day, and I told her she was welcome any time.

After she left, I sat for a while, thinking about the cottage. I picked up the letter, felt the smooth creamy paper as I slipped it from the envelope addressed to Michael.

The old man had wanted me to find this particular letter. Why else would it have been left on the mantelpiece for me to find?

I unfolded a single sheaf of loose, creamy paper. It was covered in black ink in a tight, slanted script that I recognised from the diary. Except this letter wasn't written in code.

Dearest Fen,

I thought I knew who I was before I met you. But now I know that that isn't true. Before I met you, I was a girl in waiting. Waiting for life to take the shape it always does for girls like me, while I quietly rebelled, hiding away from Celine as much as I could. My days were long, often spent in the shadows, listening to other people live their lives, wishing that I had been the boy that my parents wished for, so at least life would have been less predict-able. Sometimes I even wished that I could be like Rose, as she, for all her 'Roseness', didn't seem to recoil like I did from her life.

After I met you, everything changed. It was like the world opened up and suddenly there was space for me in it. When I found you and dear Arthur down by the creek that day, I found myself too. I realised I could be something other than the daughter of a baron. I could be, well, anything I wanted in that moment. Maybe you'll just shake that raggedy mop of hair of yours and call me a goose for saying that, but it's true.

How can I go back now? How can I go back to being the girl I was before? Spending her days hiding away from her governess behind the curtain in the library? That's what they want. Mother most of all. I've never been the daughter she wanted, not like Rose, but after I became friends with you, it's like whatever affection she had just shrivelled up and died. I don't know why I'm so shocked that they are such snobs, but I am. Especially Father — he'd called your father his friend, too, after all. I won't stand for it, Fen. I will not let them try to persuade me that what we have is wrong. The only thing that is wrong, I've come to realise, is that people who have money seem to think that they have rights over others as a result.

William Blake said he could see a world in a grain of sand, but what he never said was how you could ever see it again as sand. I don't think you can. I have found a world in my friendship with you.

'To every thing there is a season, and a time to every purpose...' X, 3:1.

I believe that there is a time for everything, and this is ours.

T

CHAPTER ELEVEN

A world in a friendship? Had I ever felt that way? I doubted it. Though I felt in reading those words that I wished that I had.

I must have read Tilly's letter three times before I finally talked myself into going to bed that night.

In the morning I woke to the sound of seagulls and a dull knocking noise. I pulled my pillow over my head, but the knocking noise grew louder. I sat up, realising that it was coming from the front door. I pulled on my robe and made my way out of the cabin to the front of the boat, my eyes widening in surprise as I saw three men staring at me.

One of them was Adam, and he gave me that now familiar lazy smile. 'Sorry, did we wake you? I tried calling…'

I blushed. Next to Adam were two young men, and all three of them were holding a rather large barrel between them. I frowned. Had I missed something?

'Fresh water,' said one of the guys. He had red hair and a very wide grin. 'Just delivered.'

'Jason and Derron offered to help bring it aboard,' said Adam, nodding first to the redhead and then to the other, darker-haired, guy.

'We live on that boat down there,' said Derron, nodding his head at a rather ramshackle houseboat near mine called *The Piston Rings*.

'You're the ones in the band?' I asked.

'The Piston Rings,' said Jason. 'Named after our boat.'

'Angie told me about you guys,' I explained.

'Angie,' he said, his face splitting into a grin. He didn't need to say much else. 'Cool top,' he added, eyeing my Def Leppard T-shirt.

'Thanks,' I said, tying my robe a little tighter. 'Come on in.' I stepped aside and they marched past me and got started on replacing the old barrel. 'This is really great of you guys,' I said, touched. This would never have happened in London.

''Tis nothing,' said Jason.

While the boys fitted the new barrel, Adam looked around. 'Wow, love what you've done with the place! Cool chair.' He pointed to my rattan, egg-shaped rocking chair.

He eyed the string lights I'd put around the kitchen and my collection of Cornish pottery on the shelves. Near the window sat the little geranium in its yellow pot.

'Gerald likes his spot by the window,' I said.

He gave me an amused look. 'Gerald? Do you always name your plants?'

'Just this one,' I admitted. 'Angie gave me the idea.'

I couldn't say for sure if Gerald had perked up because he was closer to the light or because he now had a name. I suspected what Angie would say about it though.

Adam laughed. 'She's something else, isn't she?'

'A true original,' I agreed.

There was so much I wanted to ask Adam – about the cottage, what he knew about the Waters family and their relationship with the Aspreys, why he hadn't told me that it was owned by his family – but with Jason and Derron there, I didn't bring it up.

'So you've got everything you need?' asked Adam. 'Stove okay?'

'Yeah it's great, thanks.'

I was just about to ask him if he wanted to stay for a coffee or meet up later to have a chat about the cottage when he said, 'Well, I better get going, I'm off to Truro for a few days – family stuff. You'll be alright?'

I wasn't used to this. In London you just got on and did your own thing. No one ever worried if you were fine – you just had to be.

'Course I will,' I said, perhaps more brusquely than necessary.

Adam nodded, his face impassive. Before he left he looked at me. His eyes were so very blue. 'Sorry – I have four sisters, it's hard not to play big brother sometimes.'

'Well you don't need to play big brother with me,' I said, and then wished I could take it back, as it came out not at all how I had meant.

'Oh, okay.'

I shook my head. 'Sorry, I only meant that you don't have to worry. You've got enough on your plate with your uncle and everything, you don't need to add something else to that list.'

He gave me that lazy smile, his eyes scanning mine like he knew something I didn't. 'You'll see – it's different down here, people look out for you, even if you tell them not to. You may as well start getting used to it,' he said, giving me a wink before he left. I couldn't help but smile.

After they left I thought about what Adam had said. My mother was the poster child for feminist rights, with her successful organisation, Women in Finance. I was raised to be independent and to never rely on anyone for anything, especially a man. In many ways it was a good thing – I could think of nothing worse than never being able to stand on your own two feet – but there was a downside too. If I always insisted that I could do anything, and didn't need anyone, it was hardly surprising that I found myself doing everything alone.

Something Mark had said when I'd first confronted him about Jess came to mind now. It was before the affair had started, when he had simply become friends with his personal trainer and I'd asked him if he had feelings for her. He'd said that he didn't know. 'Mostly I like talking to her. Maybe it's just that she's young and she needs someone to guide her. She's always asking my opinion. It's nice.'

I'd scoffed in response. 'So if I run every decision I make past you, will that satisfy your masculinity?' I'd regretted saying it as soon as it came out.

'No, it wouldn't. But it would be nice, as your husband, to feel maybe just a little like my opinion mattered to you from time to time. It's nice to feel needed.'

'I need you,' I said.

'Since when?'

The truth was that there had been a time when his was the only opinion that mattered. But somewhere along the way, after his career started to flail and he seemed increasingly resentful of mine, I stopped asking his advice. I stopped needing it, too, as it was almost always sprinkled with a scoop of passive aggression.

Still, I didn't want to chase people away. Was it the worst thing in the world to admit that I needed people?

After I showered and dressed, I went down to the allotment to see if Sue was still there before she headed off to the Harbour Cafe, deciding to take her up on her offer of a cup of tea and to put into practice my new vow to let more of the world in.

As I walked past rows of bare winter patches, I breathed in the rich scent of freshly turned earth. There were few people about, which I might have expected due to the cold, though here and there I spotted a light on in a garden shed and saw people leaving and entering greenhouses.

I found Sue near the middle, dressed in stripy pink wellingtons and a purple bobble hat. Her brown eyes lit up as I neared. 'Well now, this is a nice surprise. Fancy a cuppa?'

I grinned. 'I'd love one.'

She beckoned me inside the greenhouse. 'Ahh,' I said, peeling off my scarf. 'It's so warm.'

'I know, thank goodness,' she said. 'I'm so sick of winter, but at least here you can pretend it's spring.'

'Especially with this,' I said, looking at all the little seedling trays, many of which had new shoots.

'There's Swiss chard, radishes and carrots. And over here,' she said, taking me to the back, next to a small trolley on which were a kettle, a few mugs and tins of sugar, tea and coffee, 'is my winter flower patch. I have impatiens and hyacinths at the moment.'

'I love it,' I said truthfully. 'It reminds me so much of my brother. I think I told you about him – the one with the green fingers. He's got his own catering company and he grows his own produce.'

'What's it called?'

'Sea Cottage.'

She looked at me in surprise. 'You're kidding! We just ordered from them the other day. Such exotic condiments – there was even turnip chutney.'

I thought of Stuart's experiments the year before with pak choi jelly and stifled a laugh. 'You have no idea.'

'But it's good though. I mean at first you wouldn't think so, but…'

I laughed. 'That's Stuart.'

She grinned. 'He sounds nice. Are you close?'

I nodded. 'We used to be closer, but I think we'll get that back now that I've moved down here. I was in London, before,' I added, probably unnecessarily. Sue seemed to know everything around here.

'Tea or coffee?' she asked.

'Tea, please,' I said.

'Ah yes, I remember now – not an instant coffee fan,' she said, nodding her bobble hat.

I grinned. 'I know, I sound like a terrible snob.'

'No, you don't. Okay, maybe a little,' she laughed. 'But I know what you mean. I used to think a vegetable was a vegetable, you know, until me and Abbie started growing our own. Now I know the difference between homegrown, seasonal veg that has just come out the ground, and the limp, watery stuff that's been on the shelf for a few weeks. Maybe I'm a veg snob now.'

I grinned. 'Maybe. I won't tell.'

'So… you and Adam?' she asked, passing me my cup of tea.

I stood up straighter. 'Yes?'

'Well, I was just wondering… are you friends? I mean, when I met you, you were waiting outside their offices, but I got the impression that you didn't know who he was. Then next thing I know you're renting from him.' She gave me a look. 'It's just, well, he's single and you're…' It looked like she was fishing.

'Going through a divorce?' I supplied.

She bit her lip. 'Oh. Sorry. Well, it wouldn't be the worst idea, him and you – would it?'

'Not the worst, but not one of the best,' I said with a grin. 'We're strictly business, I'm afraid.' I remembered that Sue had admitted she was a little nosy at times. 'I've bought a cottage in the area that needs fixing up, and until it's ready I need a place to stay. Hence the *Somersby*.'

'A cottage, that's lovely!' she exclaimed. When I told her it was Seafall Cottage, her mouth popped open in surprise. 'You're kidding?'

I hadn't brought it up the other night over the mulled wine, but as she was the one who'd told me that they were going to demolish the cottage by the end of the month, I felt she should know.

'I couldn't let them tear it down.'

She loosened the soil in a seedling tray and transferred the new shoots into a larger pot, pressing down with her fingers and patting the soil into place. 'You know, I knew when I met you that there was something different about you. Just be warned, there'll be people round here who won't be too impressed. A lot of the locals were happy that it was finally being torn down.'

'Well, they'll just have to get over it,' I said.

She laughed. 'Yeah... Well, good luck with that.'

It turned out to be fair warning. It seemed that news of me buying Seafall Cottage had spread – and not all of the locals who heard about it were as happy as Sue and Angie.

I was in the post office in Tregollan when I ran into Gilly, the owner of the Black Horse Inn, later that week. She pursed her lips and her thin frame seemed to radiate disapproval when she saw me. I was reminded of my first night at the inn, arriving late at night, with wet hair and tracks of mascara down my cheeks from the many tears shed during the long drive away from Mark.

She made a beeline for me, abandoning the queue she was in. 'Is it true?' she demanded.

'What?' I asked. But I had an inkling that I knew what she meant.

She shot me an incredulous look. 'That you bought Cursed Cottage?'

A few people had turned to stare at me. I pulled my jacket closer to me, as if I could hide inside its embrace. 'It's not cursed,' I said.

Her brows shot up, almost disappearing into her short and spiky magenta hair. 'Oh yes, it is. I told yer not to mess with that place. It was finally being torn down and...'

She muttered something under her breath. A plump woman in a green coat tutted loudly and Gilly shot her a silencing look. 'Well, 'tis true – only an emmet would do something like that. Yer should have just left it well alone,' she said to me.

I knew that 'emmet' was the word for foreigner in Cornwall. To many locals, anyone who had to cross the Tamar Valley to get here was considered a foreigner. It wasn't an altogether bad word, but it wasn't exactly polite either.

'Gilly, I'm sorry you feel that way, but it's a lovely place – or it will be soon.'

She shook her head. ''Tisn't me you should be worried about. 'Tis yerself.'

'Well, thank you, but I'll be fine. I don't think that Seafall Cottage is cursed. I really don't.'

She gave me a doubtful look. 'Lass, for yer sake, I hope not.' And then she went and stood back in her queue, her posture stiff and disapproving.

Afterwards, I tried to shake away her words. She was wrong about it – after reading Tilly's letter, I was convinced of that. I just wished that I could know more so that I could prove it to be true. As I stood there in the post office, I vowed that there would come a time when I would.

It was that thought that changed everything. That word: time. It sat there like a pebble in my mind and it wouldn't go away.

When I went home I reread the letter. Looked at the diary, paged through it yet again. I set it down, thinking of Tilly's words, of the quote: '*To everything there is a season, and a time to every purpose.*' Then I felt a small, sharp thrill. It seemed familiar to me somehow. In the letter it was followed by an X and the numbers 3:1.

My throat was in my mouth when I opened the diary again. I skimmed the pages, forgetting to breathe. For there it was, along with the word Asprey, and it came up time and again: X and the numbers 3:1.

I took my phone, typed 'To everything there is a season' into Google and waited. It was the Book of Ecclesiastes, verse 3:1.

I sat back in shock. I took the first line of the verse, and matched the coded sentence before the word Asprey, and found that the number of letters and numbers matched.

When dawn broke, turning the sky from shades of pewter to claret and then faded denim, I'd deciphered the code. It would take days and weeks, however, for me to fully unlock the secrets of the diary, as each word had to be deciphered letter by letter, making it slow, painstaking work. It would be worth it though, as in time, I would discover that it was so much more than an ordinary diary.

PART TWO

CHAPTER TWELVE

Cornwall, 1905

Tilly

Father changed the day the letter arrived. It was an ordinary Tuesday morning, a day as unremarkable as any other, with my sister Rose reading *The Lady* and counting the days until she 'met her fate' and Mother still in bed sleeping through hers, that he found a purpose for it all. One that would change my life and Fen's forever. Although, of course, I only understood that later.

Back then I was simply ten years old, sitting in the breakfast room across from Father's distant scowl, when the footman, Edmund – the one with an ear that Rose said had been twisted by his mother so many times so that it poked out like a cauliflower – brought in the mail.

I'd been eating my two-minute egg, the shell all cracked, ready to scoop the gooey yolk into my mouth, my face set in an agony of contempt as I hate eggs and soft-boiled eggs are the worst, when he opened up the letter and all the colour faded from his face.

He was out the room before I even got a chance to ask him what was wrong. Even Rose, who is always oblivious to anything unless it is printed on a society page first, deigned to notice. 'Papa?' she called. 'Is something wrong?' But he'd already gone into his study, the door closing behind him with a distant click. 'Tilly, do you have any idea what that was about?' she asked, her grey eyes unusually troubled.

I shook my head.

Some time later, the rumours began.

It was hardly surprising that they started below stairs; I suppose they heard the news before we did. Even Mother didn't really know what was happening until the builders came, and that was only because they trundled past the house with wagons filled with bricks and stones and bags of cement, going past the west and east farms, past the sea of daffodils, to the very back of the estate where nothing grew and no one lived, to where the sea lapped at the very edges of Father's domain.

It never occurred to Father to explain his motives to Mother, or to any of us really. Even though he was building a house for someone we'd never heard of. Someone Father had, it turned out, known for a long time.

That's what I overheard Mrs Price say when I snuck into the kitchen to get a spare bit of chicken for old Bess, our Border Collie, who hadn't been eating properly for days but seemed to rally at the sight of some cold roast chicken.

Oh yes. Long before we knew, Mrs Price did. After all, Mr Waters was her sister's husband, wasn't he? Funny, at first I didn't think Father knew that. Later, I realised, of course, he did. That's why she came to work for us in the first place. Mother had wanted the Talberts' cook, Mrs Blunden, when old Mrs Carrick retired. But before anyone could say anything, there was Bertha Price, the youngest cook anyone had ever seen, who'd given herself the title of 'Mrs' solely because all respectable cooks were 'Mrs' as far as she was concerned. Who, if I'm being honest, didn't start off as the world's best cook either.

The eggs were always the wrong side of runny; she thought to cook chicken was to boil it and to make porridge was to burn it. The scent would carry itself up from the kitchen all the way to the breakfast room and lodge itself into the curve of Mother's disapproving scowl.

What was even more extraordinary was the fact that all of Mother's threats concerning her dismissal were resolutely ignored by Father, in the same way one tries to block out thoughts of being outdoors when you're cooped up in church or listening to one of our governess Celine's insufferable lectures. Mrs Price was here to stay, and no amount of meaningful scowls or burnt breakfasts seemed to make any difference.

She appeared in our lives, a new, yet enduring fixture, like the house that began to take form at the very edge of the property. Which, at first, Father attempted to deny existed. Then, when he could no longer do that, he said it was business. Though he never called it that, exactly. When I kept probing, he lost patience with me and told me that I shouldn't pry into things that didn't concern me.

Of course, Rose was convinced he had a lover and was embarrassing Mother by installing a mistress on the estate, but that was absurd. Even I knew enough about my father to know that he wasn't someone who would willingly involve the family in scandal. Or worse, ridicule.

My cousin Tim, who called me Spriggy on account of the fact that I was all elbows and knees since my growth spurt the year before, was staying with us for a few weeks while on his half-term break from school. He believed my father was setting up an illegal trade route from the old pirate cove at the end of the estate.

Years ago, the story went, the cove had been used to offload the plunder that had first led to the Aspreys' wealth – though

I couldn't believe Father was really considering giving up his farms for the life of a pirate. For starters, he turned green by simply looking at the water.

No, it was something else. I heard the upstairs servants talking about it. It was all anyone ever spoke about after the builders arrived.

I gleaned what I could by turning as near invisible as I could. The servants didn't know about my favourite hiding spot in the library, with the curtain pulled in front of the window seat, my legs tucked behind me. Dust motes flickered in the air as I learned the truth. It wasn't about business at all. Or a lover. It was something else entirely. It was for a friend. Somebody from the war.

CHAPTER THIRTEEN

Present day

Every night in the marina, the wind carried snips of music and the scent of the water, mingled with wild garlic, basil and the promise of summer. Golden lights threaded every boat, creating amber ribbons that guided me back to my waterside home each evening.

I was finding that living on a houseboat was anything but ordinary. Living on the water took away the boundaries created by land and custom and introversion. Without fences and driveways, the water provided a constant thread of connection and dependency. You soon learned that being a good neighbour wasn't merely about being nice, but was an essential part of life. Unlike land dwellers, you needed your neighbours.

Some chores simply couldn't be done alone, and everyone lent a hand, knowing that soon enough the time would come when they would need a favour in return.

It was a surprise at first – the kindness of strangers. I was used to London and the feeling of being isolated in a city of millions of people. Of never knowing the names of the people who lived across the road, though you'd seen them from a distance for years.

Jason and Derron, the guys who lived in the houseboat next to mine, were always there to lend a hand, or to show me how things worked on the boat.

Jason played the guitar, while Derron sang. He had blue eyes and an easy smile, and almost every night they sat in the bow of the boat, wrapped up against the cold while they played their music, the soft thrum of a guitar and Derron's languorous voice the backdrop to my evenings.

Boat people had their own language, and you soon learned that saying the 'back of the boat' instead of the stern would earn you some good-natured ribbing.

Easily the most interesting houseboat belonged to my favourite hippie, Angie. *The Floating Bookstore* was every bit as wondrous as its name. It was an island of books, where every available space had been given over to shelves. Some of them slid and stacked together, and you could pull them apart as you browsed, though you had to be careful not to crush anyone in the process. You learned that 'coming through' really meant 'jump aside'.

There were comfortable velvet armchairs and beanbags and a wood burner that warmed the toes and scented the air with the pine and beech that Angie collected from the forest.

There were only a handful of tables due to the size of the shop, but here you could enjoy a cup of hot chocolate and a slice of Angie's famous lemon drizzle or orange polenta cake, which paired beautifully with rooibos tea.

The first time I'd visited, I'd marvelled at the sheer volume of books in such a small space. Every available inch was stacked with books – tottering, towering and terrific.

They were old and new, first editions and the latest releases, literary and bonkbuster, all sitting companionably amongst each other. And, perhaps most interesting of all, she shelved them alphabetically. There were no distinctions of genre made in Angie's bookshop. No demarcation between non-fiction or fiction, geography or history, past or present release. No separation between thriller, sci-fi, romance or otherwise. Her only concession, no doubt due to a few horrified parents, was a plaque that said 'Old/Young', with a hand pointing left or right. On the whole, it was an anarchical system that you either loved or loathed.

It had taken me some time to see the beauty in the chaos – the genius, too. In some ways, it meant a slightly slower way of discovery, one that allowed for a bit of magic, a little like the houseboat community lifestyle itself. You took your time browsing and picked up books and stories and plays you might never have ordinarily.

Angie told me, proudly, that since she'd done away with the sections, she found more people giving different genres a chance. There were a few people who simply grumbled and left the shop altogether, complaining that they didn't have the time to waste, but they were a minority.

Some people tried to impose order on the disorder. 'Human nature,' Angie told me over a cup of coffee on my second visit. 'People like to have things make sense, and you wouldn't believe how many times someone has tried to explain to me why the system doesn't work. Just yesterday, a woman came to the counter to berate me because she came past a novel about an extra-marital affair filed next to the Kama Sutra. She said it was as if I were encouraging people to break their vows with the placement.'

I laughed. 'Seriously, she said that?'

She nodded. 'I just told her it was the shelving equivalent of kismet, and if she really thought about it, the Kama Sutra could have been a sign to spice up her marriage, not leave it.'

I giggled. 'What did she say?'

'What you'd expect.'

'She told you to shove it.'

'Yep, pretty much where the sun doesn't shine.'

Despite Angie's opposition to changing her shelving system, I noticed that people quietly curated when she wasn't looking. Occasionally, you'd find a cache of the latest thrillers assembled

in an odd corner, or a tottering pile of romances tucked behind
a potted fern (I presumed this was Frances – the fern that began
to live after it was named). These surreptitious stashes helped
similar readers to discover their favourite genre more easily, a
secret handshake amongst like-minded readers, bound together
by a covert, illicit code of order.

Despite her lack of prejudice to reading tastes, I was delighted to discover that Angie could play favourites too, as I saw, in
pride of place, a small array of my own biographies stacked on
a little table near the front of the shop. When she saw that I
noticed, she just winked.

It was the houseboat community way, I'd come to realise. They
looked after their own, just like Adam had told me, and it was
surprisingly easy to get used to. If you came into some good fortune, like Derron, my guitar-playing neighbour who'd been gifted
with a healthy supply of wood from an obliging punter at the
pub, you shared it amongst the houseboats in our watery lane.

Derron had told me that, come the summer, he'd get vegetables from Sue and Dave's allotment, and that every year the Bishop would dole out his latest batch of ginger wine along with The
Word. Though as far as I could tell the old man who wore a Russian
hat at all times and had a pointed goatee, who lived on a beaten-up
houseboat, which was in desperate need of paint and repairs, wasn't
so much ordained as deranged. I was yet to meet him officially.
Apparently there was a bit of a ceremony, according to Derron.

After Adam got back from Truro, I saw him jogging along
the riverbank, but he was too far away for me to call out.

For the most part, my days had been spent working on the
cottage in the afternoons and deciphering Tilly's diary.

It was hard to believe how much my life had changed in
such a short space of time. The first day I found myself sleeping
till nine I couldn't believe it. For years, my life had consisted of

twelve- to fifteen-hour days, often with my real work, the writing and research, squeezed into the small gaps between media appearances and book tours. In many ways, it was a wonderful way of life, but for the first time in years, despite the fact that I wasn't in fact working on a book at the moment, I was doing what I loved – researching and uncovering a mystery.

Some mornings I went past the allotment and helped Sue. Getting my fingers dirty and planting seedlings was therapeutic, and as a bonus I went home with some of the produce, not to mention some of her recipes – though I was yet to try them. I was a bit of a disaster in the kitchen department, but it was one of my new goals. I wasn't aiming for anything besides the ability to make something edible. Still, I was enjoying the slower pace of life, the little luxuries like falling asleep with a novel. Listening to the rain as it fell on the boat. Waking up to a view of the endless blue river and not having to rush off anywhere, not living life according to a rigidly organised calendar. The shadows under my eyes had begun to fade, and though I was putting on some weight, for the first time in forever I didn't care. I was discovering that despite popular belief, it wasn't blondes who had more fun – it was women who ate carbs.

Still, old habits are hard to break and it was difficult to circumvent my workaholic tendencies. I had to discipline myself not to spend all my time deciphering Tilly's diary. Well, I called it a diary, even though it didn't seem to follow the general day-to-day structure of most journals.

It was painstaking work and often had to be done word by word, but as I became more accustomed to the code, it was getting faster and easier to decrypt.

This past week had been filled with late nights. It was an odd sort of providence that the diary began with Tilly finding Seafall Cottage when, more than a hundred years later, I'd stumbled across it myself. It couldn't help but colour my time in the cottage, and I thought of her often while I was clearing out and cleaning. But the real work was only just about to begin.

From Angie I'd gotten the name of the renovators who were responsible for the creation of her fabulous moveable shelves in *The Floating Bookstore*. They were a father-and-son team – Jack and Will Abrams. I was to go down to the cottage that afternoon to meet them.

I'd given Jack directions and explained how to find the cottage on the phone. 'What's this, me lover, Narnia?' he'd joked.

'Almost,' I laughed. Me lover! I'd been coming to Cornwall for years, but this was the first time I'd actually heard someone use that expression on me. I counted it as a victory, like a baptism of sorts.

As I waited for them to arrive, I pulled one of the brass handles of the chest, grateful that I'd now have some help in clearing the stairs of all the heavy furniture, which had prevented me from seeing the rest of the cottage. To my surprise, it shifted until there was a sudden gap between it and the armoire. The space was just big enough that I'd be able to squeeze past, up the stairs. When I'd spoken to Jack, the renovator, on the phone about the stairs he'd told me to be careful as the weight of the furniture – combined with the damp – could mean that it was unstable. He advised me to wait for them before I tried going up there myself, but I'd been so curious about the rest of the house which in all these weeks I hadn't yet seen – surely a little peek couldn't hurt – if I were careful enough on the steps?

I felt a surge of excitement, laced with trepidation – what was waiting for me upstairs? Especially as it was clear that no one had been up there for years.

I made my way gingerly up the stairs, careful as I ascended. At the top, I found myself staring into a room that looked as if it had slipped back in time.

A thick layer of heavy dust had settled around it, like a co-coon. The bed was dark, ornately carved, a wooden four-poster, perfectly made up with faded, once-white sheets, as if it were still waiting for its occupant's return. I stepped into the room and saw a butler's stand, where a pair of men's trousers had been folded.

A poster on the wall, the tape yellowed and curling, said 'Welcome to Idyllwild', and advertised a spring festival at the daffodil farm in 1912.

On the bureau was a hairbrush with a silver handle and a matching comb; there were still fine, dark hairs in the teeth. Next to this was a small, hand-tied posy of dried, blue flowers.

I moved closer to see what they were; it looked like a kind of blue heather. It was wound with a familiar ribbon. My heart began to thud. I touched the thread, and found, wrapped around the fabric, a small scrap of paper, almost like a message intended for a pigeon carrier.

I unwound it, fingers shaking. Inside were letters and numbers I recognised. It was the same code as the diary, only now I had no trouble deciphering it. It read, simply, 'My love'.

A noise downstairs startled me. I put the note, along with the posy, carefully in the pocket of my hoodie and hurried down to the ground floor – my foot crashing through the rickety wood of the well-worn stairs.

'Aaagh!' I yelled, trying to pull my foot out. The pain was tremendous; several splinters from the wood had torn through the fabric of my jeans.

'Oh my God, are you okay?' came an American voice from below. I tried to stand up, wincing in pain. My foot, however, wouldn't budge. I craned my head forward and peered down the stairs. 'Adam? What are you doing down there?'

A pair of very blue, very wide eyes gazed up at me. 'What are you doing up there?' he asked. 'Are you hurt?'

I nodded. 'Yeah, my foot went through one of the steps. I came down too fast and it just gave out. I'm an idiot.'

He ran a hand through his dark blond hair. 'No, I'm sorry I startled you.'

He put something down on the floor and then made his way carefully up the stairs towards me, grimacing when he saw my leg. 'Ouch!' He bent down and began breaking away the rest of the wood around my leg.

'Let's see if we can get it loose rather than trying to yank it out,' he said with a grin.

I sighed and gave a short laugh. 'Yes, that would be the smarter approach.'

This close, I could smell his aftershave. It was light and spicy. Without thinking, I leant forward to breathe it in. He looked up at me, and I was sure he could sense my thoughts. I looked away, my face colouring.

He was saying something, and it took me a moment to re-alise that my foot was free.

As if from a distance, I found my voice. He was staring at me, slightly puzzled.

'Thanks,' I said, wiggling my foot and wincing at the tender-ness. Luckily, there was no real damage, just slight broken flesh, and the start of what would no doubt be an impressive bruise.

He helped me down, half carrying me as I hopped on my good leg.

'I just wanted to see how you're getting on. Brought us some cof-fee from the Harbour Cafe.' He handed me a cappuccino, which I took with a grateful groan. Sue's cafe made the best cappuccinos.

'Thought I'd come past and see how you're doing, hope you don't mind.'

The last time I'd seen him I'd seemed to imply that I didn't need his concern – something I regretted the second it came out. 'I don't mind at all, thank you so much,' I said pointedly. 'How was Truro?'

'Not so great, my uncle's treatment hasn't been working all that well.'

Though I knew that Adam's uncle hadn't been well, I hadn't realised that this was why he'd been out of town. 'I'm so sorry,' I said.

'He's had a bad run of it with the chemotherapy lately. They might try something else. Not sure if I told you that he has cancer?'

I felt my stomach twist and shook my head. 'I'm so sorry, I had no idea.'

He ran a hand through his hair again. 'Yeah, thanks, it's been a rough few weeks. Anyway, I'm trying not to think about it today, keep picturing my aunt's face, you know.'

I nodded. 'That's – that must be really hard to go through. Are you very close?'

'Yeah. I mean, as close as we can be. We moved to the States when I was quite young, but we'd visit every few years. This is the longest I've been back in the country though. My mom was here for a while, but she's had to go back – my dad's hopeless without her, can't even work the toaster.'

'Oh, I never realised you were born here. So you're British?'

'Half. My dad's American. The funny thing is, it's only now that I'm here that I realise that I actually *am* American.'

'Didn't you know?' I teased.

He laughed. 'Well, yes, but when you're surrounded by people who sound like you but don't exactly share the same ideas or interests you don't think of yourself as that, you know? It's only now I'm here that I see what makes me American.'

'Like what?'

'Well, like our enthusiasm, for instance. Americans are pretty passionate, and we show it. And, well...'

I grinned. 'The British are well known for their reserve. I get it, we can be a boring bunch at times.'

He laughed. 'Yeah. Well, not boring exactly, not when you get to know them anyway. And I suppose we can be a bit too enthusiastic. I've learned to tone it down a little, otherwise people think you're coming on too strong, or maybe a little false.'

'False?'

'Sometimes.'

I laughed. 'Well, I like that. You'd love my sister-in-law, Ivy. She's like that, very high energy, and she's a Brit so it does happen here too sometimes. But I know what you mean. I've had a few American friends and I love their energy. My editor in New York really makes writing fun – her emails are always full of exclamation points about the things she likes.'

'Let's hope she doesn't do it with the bits she doesn't.'

I laughed. 'No, thank goodness. But, you know, coming here made me realise that I'm a Londoner, even if I don't always want to be. I didn't really think I was – I'm not a city girl at heart – but at the same time, I'm not from here.'

'That's it, yeah. I love it here, but I just can't escape the fact that I'm a bit of an outsider too. Nice to know it isn't just me. I wonder when that'll start to feel different.'

'Maybe when you get called "me lover", like I was today?'

'What? I'm jealous!' exclaimed Adam with an irrepressible grin. 'I've been here six months and it hasn't happened yet. Do you think it's because I'm a guy?'

I shook my head. 'No, as far as I know they don't discriminate.'

'Well, that's good to know. So I'll just wait in hope.'

Just then, the person who'd given me my distinctly Cornish greeting called out from the front of the house.

'Hullo?' came a West Country brogue from the kitchen passage.

'Here,' I said, limping into the sea room with Adam at my heels.

'Will! You've got to see this window,' said a heavyset man with a balding head who was whistling at the view while he rocked on his paint-spattered heels.

'Hello,' I greeted. 'I'm Victoria – we spoke on the phone?'

'Hullo! Jack Abrams. This is Will, my son,' he said as a young boy barely out of his teens came inside and stuttered a hello. He had large goggle eyes and was almost painfully thin. I couldn't help hoping that there was more to this team than the two of them.

'Pretty view, would have been half-tempted myself to buy this if I'd seen that. Looks Art Nouveau,' continued Jack.

I grinned. 'I think so too. It was the period, I think.'

Adam nodded. 'My uncle said it was built in 1905, it didn't say on the deed though when the construction started.'

Jack looked at him. 'Graham Waters' nephew?'

Adam nodded.

'Ah, well, you'll know all about this place then.'

I was about to ask Adam about the house, about his family being the owners of the cottage, when his phone started to ring.

'Excuse me,' he said. 'Got to take this, it's a client.'

'There's nothing like an old house for secrets,' said Jack, as I pointed out the site of my accident on the steps. 'Probably best to avoid these stairs, me lover, till we can get them seen to, alright?'

I grinned, glancing over at Adam, who was standing by the kitchen on the phone. His mouth had popped open and when Jack turned he gave me the victory sign. I stifled a laugh.

'I'm going to have to take care of this, sorry,' said Adam, after he finished his call. 'But I'll see you soon.'

'If you're free, come past the boat later,' I said. Then I found myself blushing at how suggestive it sounded. 'I, er, there's something I wanted to discuss with you about the house, but I can give you a call if you'd rather.'

'Oh?' He looked concerned.

'It's not serious... just something I wanted to know a bit more about. It's not important. No rush or anything.'

'It's no problem. I can be there about seven if that's good?'

'Great,' I said, while Jack gave me a beady, knowing look that I tried to ignore.

'So, I suppose what I've been wanting to ask is why the house was left abandoned, when it belonged to the Waters family,' I explained a few hours later.

Adam was sitting in the egg-shaped chair next to the sofa, where I was curled up with a cup of coffee. His long legs were stretched out in front of him, soaking up the warmth from the wood burner, and a cup of tea rested on one knee.

If I'd felt slightly nervous about asking him over, in case he got the wrong idea, I was quickly disabused of the notion. There was something disarming about Adam. Perhaps it was the fact that he was rather direct, so you felt like you knew where you stood. Though there was something about his past that he seemed to be holding back. When I'd asked him about what he did before he came here, he'd been rather vague.

'Sorry,' I said. 'I hope that doesn't sound like an accusation or anything – it's really just curiosity. When Angie told me that the house actually belonged to your great-grandfather and not the Aspreys, well, I was surprised, to be honest.'

He nodded. 'That's completely understandable. It was a question I asked too. I mean, it would make sense that the cot-

tage belonged to the Aspreys and for it to have been left in the
state it was because they'd fled the country some time during
the First World War, but it doesn't make sense when the owners
have lived in the county the whole time.'

I nodded. 'Exactly.'

'Well, the answer is simple. Like you, everyone thought that
it belonged to the Aspreys.'

'What? So you mean your family never knew it belonged to
them?'

He shook his head. 'Well, most of the family anyway. My
uncle didn't know about it until it came into his hands in the
seventies. And I didn't know about it till I found the deed. Maybe the secrecy was something to do with the "curse" – I'm not
sure. I do know that even my uncle can't talk about the cottage
without getting the shivers. I think that's why it was left... To
be honest, I think there's more to the story, but no one in the
family speaks about it.'

'But don't you think it's strange?'

'Definitely. I mean, even if there are some old rumours floating about, you can't help but see that it was a lovely place once.
The idea that my uncle actually wanted to demolish it, well, it
seemed rather awful. To be honest, I'm rather curious about the
place myself. I didn't know who the Aspreys were until I found
that deed in my uncle's office and since then I've tried to find
out about them, about what happened to them,' he admitted.

I looked at him in surprise and set down my coffee cup. 'Me
too. I thought it was just a professional hazard, you know, but
I'm glad to know I'm not the only one who's curious.'

His eyes fell upon the small stack of biographies I'd written,
arranged on the bottom shelf. He grinned. 'I googled you, you
know.'

I put my hands on my cheeks. 'Ah, no!'

'Sorry,' he grinned. 'I wanted to know why someone would buy an abandoned cottage… It made more sense when I found out that you were – are – a biographer.'

I nodded. 'Yeah, I guess so. It's still a mad thing to do though, even for me. All I can say is that I felt in some way like it was calling out to me when I saw it.'

'What do you mean?'

I told him how I'd found it, while out walking. I didn't tell him, though, that it was in the immediate aftermath of the implosion of my marriage. My fingers touched the place where my wedding ring used to be, felt the pale emptiness. 'I looked up and I saw this house in the cliffs and I decided to go and look. It was trespassing, of course,' I said with a grin. 'Sorry.'

He waved a hand. 'I'd probably have done the same thing.'

'But you're a lawyer!' I said in mock horror.

He shrugged. 'Still human, mostly.'

I laughed. 'Well, I'm glad you'd also have done it. It's hard to explain, but I felt drawn to it…' I cleared my throat, and decided to come clean. 'Also, it's how I found this,' I said, picking up Tilly's diary, which had been sitting on the coffee table, surrounded by loose sheaves of paper upon which I'd painstakingly started to decode the diary, page by page.

'What is it?'

'Open it.'

He unwound the turquoise ribbon and I pointed out the name embroidered on the thread. 'Do you see the name?'

'Tilly?'

'Tilly Asprey. It's her diary.'

He looked at me in surprise, his blue eyes wide. 'Asprey? But what was her diary doing at the cottage?'

'That's the question I keep asking myself.'

He opened the diary, his mouth falling open slightly as he scanned the pages. 'It's in code?'

I nodded, then lifted the sheets of paper with my transcriptions. I showed him the letter I had found and how I'd worked out the code. I never mentioned the old man. He was the one secret I wasn't quite ready to divulge, mostly because I knew that he would probably want to call the police and I didn't want to do that, at least not until I'd found him and spoken to him.

His eyes went huge. 'This is incredible. And you've done this all yourself?'

I thought of my old professor, Stan. 'I had some help, but the theft – well, that was all me, baby,' I said with a wry smile, and a slightly nervous laugh. 'Technically, these belong to your uncle,' I admitted apologetically.

Adam shook his head. 'Don't worry about that – my uncle's instructions were that you could have the house as it was, with everything inside. He never wanted any of it, and if we'd demolished it, everything would have been destroyed, this along with it.'

I looked at Tilly's diary and thought of how sad it would have been never to have read her words. Even though we'd lived over a hundred years apart, I felt like I was getting to know a friend.

'So how does the code work?'

I explained the system. 'I've written it here to make it easier for transcribing,' I said, pulling out a scrap piece of paper. 'It's hard going though, as each page can take ages.'

He took a sip of his cold tea and gave me an appraising look. 'What if you had an assistant?'

'You'd want to do that?' I said in surprise. Part of me had relished it as my own delicious secret. I always worked alone – it's what I enjoyed. But the thing about secrets, I've often learned, is that they are almost always better once shared, and I had to admit that having someone to discuss it with would help.

'Yeah, I mean, you can say no, of course, but for me, it would be really interesting to learn more about my family, and about why the cottage was left like it was. It's so covered up that even now my uncle won't speak about it, you know?'

'That's so strange, when you think that the cottage was built for them. I mean, the Waters and the Aspreys must have been friends for John Asprey to have done that. It makes you wonder then what went wrong.'

Adam looked at me in surprise. 'I don't think they were friends – not exactly. From what my uncle has said about it, I think the house was about something else.'

'Like what?'

'A debt.'

'A debt?' I said in surprise. 'For what?'

'The war.'

CHAPTER FOURTEEN

Cornwall, 1905

Tilly

Father never spoke about the war. I just saw the medals, and later, the scars. Like the long purple welt that puckered like a kiss where his hand had nearly been sawn in half. Sometimes, when he's angry and his fist is clenched, it glows white. Like whenever anyone asks him about his time in South Africa. The first time he'd ever seen the country was when he was asked to go and fight for it. To defend 'The Empire', something I don't think he believed in all that much by the end. And now here was this growing reminder at the end of the estate, starting to take shape.

I asked too many questions. Questions no one else dared to, something only a child would do. I couldn't seem to help myself. I must have asked Father a thousand times before he finally told me that the house was for someone who needed a place to stay. As if it was the most natural thing in the world to build someone a home right at the end of your property.

Maybe it was for people like my aunt Cassie and my uncle Win, who looked after their estate in Hampshire as if it were a charity, which Mother had once told us as if it were the very worst thing a person could do. Perhaps, to her, it was. Asprey is a name that has never been on more than nodding terms with the idea of charity. 'You don't make money by giving it away,' was something Father was fond of saying.

My cousin Tim said this just proved that in his heart Father was really just middle-class, even if his wealth, title, and privilege said otherwise. His attitude, if nothing else, showed that the Aspreys remained resolutely self-made men, and this wasn't something my Father was ashamed of.

I was brought up learning about the family business, about the estate, the farms, the tenants and all two thousand acres of the agricultural land which the Aspreys and their tenants have worked for over two hundred years. Most of all I learned about Father's pet project, Idyllwild, the passion of his life – the daffodil farm into which he'd sunk every last penny. Growing and cultivating keeps him busy every day of his life, fighting the wind and the rain and the snow – and God, if he has to. It's kept us in last season's dresses and my mother in a steady state of simmering rage, because he refused to invest in tin or copper or the railway instead, like all of their friends.

Which is why it was so strange that he did what he did.

'This house,' I asked, when we were alone at breakfast. 'It's for a friend?' Somehow, Father wasn't the type I'd ever imagined to have friends. Colleagues, associates, allies, perhaps, but never friends.'

'A friend,' he agreed.

When I asked why he had to build his friend a house, instead of giving him a cottage from one of the farms on the estate, he just shrugged and said it wouldn't be right.

Up until then I had thought I understood my father – his austerity, his black moods, his sense of duty to Asprey House, its farms, his contradictions, the frankly befuddling love he had for his daffodils and the way he wouldn't budge for anything or anyone. But I didn't understand at all, really.

The thing that was odd, even then, was how normal Mother was about it all. How accepting. A woman who'd waged war against her husband about the appointment of Mrs Price for an entire year, before she finally let it go, just simply accepted it without fuss or ceremony.

'Just leave it be, Tilly,' she said, a few weeks after the builders arrived. 'You don't need to know *why*, just accept that it's happening – and do not go down there. Do you hear me? It is forbidden.' And she headed up the stairs, her back starch-stiff.

'But why?' I'd asked.

'Don't ask questions. Go, Celine is waiting for you. She says she is always having to find you and that your French is appalling. Six months without any improvement – it's shocking.'

I sighed. That's all Celine taught. French – *in French* – all day. It was *je suis, tu es, vous etês* as soon as you walked in the nursery door – who wouldn't run away?

'Mother, honestly, why can't I just go to a school?' I asked for the millionth time. 'I'm so bored with Celine. I love her, but I want to learn something besides French!'

'The village school?' she said, eyes popping as she turned to look at me, her heel coming to a halt on the polished mahogany staircase. 'Over my dead body! Your father may run this place as if we were cut off in some blasted colonial outpost, but I insist upon a proper education, at the very least.'

'There's nothing proper about my education. By my age Tim was learning mathematics, geography and Latin.'

'Even if I pointed out the obvious – which is that Tim is a boy and therefore has had an education vastly different to your own – do you honestly believe you could attain anything like it from the village school? I fear you'd be sadly disappointed.'

'Well, maybe not, but at least I could be spared from reading Chaucer in French. And there are schools for girls now.

Rose said that Lady Hammond's girls have gone to one in Surrey.'

The Hammonds were a trump card. They were the sort of company my mother wished to keep – if only she could persuade my father to behave himself accordingly.

Her mouth twisted. 'I'll think about it. In the meantime, stay away from that house and stop hiding away from Celine.'

I did my best, for a while at least.

The buggy arrived after dark, while Mrs Price was preparing dinner and the staff were getting the dining room ready. As it rolled through the grounds and past the house, the tarpaulin rustled in the wind and flapped open, and I saw a pair of trousers before they were whipped out of sight, on to a destination I wasn't allowed to investigate.

The new rule came at breakfast, after Father was done with the toast, and Rose had complained about Mrs Price's salt-ridden marmalade, and Mother – who'd come down to join us for a change – had sniffed disapprovingly all through her second cup of coffee.

'Girls,' Father said, barely looking up from his newspaper as he turned the page. 'The south part of the estate, near the cove, is now out of bounds. Don't let me hear that you've ventured there. The consequences will be serious.' At this he looked up, pinned a dark eye on me, and said, 'Understood, Tilly?'

'But why?' I began.

'Don't ask ques—'

'Questions,' Rose and I repeated resignedly.

'Quite,' said Father.

My cousin Tim was the only one who looked smug. That is, until Father cleared his throat and said, 'You too, Tim.'

Rose and I shared a short-lived moment of sibling triumph, before she went back to ignoring my existence as usual.

Later that afternoon, while Tim left with Father to see about some matter on the estate, I visited Rose's room to find out what she thought about the rule. She was sitting at her dressing table when I asked. She rolled her eyes at me in the mirror then went back to adjusting her riding hat against her bright curls. 'Why do you even care? It's some fellow soldier that he feels sorry for – that's what Mother said.'

'A soldier,' I repeated. 'When did Mother tell you that?'

She sighed. 'When I asked. Perhaps as I'm older they tell me things.'

I pursed my lips at the barb, but Rose just shrugged. 'Just forget about it. Whoever it is just wants to be left alone – so stay out of it.'

CHAPTER FIFTEEN

Present day

Old houses have their quirks, and Seafall Cottage was no exception.

While there weren't as many foundation issues as one might expect, the amount of structural ones more than made up for that, according to Jack Abrams. Which meant that my initial estimate of moving in by the end of the year was most likely a gross underestimation. On some level, I had harboured visions of doing up the house alongside the builders, like Diane Lane in the fictionalised version of Frances Hayes' memoir *Under the Tuscan Sun*. Though an English countryside version, of course. In the summer there would be berries picked straight off the hedges, elderflower cordial, and lunch (I'd miraculously turn into a superb cook) eaten al fresco in the restored kitchen garden on a table constructed out of one of the doors that had been left outside, yet had somehow developed a beautiful patina with age… But alas, all those romantic imaginings were dashed with two words from Will, Jack the builder's son.

'Got rot,' he said, poking at the kitchen wall, where the smell of damp was indeed overwhelming, as a large piece of plaster and wall came tumbling down. Will's eyes were of the bulbous variety, like two pickled onions in a beetroot face, and they seemed to magnify the problem. 'Worst case I ever saw,' he added, as if somehow I should feel a sense of pride about that.

He popped his headphones back into his ears and got back to ripping up the kitchen.

Most of the wooden floors were affected too and would need to be replaced along with a large portion of the roof and the stairs.

Then there was the matter of not having any running water or electricity. Plumbers could be called for the former, but wiring a house that had never had electricity was a sizeable job.

'Yep,' agreed Jack, rocking on his heels at the bottom of the stairs a few minutes later. 'This is going to be a big job.'

Which Angie told me later was a slightly worrying sign, as builders often underestimate how big a project is, or how long it will take.

'Here, have the last slice of pecan pie, your need is greater,' she said in consolation.

What I needed was word that our London house was sold. I had some money left from my royalties, but not a lot, and there was no way I was going to go to my mother, AKA The Terrorist, for a loan. My brother Stuart and I had named her as such when we were children, and like the US government we had a pact to never negotiate with her – mostly because we would lose every time. Our strategy was simple: when she called one of us, often on some pretence, and tried to sniff out information, we denied everything. It was an effective plan, most of the time.

Since I'd left London and walked out of my marriage, I'd been avoiding her calls like the coward I was. I was planning on telling her about the new direction my life had taken – some time. Preferably when I had enough liquor in my system to float a small island.

Avoiding Mum, however, is like trying to dam a river with a finger. Even if you try to convince yourself that you can't feel the pressure building up, sooner or later it will burst.

My mother has never been on more than the loosest terms with the idea of subtlety and when she phoned early the following week, it was no exception. 'Have you gone insane?' she demanded.

'Well, hello to you too, Mum,' I said, feeling the need to sit. I put my coffee cup down, turning my attention away from the family of ducklings that were swimming past my narrowboat, and took a seat at the sofa. It was covered in stacks of notes from deciphering Tilly's diary, along with the two novels I was simultaneously reading in my new pursuit of leisure time.

'I didn't think it was possible,' she continued, 'but you've actually made Stuart seem like the sensible one in the family.'

I sighed. 'That's because he *is* sensible, Mum.' Apart from his exotic jam fetishes, that is.

She snorted. 'Your brother is not the point of my call. What I want to know is when were you going to tell me?'

'About what?' I asked, feigning innocence, and deciding that Stuart was in big trouble.

'Are you serious? About everything!'

That was the trouble; so much had happened in the past few weeks I didn't quite know where to start – or just how much Stuart had spilled. 'Mum, look, it's been a rough start to the year, I've been really busy, then things with Mark—'

'But not too busy to buy a house!'

'Ah,' I said. 'Well…' I swallowed, chickened out again. 'It's a long story, and you were in China, so I didn't want to bother you—'

'I wasn't in China!'

'Oh? Well, I know you had a trip. In Asia somewhere?'

'Bangor – it's in Maine,' she explained, snorting. 'And that was weeks ago and you could still speak to me. That's what mobiles were invented for, Victoria. Why haven't you returned my calls? Stuart said that you and Mark—'

I was going to kill Stuart. 'Sorry, Mum. Like I said, I've been swamped. I'm sorry I didn't tell you about the house, but I'm actually in a meeting at the moment, so can I phone you back?'

'Nice try, Victoria. Open the door.'

I frowned. 'What? Mum, I'm not in London—'

'Yes, I know. Not that you had the grace to tell me you were leaving or actually moving cities.'

'Mum, I'm sorry. Look, I'm coming up to London next week for a meeting, maybe we can catch up then? I can tell you all about the house?'

There was a second's silence, during which I enjoyed a short-lived moment of relief.

'Maybe you can tell me after you open the door?'

My heart skipped a beat. I looked up, my eyes scanning the living room, then widening in horror as it took in the porthole window – she was standing on the gangplank outside.

'Oh God!'

'Indeed.'

My mother held onto her blue leather Hermès bag with both hands as she stepped inside. Her helmet of bobbed, pencil-straight, iron-hued hair didn't move, and neither did her mouth, which remained in a fixed grimace.

She raised an eyebrow at the surroundings, her eyes raking me in the process. I found myself smoothing down my T-shirt, wishing I'd run a comb through my long, untidy curls.

'Did you actually sign a lease for this?'

I resisted the urge to move my abandoned coffee cup and tidy up the overflowing table and sofa. I hated that she had this effect on me.

'Look, Mum, if you're here simply to be insulting or cruel then I suggest you go.'

She set her bag down on the table. 'Cruel? That's a bit rich, don't you think? I haven't heard from you in weeks. I've only now recovered from what happened to your brother, and then I find out that you've decided to run away from your life and that you never even thought to let me, or your father, know about it. I mean,' she said, looking around with distaste, 'what exactly were you thinking?'

I loved my father, but he hardly ever phoned me, relying on getting any family news from my mother. The last time he'd called was to ask me to bring the spare keys round as he'd left his at his office. That was almost a year ago. It wasn't that he wasn't a good father – he was. He just wasn't the best communicator. Maybe it was an inherited trait.

Before I could retort, she held up her hand. 'I'm not here to fight.'

'You're not? Well!'

'No, I'm not. I love you, and I'm worried about you.' She sat down and gave me a searching look. 'I just want to understand.'

How did she do that? Go from being the most frustrating human being I knew to the person I most wanted to speak to all in the space of a minute?

'I know you and Mark have had problems – I've been worried about you both for a while. It hasn't been the happiest time.'

I sat down and sighed. 'How much did Stuart tell you?'

'Not everything, but I gather it's a permanent separation this time?'

I nodded. 'Divorce.'

She took my hand. 'I'm so sorry.'

I squeezed her fingers.

'I didn't realise it had got that bad.'

I gave a sad laugh. 'Neither had I. After Stuart's accident, I came home thinking that I understood what was important, that nine years of marriage was worth fighting for. Turns out he'd been doing some thinking too – just not about me.'

She closed her eyes. 'So there *was* someone else.'

Mum had heard a while back that I'd suspected Mark was cheating. But of course he'd denied it *then*.

'Yeah.'

'God, he's an arse! I mean, he was always a pompous sort, you know, but this?'

'Yeah, well. Look, I'm not defending him or anything, but he had a point… I haven't spent almost any time at home in the past eighteen months – if I haven't been on site doing research, I've been on tour. It hasn't been easy on us.'

She shook her head. 'You know, Victoria, he played that card a lot, but there was nothing stopping him from coming with you, especially when he wasn't that busy himself. It's not like you had children, or he worked in an office and couldn't get away. He didn't need to be at home. Most of the hotels would have accommodated him as well while you were working. I mean, when you first got together, in the beginning, you used to do it for him. You rather enjoyed it, too. You got to travel, see the world.'

She was right, of course. Mark and I had met shortly after I'd gotten my first book contract, at a Christmas party thrown by our publisher. Back then he was the most encouraging person I'd ever met.

I'd been attracted to the confident, intelligent man who wrote biographies on some of history's most prominent war leaders. In the beginning of our relationship, I found it exciting to tag along to book tours, visit exotic locations and dream of one day having him come along to some of my own.

And he was supportive, in the beginning. He joined me for my first tour in America. He wrote the foreword to my second biography. And on our first wedding anniversary he suggested we go to India so that I could get primary research for my book featuring the love story that surrounded the Taj Mahal.

Things started to change for us when the recession hit. There were fewer people buying books about war generals, and it was the first real setback in his career. My books, however, held more of a general interest and had an enduring appeal. I didn't know why that was. I wrote and researched what I cared about. To me, that was the important thing. It wasn't about how much money I could make. But then it's easy to think that way when you're doing well.

Mark didn't start off a bitter man, but somehow, in the last five years, that's what he'd become. I don't think he liked it any more than I did.

I didn't know what I thought about the whole situation any more. All I knew was that I was tired of feeling like we were on opposing sides, tired of feeling guilty, tired of always underselling myself, dimming a light that perhaps he hadn't really wanted me to dim in the first place.

'I don't think it was that he was resentful of my success so much as he was resentful of his own failures. By tagging along with me, I think he saw it as admitting defeat.'

'But couldn't it have just been a show of support?' Mum asked.

'I don't know, Mum. Maybe. He tried, but I don't think he could let it go. They say you can't have two cooks in the kitchen, maybe it's the same thing.'

'I don't know if that's true.' She shook her head. 'There are lots of famous artist couples.'

'Maybe it depends on the person.'

She sighed. 'Maybe, but don't you think that he could have just sucked it up? Haven't women being doing that for years?'

I laughed. Typical Mum! She ran a business that supported female entrepreneurship and was all about equal rights, but sometimes she could be rather sexist herself and didn't realise that it was a two-way thing.

'He tried to do it, you know.'

'Tried what?'

'To put his own ambitions aside.'

'Did you ask him to do that?'

'No.'

She shrugged. 'Well, just because you were achieving some level of success—'

'Look, Mum, it wasn't just about success or failure or our careers. It was that once you took that out of the picture, we didn't have very much. You know, Ivy said something to me a while back that has haunted me ever since.'

'Ivy?'

'Your daughter-in-law?'

'Yes, I know who she is. What did she say?'

'Well, she said that love should feel good. Actually, she said that Oprah had said it, but you know what I mean.'

'Love should feel good?' she repeated. 'What does that mean? Typical bloody hippie!'

I laughed. If it wasn't quantifiable or on a spreadsheet that she could scrutinise, my mother didn't have time for it.

'It means that if you love someone, and they love you, for the most part it should feel good. Obviously you can't have it that way every day, and there's bound to be tough times, but on the whole that's how it should be.'

She looked at me. 'And your marriage... didn't?'

I shook my head. 'Not for a very long time.'

The expression in her eyes was sad. 'I'm sorry. But,' she said, looking around, moving her linen pants away from my stack of papers, 'did you really need to come here, of all places? I mean, whose boat is this anyway? And what's this about buying a house – did you really? This isn't like you, you know.'

As if I didn't know. I was her daughter, wasn't I? Other mothers teach their children 'Mind your manners' and 'If you don't have anything nice to say, don't say anything at all'. Mine taught me the difference between long- and short-term investments, and why cost and worth are two separate issues, long before the age of ten.

'You should have come to us. You didn't need to come and live here, for goodness' sake!'

As if 'here' was a drug-infested housing estate instead of a pretty marina in a picturesque part of western Cornwall. I rolled my eyes. Apparently, Mum's sympathy was only good for ten minutes.

'Mum, I like it here – a lot actually. It's small but—'

'That's an understatement!'

I ignored that. 'It's temporary. I've signed a lease for a few months and I've taken a break for a while. It's doing me good while I get on with the work on the house.'

She shook her head. 'So you did buy a house?'

I nodded. 'Mark and I are selling our London home – it's on the market now.'

'I know.'

'Oh?'

'And how do you think I found out? I drove past and saw the bloody sign!'

'I thought maybe Stuart told you?'

'He did eventually. I tried to call you, then I tried Mark, and finally Stuart.'

I sighed. She'd no doubt bullied it out of him.

'Well, I could have a chat with this leaseholder of yours – clearly you weren't in the right frame of mind. And the house…'

'No, Mum.'

She raised an eyebrow.

'I appreciate it,' I said, putting my hand on hers. In a weird way I really did appreciate how hard she fought for all of us. 'But I'm a grown woman. I like it here, I've bought a house that I'm going to fix up – it'll be good for me.'

'Good for you?'

'Yeah, who knows?'

She seemed to be fighting some sort of internal struggle, probably the need to go on the warpath versus the need to still have children who spoke to her.

She half laughed, half smiled. 'Okay, I will be supportive. If that's what you need.'

I nodded. 'It is. And if you're really good I'll show you all my rot…'

'Good God!' she balked.

Later that afternoon, after Mum left, I phoned Stuart.

'Hello, Judas,' I said.

'Ah, Smudge, I'm sorry.'

'And you gave her my *address*! I'm tempted to come past and inflict a few new injuries. Couldn't you have even warned me?'

'I did!'

I checked my phone and saw that I had one new message. It read, '*Terrorist attack alert, descending on your doorstep as we speak.*'

'Ah.'

'I thought it gave you an hour at least to make a run for it…'

'Sadly not.'

CHAPTER SIXTEEN

To make it up to me, Stuart and Ivy came past a few days later, along with my little niece, Holly, and a houseboat-warming gift – a set of herbs in containers and a rather impressive supply of homemade vegetable beer from his Sea Cottage label.

The idea of vegetable beer didn't sound all that appealing, though I was thrilled to see Holly, who had grown so much in the past few weeks.

I showed them the boat while I held onto my niece, loving how she gurgled up at me.

'Love the portholes!' Ivy exclaimed, looking at the one in the living room.

'Yeah, they're the best,' I agreed, showing her the cushion curtains.

'What's this?' asked Stuart, eyeing the small posy that I had taken from the upstairs room at the cottage, tied with the sea-green ribbon. It was sitting on top of the diary.

'Some sort of posy, I found it at the cottage.'

I didn't mention the rolled-up note that had been with it, or the coded diary. I wouldn't know where to begin.

'It's amazing how preserved it is,' said Ivy.

'Blue thistle,' said Stuart. 'Really cool – quite rare.'

'Blue thistle?' I asked.

He picked it up and examined it closely. 'Yeah, definitely. You got this at the cottage, you said?'

'Yeah.'

'Strange.'

'Why's it strange?' asked Ivy, sitting down in the egg chair.

'Well, it's not a common flower, is it? I don't think it grows here at all. I mean, nowadays you can get almost anything online, or at a flower market, but this would have been, what, thirty, forty years ago?'

I shrugged. 'Longer, I think. From what I've heard, the cottage hasn't been occupied since the thirties.'

'Wow!' whistled Stuart. 'I can't believe it's so well preserved. And, yeah, someone had to have gone to a lot of trouble to get this. Especially back then. It's really beautiful. Different.'

I thought of the code. The words 'My love' written in Tilly's cipher text, the unusual flowers. It spoke of a devotion that, along with the secrecy that surrounded it, was perhaps as unusual as the blooms accompanying it.

CHAPTER SEVENTEEN

Cornwall, 1905

Tilly

It was spying, and I'd get in trouble if anyone found out, but I had to know if he was real. If any of it was.

I'd tried to put the house out of my mind, along with the soldier, and the pair of men's trousers in the buggy that was going somewhere I wasn't allowed to visit and no one else seemed to be all that bothered about. For everyone else, life had gone back to normal. It's what I was trying to do too.

But that was until I saw the boy. No one had said anything about *him*.

I was lying on the grass by the little brook, far away from the house – my ritual escape from Celine – reading an illicit chapter from a novel that she disapproved of when I saw him.

He was around my age, with dark curly hair, standing in the middle of the water with a fox in his arms. But he couldn't have been standing *on* the water, could he? And it wasn't an actual fox, was it? As soon as I stood up, he turned towards me in surprise, his eyes wide and so very blue. By the time I'd managed to wade through the ice-cold water to get to the other side, my skirts dragging me down, boots filled with riverwater, there was no trace of him. He was gone.

When I got back to the house, my lips were blue and I was shivering rather theatrically. Celine gave me a scolding that lasted half the evening, and ended with her favourite admonishment, one I heard at least twice a day. 'Your sister was never like this.'

'She was always a lady,' I echoed, while I defrosted by the fire. I was wary of this admonishment. Wary of Rose's perfect example.

In the morning I'd made up my mind.

When Edmund had spoken about the house while they were lighting the fire in the library, and I was hidden in the window seat behind the curtain, he told Martha, the parlour maid, that they were building it at the very bottom of the estate, past the fields and gardens to where the land met the sea and sky. Exactly where Father had forbidden us to go.

Martha had told Edmund that he couldn't be right. 'Nothing but cliffs there – that's no place for a house. Someone's pulling your leg.'

I told myself I wouldn't linger long enough for anyone to see me. I'd go just as far as I could so that I could find it – just so that I could see it for myself. See if the boy was part of it. *Then* I could come back and forget about it.

The next morning, I set off before anyone was awake, slipping past Celine's room on tiptoes, my heart thrumming in excitement. There was frost in the air, and my feet were half-frozen when I slipped my boots on outside and set off.

If I were brave, like one of the children in the stories I read – in the books that Celine disapproved of – I'd saddle up a horse and ride out. But I wasn't, nor did I know how to saddle up a horse all by myself, or ride well enough to go without a saddle. I wasn't a natural horsewoman. Not like Rose anyway, who was jumping fences by the time she was seven, while I could barely keep Jewel on a straight path.

So I walked all along the brook, where I'd found the boy, past the empty daffodil fields, to where the cultivated earth changed from perfect rows to wild scrubland, full of wind-battered seagrass and plants that bent sideways in the wind, like old men walking in a storm to the very edge of the earth, to the sheer cliffs and the green sea that churned beneath.

Not a house for miles; nothing but cliffs.

If I hadn't seen the builders trekking their materials past the fields, I might even have thought they had made it all up.

'You're looking for it, aren't you?' asked a voice from behind. I whipped around.

It was the boy, the fox at his heels, like a dog. They were both staring at me. The boy's eyes were very pale and blue, like two chips taken out of the summer sky. His hair was messy and wild, dark curls fell all across his forehead. The fox sat at his heels as if he were contemplating his words. 'Aye, you'd almost think from 'ere that there was *no* house.'

My mouth flopped open.

'But that's the whole point, ye ken?' he said, smiling like he was letting me in on a secret. Which, I suppose, he was.

'Who are you?' I asked.

The boy smiled widely, his teeth even. 'Who are you?'

'I'm Tilly,' I said, holding out a prim hand so we could be properly introduced. 'Tilly Asprey.' I wanted him to know that I wasn't completely trespassing, even if I was.

He shook my hand, his fingers warm, and introduced me to the fox. 'This is Arthur.'

'Arthur!' I said, delighted that the creature had a human name.

The fox looked at me with solemn eyes, then turned and walked away.

'Oh no, please come back,' I said, watching him leave.

The boy shrugged, nonchalant. 'He can't be hanging about all day. Got fox business to take care of.'

I wondered what a fox's business consisted of. 'Like what?'

The boy waggled his brows mysteriously. 'Oh, I've never asked.'

I laughed but then pulled a serious face. 'So there *is* a house?' I asked, looking at the cliffs in doubt.

'Oh yes… with a secret entranceway and everything.'

I looked at him, and then narrowed my eyes. 'You're just making fun of me.' I didn't like it when people did that.

'I'm not!' he protested. 'Look…' He pointed to the cliff wall. 'See there, in the middle.'

I looked. For a long while I saw nothing. Then, suddenly, I saw a hairbreadth's gap.

'See it?'

I nodded.

'That's how you get in. Though you could get in from the sea, I think, if you came by boat. There's steps in the cliff that take you down to the cove. I'm sure that's what the old pirates used, back in the day.'

I looked at him in surprise. I'd lived here my whole life and I didn't know about those steps. He smiled and shook his head. 'I shouldn't have shown you the cliff entrance, you know. My Da won't like it. It's meant to be a secret.'

'What's meant to be a secret?' I asked. 'The house?'

He shook his head. 'Not the house, exactly, just where it is.'

'Why?'

He shrugged.

'Why did you tell me where to find it then? What if I told?'

He looked at me. 'You won't,' he said.

'How do you know?'

'Because Arthur trusts you,' he said, as the fox came bounding up to him, back from his fox business, and climbed the boy's legs and arms like a tree, till he came to rest on his shoulder, as though the boy was some forest-dwelling sprite. He was a world away from deportment lessons, Father's rules and Celine's tireless crusade to turn me into a replica of my sister.

'I'm Fen,' he said. 'You've already met Arthur. Go on, you can touch him – he won't bite.'

I held out a hand in trepidation and touched his tail, which was springy and silken all at the same time. I was surprised to see the fox close his eyes. I didn't know foxes could be like this. Maybe they weren't. Maybe it was only with Fen.

'Do you like boats?'

'What?' I asked in surprise, looking from Arthur to Fen.

'I found an old dinghy near the river, want to see it?'

What I wanted to do, of course, was to see the house. To ask what he knew about it. Did he live there? Did he know who did? But more than anything, I realised, I wanted to spend time with this odd boy who charmed foxes and knew secrets that I didn't, and who wasn't afraid of sharing them with me.

We walked over the scrubland, through tall seagrass that rustled in the wind. When a flock of seagulls cried above, Fen whistled in response, his call a perfect imitation. I stared in wonder as they came swooping low.

It was only as we got to the brook that I saw that there was something wrong with his leg, which seemed to twist ever so slightly inward. I hadn't noticed while we'd been walking side by side. It was only as he got onto the rocks ahead of me, crossing the little stream, I saw. He caught me looking.

'It was an accident, when I were little,' he explained. 'It's not normal looking, I suppose, but it works fine. Only gets sore in winter, when the muscles get cold, but it's never slowed me down or nothing – wouldn't let it.'

I looked at his blue eyes, at the fox on his shoulder, his wild, curly hair, the way he seemed to be made of magic itself, and I thought of how everyone seemed hell-bent on making me just like Rose. 'Normal is boring.'

CHAPTER EIGHTEEN

Cornwall, present day

The old photocopier in the Waters Solicitors Office made a sonorous hum as it spat out page after page of Tilly's diary.

We'd decided to split it every four pages and to swap it as we went. Adam came up with the idea that we could take photographs of the work we'd transcribed and send them to each other. I was touched by his enthusiasm.

I was surprised that he wanted to get started straight away, but he explained that it was like solving a case – and around here there were very few of those.

Adam made us coffee from an ageing percolator while I divided up the pages. There was a part of me that still felt a small residue of apprehension at the thought of having someone else look at her diary. I'd developed a soft spot for Tilly and was reluctant to have her over-examined. I didn't know what Adam would think of her. What he'd feel about reading her private thoughts. It had been a safe place for her, something she had never intended anyone to read, and now she had not one but two unintended readers.

It turned out to be an unnecessary fear, as Adam took to Tilly straight away.

One evening, after a long day of working on the cottage with Jack and Will, I got a text at 11.15 p.m. from Adam: '*You've got to read this!*'

Attached was a picture of two transcribed pages of Tilly's diary. This was followed quickly by another, more apologetic, message: '*Sorry. Hope I didn't wake you? Bloody Americans and our enthusiasm…*'

I texted back quickly.

'*Don't worry about it. Never get to sleep before 1 a.m. on the best of days.*'

'*So you're a night owl?*' he asked.

'*Always, only way I get anything done.*'

'*In that case, feel like company?*'

I blinked in surprise, feeling my throat go a little dry, and then I had to remind myself that we were simply friends. What was wrong with a bit of company? I had a quick mental flash of his lazy smile, and the way it made his blue eyes crinkle, but pushed it aside. I wanted to find out what had got him so animated, that was all, I told myself firmly.

'*Why not?*' I replied.

My pulse began to race. I poured myself another glass of wine, drank half of it for Dutch courage, and then quickly went and changed my pyjama bottoms for something slightly more appealing.

A few seconds later there was a soft knock on the door and I let him in, noticing, as I opened the door, the gentle sounds of the river at night – the lapping of the water, crickets on the banks and, in the distance, a low, still hum.

'Evening,' he said with an easy grin.

'Evening,' I replied.

'Wine?' he said, managing in his confident, American way not to seem at all bashful.

'Why not?'

I went and fetched him a glass from behind the multi-coloured curtain in the kitchen. When I came back and filled up his glass from the bottle on the coffee table, he said, mock seriously, his blue eyes solemn, 'So, what exactly have you done to me?'

I blinked, suddenly nervous. 'I'm sorry?' I said, eyes wide, reddening slightly.

He handed me a few sheaves of paper. 'Here's my sleep-killer. It's a bit like a spy novel, in that every time I think I'll stop, it keeps getting better and I find myself unlocking more and more. I never knew my great-grandfather had a disability. Or that he was originally from Yorkshire.'

I breathed out. Of course he meant the diary. 'So you caught up,' I said with an approving nod.

'Yeah, I was meant to be filing something and lost track of time at the office,' he laughed.

I grinned. 'I can see how that could happen.'

He took a seat in the egg chair and I handed him his glass of wine.

'You know,' he said, with a self-deprecating laugh, 'in the beginning, when I was reading it, I really thought that it might have been a secret cottage, the way she seemed so convinced that it was, but that doesn't make sense, does it? I mean, especially now.'

'Yes, I know what you mean. I think you have to remember that she's telling the story the way she remembers it, from when she was a child. The cottage was unlikely to have really been a secret.'

He nodded. 'Yeah, it was only later, after I read those' – he pointed at his freshly transcribed sheets – 'that I saw that it wasn't intended to be secret so much as private.'

That made sense. Especially considering that most of the staff knew that the cottage had been built. There were certainly enough rumours circulating. It would be easy, as a child, to see the house in the cliffs as a place of mystery and secrets, even now.

'What did you find out that made you think that?' I asked, taking a sip of wine.

'After I found out that my great-grandfather had helped run the flower farm.'

I sat back, closing my eyes as I realised. 'Oh God, I should have remembered…' I said, getting up and fishing around in my backpack. I pulled out the book on Victorian farming that I'd gotten from the London Library, and flicked to the page with the photograph of the Aspreys.

'This is a photograph of John Asprey with his daughters, Rose and Matilda. Standing next to them is Michael Waters,' I said, handing it to him.

'So that's him?' he said in surprise, staring at the grainy image of the tall, strong-looking man. 'My great-great grandfather.'

'Did you know he worked at Idyllwild?'

He shook his head. 'I had no idea.'

CHAPTER NINETEEN

Cornwall, 1905

Tilly

For weeks I had been hearing about the new head gardener at Idyllwild, but a fresh whisper pricked my ears while I was reading Walter Scott behind the velvet curtain in the library one wet afternoon.

At first they were the ordinary rumours, the ones that always surround a new appointment. The usual grumblings that always seem to accompany change when the newcomer was that most dreaded of things – an outsider.

Edmund, the footman, said that many of the workers complained that he was full of new ideas – particularly for someone who had never worked with daffodils before.

'Well, I heard Mr Davies tell our William,' Martha whispered, 'that he likes to disappear.'

'Disappear? Where?'

'No one knows.'

It was only later that I realised they were talking about Fen's father. It should have occurred to me much earlier. Father was nothing if not practical. If Fen's family moved here, there was bound to be a reason. It appeared that everyone downstairs was wondering why my father had replaced Mr Rivers, the previous gardener, and appointed someone whose background had very little to do with horticulture.

'Mr Rivers has been given the tenancy of the east farm,' said Edmund. 'Apparently he's happy with it, but he was surprised. The move was rather sudden, so I hear.'

'What I don't understand is why couldn't Lord Asprey give Mr Waters the east farm instead of moving Mr Rivers?' said Martha.

'Search me. My uncle – you know he works at Idyllwild? – asked his lordship. He just said they were trying something new. Something that would put the farm on the map.'

'Do you think that's likely with someone like Mr Waters, someone who has never worked on a flower farm before?'

'I don't like to speak against someone who has done battle for his country, but I do believe in having the right man for the job. If it goes wrong, his lordship will only have himself to blame. Apparently, Mr Waters was happy to work on the east farm, but it was Lord Asprey who insisted that he head up Idyllwild.'

'But why? Why would he do that?'

'Lord knows. I just hope it doesn't blow up in their faces. It's the biggest earner on the estate. I can't see why he'd risk it, myself.'

'Nor I,' said Martha, before they left.

I peeked out from behind the curtain with a frown, wondering about all I'd heard. Why I hadn't realised that Fen's father had been brought here for a purpose after all.

It wasn't only the staff who were wondering about Father's new appointment. A few days later, when my grandmother came to stay, I realised that even she had heard the rumours.

'So I hear you've gotten rid of Mr Rivers?' she asked.

Father looked up from the latest efforts of our cook, Mrs Price, and what we'd been told was bouillon, and raised an eyebrow. 'I haven't "gotten rid" of anyone. Mr Rivers has simply been assigned the east farm. He is more than up for the task, and I'm delighted to have someone with his background championing a rather difficult piece of land.'

Mother made a disapproving noise in the back of her throat. 'Yes, and in turn we now have a former turnip farmer as the new head gardener of Idyllwild. But John does enjoy his little experiments,' she said, placing her spoon in the bowl, which came to rest, upright and dead centre, like an arrow in a target in the tar-like soup. 'If only we didn't have to endure them quite *so much*.'

'Helena,' Father said warningly.

She gave him a tight, cold smile. 'It's only the family business, darling,' she said, arching an eyebrow. 'Heaven forbid I make any attempt to take the fruits of our labours seriously.'

The real difference about having Fen's father work at the farm was the difference it wrought on Father. He had always been studious. Words like formidable, intractable and hardworking had always applied to him. But now it seemed like there was a greater purpose in his step, and a lighter cast to his features. The only thing that we could really put it down to was the fact that Fen's father had started at the farm, and perhaps, at last, he had someone who believed in his vision for Idyllwild.

We'd find Father in his study, surrounded by plans for expansion. Every week there appeared to be new partnerships and ideas for hybrids. Behind closed doors, my father had long been accused of being a businessman, but now it was a title he wore with more than a degree of pride.

'Honestly, it's like he's forgotten that he's meant to be a gentleman,' Rose complained one morning over toast, after Father got up to check on some new farm equipment that he said would improve the harvest.

'Why does he keep on with this, Helena?' asked Granny. 'Susan Prester-Harvald says in her letter that you've twice declined dinner due to that farm. I mean, people will talk.'

'Don't be ridiculous,' I said. 'Surely no one expects him to abandon his business for the sake of a dinner?'

Mother pursed her lips. 'Matilda, you are far too young to understand this now, but the truth of the matter is that people are already starting to talk.'

'Father is in over his head,' agreed Rose.

'Rose!' said Mother.

Granny shrugged. 'No, I think she's right. He's appointed someone who doesn't really know what he's doing, and he himself hasn't got all that much practical experience.'

'I should hope not!' said Rose, horrified.

'Oh, Rose, you're insufferable,' I sighed.

'Well,' continued Mother, 'he's getting enough practical experience now, as he's having to carry the load. He won't say it, of course, but I think his sense of duty to this awful man may just be the ruin of us all.'

I shook my head at her. 'I think that's a bit melodramatic.'

Mother sipped her tea. 'I doubt I am being dramatic *enough*.'

CHAPTER TWENTY

Present day

When I was at university, my friends and I made a pact. Which was that no one ever lets a friend phone or message their ex after they've been drinking. This rule was especially enforced after midnight.

Someone should have told my husband this.

'I know I'm not meant to do this. I'm an idiot. I'm so sorry, Smudge. But it's the truth. I'm in hell. I miss you so much.'

I drank two glasses of whisky and tried to get the text out of my head. When I had convinced myself that what I was feeling wasn't pain but simply mild curiosity, I phoned Mark back. I am, of course, an idiot too.

He answered on the first ring.

I didn't realise that I was mildly drunk until I began to slur. 'So whys – I mean, why – did you do' – I paused, concentrating hard – 'why did you just do that? Send me that. You're right, it *is* mean.'

'I never said it was mean.'

'You said stupid.'

'I said I was an idiot.'

'Oh.'

'Are you drunk?' He sounded a little amused. I pictured his smile. I hated how I missed his smile.

'*Of course* I'm drunk. Aren't you?'

'No, I said it because I love you. I never stopped loving you and I'm an idiot.'

I found myself sobering fast.

'So, um, does that mean that you and her—'

'I miss you, Smudge. I don't know what I'm doing.'

I tasted the tears before I even realised that I was crying. In my fog of booze and pain, I sat with the phone by my ear. Almost a full minute passed before I realised that he hadn't said anything real, anything new – not really. 'So, what you're saying is that you're still with Jess, but you miss me, is that it?'

There was silence for some time, and then he said, softly, 'Yes.'

I took a shuddering breath of air. 'You know, Mark, I don't know what I want either. I tell everyone that I have it all figured out, and at the time it feels all figured out.' I gave a grim laugh. 'I had a surprisingly insightful chat with Mum about it.'

'Oh God, sorry.'

I took a breath. 'Mark, I don't know why I can be fine until I hear your voice. I don't know why it is that I still care what you have to say, or why for even a second I thought you were going to say something else, that you would honestly—'

'So you want me to leave her, is that it?' he asked baldly.

'Mark, I know what I want and it's not this at all – this horrible, messy thing that you've created between us. We need to file for a divorce, please, so we can move on.'

I hung up and crawled back onto the couch.

In the morning, I woke up to find Adam shaking my arm. 'Victoria?'

'Hmm?'

'Victoria?'

He had a very nice voice, I realised. Very deep, rather husky. The sort of voice that could advertise athletic men zooming along mountains then storming into a casino in a suit, all the while smelling supposedly of Aqua Velva. I had a little laugh, and then groaned as my head felt like it might split apart.

I looked up to see a pair of very concerned, blue eyes. He was wearing faded denims and a navy jumper that made his eyes ever bluer still.

'You look nice,' I said, somewhat sleepily.

'You alright?'

I frowned. Then I looked down. I was wearing one shoe, and had gone to bed with the whisky bottle, which was wedged beneath my chin like a rather sad teddy bear. It had left behind a large, wet puddle on the sofa, which I had slept upon in my drunken, pain-soaked funk.

I didn't need a mirror to know that I had mascara tracks running across my cheeks. I sat up. The world spun. I could only imagine the bird's nest that was my hair.

'I'm fine,' I said with a wry grin. 'Why do you ask?'

His mouth curled up in a half smile. 'Yeah, sorry. I was knocking. Apparently Jack Abrams came past but you didn't answer.'

'What?'

'The builder. Said he was dropping off the sample tiles for the kitchen. Apparently he tried knocking, shouting…'

I cringed.

Adam laughed. 'Said he could hear snoring, so he wasn't worried.'

'Oh my God,' I said, burying my face in my hands. 'No!'

Adam waggled my foot. 'Don't worry about it.'

'Aaagh!'

'Okay, right. First things first, here's a coffee.'

I opened my eyes and held out my hand. 'You are a saint, thank you,' I said, setting it down on the coffee table. I got up, fetched a kitchen towel and attempted to soak up some of the spilled whisky.

'It smells like a distillery in here,' I said. 'Exactly the type of thing you want your landlord to find.'

He winked, and gave me that lazy smile of his.

I felt my stomach flip, an unbidden reaction to his smile.

'Don't worry about it,' he said. 'Drink your coffee.'

I sat on a bit of the sofa that wasn't wet and took a sip. It was good.

'So...' he said, his blue eyes pinned on me, 'wanna tell me about it?'

I looked at him above the rim of the styrofoam cup. 'Ah, that. Well, that was simply the result of a chat with the soon to be ex-husband last night...'

He snorted. 'Looks like it went rather well.'

I had a short laugh. 'Yes. Have I told you about him? About what happened?' I felt I owed him some sort of explanation at least, in payment for the coffee and the sympathy.

He shook his head. 'Not really. I gathered you were separated...'

When I gave him a curious look, he said, 'Well, when I researched who you were, I saw you were married. But when you bought the cottage and signed the lease for the boat it was only for you.'

'Ah, you're a good detective,' I said.

'Years of reading crime novels,' he agreed.

'Anyway... Well, divorce is the plan, and after last night, well, it can't happen soon enough.'

'Is that why he phoned, to ask for a divorce?'

'No, actually. I think he wanted us to get back together.'

'Oh,' he said, with a frown. 'Would you?'

I wondered what he must have thought. If my ex had this effect on me, surely there were still feelings involved?

I shook my head. 'No. I think this was me realising that, even if I wanted to, I couldn't be in that relationship any longer. I've known it for a long time, but last night it was just really driven home to me that we aren't good for each other.'

I told him a little about what had happened, what my life used to be like before.

'Since I've moved here, I feel like I'm finally living, you know? Like there's room for me,' I said, unconsciously echoing Tilly's words from her letter describing how she had felt when she'd met Fen. The same thing had happened to me since I'd left my marriage.

'Room?'

'Yeah, for a long time, it was like I wasn't able to be me.'

I told him about how I used to sleep in Stan's spare room for a little longer than was strictly necessary when I was on a research trip, just to avoid going home. That sometimes I booked extra-long trips or convinced myself that I actually did need to see something in person for my work, when a photograph or a transcript would have worked just as well, just so that I could avoid going home and facing whatever he'd had time to fester on in my absence. Even though I was making things worse, doing the very thing he accused me of so that we kept repeating the same toxic pattern we'd created, I couldn't help it. I was tired of being the target for his disappointments instead of what I wanted, which was to be the soft place he could fall.

'I don't think I've told anyone else that,' I admitted. 'For the first time in years, I'm enjoying my life. I know that a lot of it has to do with finally having time to myself, time to lie in past five in the morning, but it's more than that. I think the main reason I could never get back with Mark now is that I'm tired of the constant pain, you know?'

'I do.'

I looked at him. Adam had been silent about why he was really here in Cornwall. I knew he was helping his uncle shut down the business, but I had always sensed that there was more to it than that.

'Has that got to do with why you're really here? In England?'

He closed his eyes for a second and nodded. ' I was supposed to be getting married – this week, in fact.'

'What?' I said, sitting up, my eyes huge.

'Yeah, if things had gone the way they were meant to I'd be back in Connecticut, getting married this coming Friday.'

'What happened? Did – did you get cold feet?'

His laugh had a cracked sound to it. '*Me?* No. But she did, about seven months ago, just after we'd bought a house together, fitted it out with furniture that we'd hand-picked. She told me that she was leaving me to go and live with her boss in New York.'

'What?'

'Yeah, it seems she'd been having an affair with him for years, and now that she had decided to move on with me, he'd finally worked up the courage to leave his wife. A New York sort of fairy tale, just like the movies. *Oh wait,*' he said, a sarcastic edge to his voice.

'Oh my God, I'm so sorry, Adam.'

He shrugged. 'Yeah. It wasn't – hasn't been – a great time.'

'I can imagine.'

'And the house?'

'Had to sell it. Couldn't live there, you know.'

I did know. I was tempted to offer him his own whisky bottle. Thankfully Adam had a better idea.

'Okay,' he said decisively. 'Why don't you get showered – depanda yourself – and we'll go out for breakfast? Forget about exes and discuss instead how on earth someone goes about taming a fox?'

'Or a wild little girl?'

He nodded. 'That too.'

I grinned. 'I'd love that.'

In the streets of Tregollan spring was like a whisper everyone was straining to hear. There were colourful pots outside shops brimming with flowers, and a few hopefuls had put tables and chairs on the pavements.

We had breakfast at the Harbour Cafe watching the leisure boats in the distance, and spoke about our lives before we moved to Cornwall.

'Did you always want to be a lawyer?' I asked.

'Yes.'

I looked at him in surprise and started to laugh. 'No one ever says yes to that question!'

His eyes crinkled at the corners. 'I told you I had four sisters growing up, right?'

I nodded.

'Well, as you can imagine, there was a lot of fighting, scream-ing, hair-pulling, people sitting on you – my sister Stacey's trademark. So one day I watched some movie where a lawyer goes to prison and starts settling all these fights, and that was it, it's what I wanted to be, if only to avoid being sat on again.'

'Seriously?'

He laughed. 'No. But when you grow up with four conniv-ing siblings, justice does become rather important. And you, did you always want to be a writer?'

I took a sip of my cappuccino. 'Not a writer exactly, though I do love that part. I've always loved history; it feels very alive to me. Though if it had been up to my mother I would have done something in the sciences.'

'Really?'

'Yeah. I, um, did really well at it, but just because you're good at something doesn't mean you have to do it,' I said, not mentioning the scholarships I'd turned down, the IQ tests that had all my teachers and family wildly excited for years, steering me into a path I didn't want.

'I agree with you.'

I looked at him in surprise.

'Yeah, well, in America it's a big thing – "What will you become?" Everyone is so focused on it. I think people laugh at the idea of being passionate about what you do – it's almost a cliché nowadays – but the truth is, when someone *wants* to do something, that's when the magic happens. You hear about breakthroughs in science only because the people behind it were devoted to it. That's what it takes.'

I looked at him. 'You're a good lawyer. You know, for years I've always felt a little guilty about "wasting my potential", as my careers advisor put it.'

'You haven't wasted your potential, Victoria. We need stories in order to understand ourselves, for good or bad, to be inspired or horrified, it's how we cope with being human and how we decide what type of person we will become.'

I looked at him in surprise. 'I agree completely.'

He grinned. 'I'm not just a pretty face, right?'

'Well, it is rather pretty,' I said, then blushed like an idiot.

CHAPTER TWENTY-ONE

Cornwall, 1905

Tilly

That winter, despite temperatures that hit well below freezing, I had something I'd never had before, something that kept me warm, even on those cold nights.

I had a friend – I had Fen.

The first friend I'd had who lived in the village. The first friend who wasn't a girl and wasn't a relation.

I'd never had a brother. Only my cousin Tim – and he'd been a young man when I was a little girl, with no time for adventures and games.

Rose and I, as the two only siblings, should have been close, but our opposing personalities put us at war more often than not. Perhaps it would have been easier if every step I took wasn't found wanting in relation to Rose's, or if I'd had less of a rebellious, questioning nature. 'Why do you feel the need to question everything?' Father once remarked. 'You make your life harder.'

But for once, this wasn't something I was overthinking. As soon as Celine was done with lessons, I'd tear off, her calls to me to 'Take another jacket, child', or 'Wear your wellies if you're going out' fading into the distance as I joined Fen and Arthur by the brook, where he'd show me how to bend a reed, blow a

tune through the grass pipe, or climb a tree just the right way to
see a squirrel skating past.

Afternoons became our time, because that was when Fen was
done with his chores. Many of our expeditions centred around
food, as he was always hungry.

Unlike Rose, who cut her food into the smallest bites and
chewed each morsel with slow deliberation, Fen ate while we
walked, taking hungry bites out of the still-warm jacket potatoes I'd wrap up in newspaper, stolen from the kitchen, or the
hefty wedges of apple pie I'd sneak out, wrapped in tissue, bulg-
ing the pockets of my dress.

Fen was the only one who didn't seem to mind Mrs Price's
cooking. 'Hunger makes everything taste good,' he assured me,
even when I handed him her latest experimental pie, which tasted of cabbage and fish.

When Mrs Price found out that I was the one stealing
from the kitchen she began leaving out small packages, neatly
wrapped up for me to take outdoors as my afternoon tea. I think
she was that glad to find someone who appreciated her food.

I was full of questions for Fen about his house, his father
and how he was getting on at the farm. Fen seemed to know the
countryside so well; it surprised me to know that he hadn't lived
there his whole life.

'Da's from Cornwall originally. Mum's from Yorkshire. We
lived here when I was little, then when Da got sick we moved in
with me gran – until she died. That was a few months ago. Then
we moved here.'

To the house. I still longed to visit it. I'd only got as far as the
wall, and hadn't had the courage to ask to see more.

'So it's just you and your parents then?' I asked.

He nodded. 'Had two older brothers and a sister when I was
little. Consumption,' he explained. One word that said so much.

'I'm so sorry,' I said.

His eyes grew sad. 'It was a while ago. But I still hear Tommy's voice now and again.'

'Tommy? Your brother?'

He nodded. 'The eldest. He took care of us when Da – well, when Da was away. Still miss him.'

'I'm sorry,' I said. 'Why did you move back here? If you've still got family up in Yorkshire, I mean?'

Fen shrugged. 'Me da, he wanted to come home. Missed the sea. Never thought we'd have a place like this, though. It's all thanks to the kindness of yer da.'

I blinked. 'My father?' I wasn't sure I'd ever heard anyone speak about him in that way. He'd been called hardworking, tenacious, formidable, but kind? There was a loyalty to his family and to those he cared about but I'd never heard him described that way.

I looked at Fen. 'He said they were friends, your father and mine, in the war.'

Fen didn't say anything for a moment. 'Something like that. He's a good man though, yer da. Not what I would have expected from a lord, if you know what I mean. Not that I've met that many, or any, really, mind.'

I looked at him in surprise. 'Have you met him?'

He nodded. 'Sure. On our first night. He came round, asked if everything was okay. Like it wouldn't be. Seemed real concerned that it was comfortable. To tell you the truth, till we lived here, I didn't even know people had their own rooms. Couldn't believe this was all for us.'

I blinked. Up until then, I hadn't realised that people really shared before. It was a moment when I understood, perhaps for the first time, how blind I was to my own privilege. It was the first time I felt a stirring of shame for it.

He looked at me, and then coloured slightly. 'You probably have a big room—'

'No, not at all,' I lied. 'I know what you mean. Rose and I shared the nursery for years, and she drove me insane. She used to take away my books and tell on me to our governess, Celine. She still does, actually,' I sighed.

'Tell on you? Why?'

'They weren't always the best books…'

'How can a book be bad?'

'Well, when there's pirates and loose morals…'

He looked rather impressed. 'Really? How did you get them, then, if no one wanted you to read them?'

'My cousin, Tim. He can always be relied upon.'

'He sounds fun,' he said with a grin.

'He is. I'll bring you one but you'll have to read it at night. I don't want you to get in trouble with your parents.'

Fen laughed. 'I think me mam would be that impressed to see me reading a book!'

I grinned. 'Not this kind.'

While the new title of Prime Minister of the United Kingdom, which had been officially recognised by a Royal Warrant from the King, filled up the leading spaces in newspapers and discussions that March, Celine was growing increasingly suspicious of what I got up to in the afternoons, and I was finding it harder to come up with excuses for the leaves in my hair and the grass stains on my hands and knees.

She'd warned me that if there were any further transgressions, I would have an audience with my father.

The trouble was that it was hard to remember to worry about such things when your best friend said things like, 'Don't be a goose.'

'I'm not!'

'Suppose you're worrying about your dress and what that foreign woman will say if it gets all dirty again? Anyway, why can't you just wear some normal clothes, if you're worried?'

We were looking up at Old Tom, the wild pear tree that bordered the river. It was over twelve feet high and had a trunk about as wide as two carriages sat side by side. Over two hundred years old, it still bore the tastiest fruit to be had. The only trouble was that, to get there, you needed to climb like your life depended on it.

I huffed. 'I am not worrying about my dress,' I said, though of course I was. I'd already gotten a severe scolding from Celine. 'My governess is French,' I pointed out. 'And these are normal.' I peered down at my ankle boots, stockings and knee-length dress in doubt.

He shrugged; there was a dare in his eyes. 'Fine, she's fancy foreign. And o-kay, if you say so. Though I could just lend you some of my things for the tree climbing. I have a spare.'

I folded my lips; I wouldn't smile. 'A spare what?'

'Pair of trousers.'

I laughed. 'I think I'll pass, thank you…'

He grinned. 'Well, alright, but you won't fall, I'll go up after you. Here,' he said, folding his hands together and making a little step for me to climb.

I stepped around him and made a leap for an overhanging branch, catching it with my arms, then pulled myself up, my legs kicking beneath me. Fen followed, and we climbed higher and higher, coming to rest in a deep branch, where he clambered across to get to the ripe, juicy fruit. He sat down next to me and we ate our stolen pears, grinning as the clouded juice ran down our chins.

We were leaning against the trunk when he picked up my hand and laughed. 'Yep,' he said, looking at my new collection of scratches, 'should have just used my boost.'

'Shut up,' I said, laughing. My hand tingled from his touch, and I felt my cheeks reddening slightly as a result. 'Rather have that than be a goose.'

'I like geese. You don't want to be around one that decides it's out for blood. You know, actually, they look just like you do when you're cross.'

I scrambled after him as he slipped down the tree. 'Yes, you'd better run!'

Later, Celine sighed over the scratches on my hands and knees. 'Haven't you been wearing gloves?' she asked, appalled. I shrugged. She picked up my dress, which though free of grass stains from the scrub I'd given it when I came in, was puckered and torn.

'When did you become so rough?'

I shrugged. 'We do live in the countryside,' I pointed out. 'Surrounded by trees, fields, rocks…'

'Yes, but is it absolutely necessary to catch all of it upon yourself?'

I held my hands palm up.

Her face changed. 'William said that he saw you down at the river the other day, talking to a boy. He thought it was strange.'

'Strange?' I said, but I didn't meet her eyes.

She nodded, and I felt a prickle of trepidation.

'Yes. He thought it was rather odd for a girl like you to be speaking with a boy like that…'

'A boy like what?' I asked. 'And what's the harm in speaking?'

She gave me a stern look. 'Tilly, of all people, you should be aware of the differences between the two of you – the class distinctions.'

'That doesn't bother me!'

She raised a brow. 'No, class never does bother the ones it privileges, does it?'

I looked away. Her eyes softened. 'I know that it doesn't make a difference to you – but you must realise that it does to everyone else.'

Why did that matter, when we weren't hurting anyone?

'I hope that's not what you've been doing with all your time in the afternoons.'

'And if I am?'

Her eyes flashed. 'Consider this a warning then. It's not you who will suffer the most. If you continue, I will have no choice but to speak to your mother.'

My eyes met hers. I was often threatened with being reported to my father, which I knew to be an idle threat, but being reported to my mother was not.

I looked away, the challenge dying on my lips, her words echoing in my head that it wasn't me who would pay the price. Why did anyone have to suffer, simply because Fen and I were friends? What harm was there in it? What did it matter if he was born into a world where no one ever had a room of their own and I had been born into one where hardly anyone ever shared theirs? Why was the world divided over material things? And couldn't I, for once, just have a friend?

CHAPTER TWENTY-TWO

Present day

The water was colder than I'd expected, the sound of the waves amplified against the rocks. In the sand, like so many jewels, pebbles of sea glass were scattered along the beach. I marvelled at them, picking up ones that were aquamarine in colour, others like emeralds and sapphires.

Sea glass has always fascinated me. There's poetry in nature, but poetic justice too. Glass is made from sand, yet the ocean claims the glass from boats, shipwrecks and things left on shore; it takes it into its embrace and over time transforms it into something wild once more.

'They're beautiful, aren't they?' I said to Adam as he came over, his dark blond hair tousled by the wind, trousers rolled up. In the sun, his eyes were an almost electric blue.

He nodded. 'I'm sure this is what was used in your staircase.' He was speaking about the beautiful spiral staircase in Seafall Cottage, which was currently being restored.

'I'm sure you're right,' I said, marvelling that I might be on the very beach that had inspired my seashell-like staircase.

Adam had popped into the cottage after work to see the progress the builders had made after I'd last shown him around. We'd decided to take a walk down the steps from the cottage to see if we could find the cove.

'Do you think the Aspreys really made their money as pi-rates?' I asked.

He shrugged. 'I don't know – but it was common back then. There were even plundering rights for locals, as Cornish seas were so treacherous to ships because of all the rocks. If they had made their money that way, I'm sure they weren't the only ones.'

Since we'd begun decoding Tilly's diary, Adam and I were spending a lot of time together. Most days he'd come past with a coffee or pop into the bookshop, where I would be having a chat with Angie. Before long we'd be discussing the diary, going off for a walk or deciding to grab something to eat.

I had tried not to overanalyse it. Everyone needs a friend, even if that friend is six foot something, has a smile that should come with a health warning and is also utterly gorgeous to look at.

Angie, of course, was having none of that. The day before, she'd flat out asked me, 'So you and McAmerican – have you jumped his bones yet?'

'Angie!' I'd exclaimed, looking around *The Floating Book-store* in case anyone had overheard her, though I knew we were alone.

'Yes?' she'd said, looking amused. She was using her finger to keep her place in her novel – currently Lemony Snicket's *The Bad Beginning*. She'd made me sit down with my lemon drizzle slice while she read some of the funny bits aloud, until she inter-rupted herself and asked about Adam.

Her feet had been propped up on a beanbag and she was the picture of a relaxed hippie, her long grey hair falling behind her. In the background, Creedence Clearwater Revival were singing 'Green River'.

'You can't go around asking people things like that!'

'Oh, I'm sorry, I had this accident that affected part of my brain so now I'm never sure if what I say is rude or not,' she'd said, her face serious, green eyes repentant.

'Really?' I'd asked, sitting forward in my beanbag. This would explain a lot.

'No,' she'd laughed, chucking the book at me. 'Stop being so bloody prim.'

I'd straightened up primly, stifling a smile. 'Angie, I did not grow up in the sixties.'

'More's the pity,' she had said. 'You poor eighties kids... Punk, like that made the world go round.'

I snorted now, thinking of her phrase 'McAmerican'.

'What's so funny?' asked Adam.

'I was just thinking of something Angie said—'

'Oh wait, you've got something on your face,' he said, gently trailing a hand across my cheek.

I blinked. My heart began to race. Up close I could smell his cologne. 'W-what was it?' I asked.

'Just sand,' he said, smiling that lazy smile.

'Oh,' I said, feeling suddenly as if something had shifted, beyond the sand beneath my feet. When he started walking back, my hand crept up to the place where his fingers had been. Like it had been gently burnt, I could still feel his touch.

'Have you ever watched the movie *Waterworld*?' I heard Angie call outside my window later that evening.

I peered out the window. 'Um, no?'

Her long grey hair was loose, and she had on stripy purple and pink bellbottoms and a mustard-coloured T-shirt. There were silver swallows dangling from her ears.

She held up a DVD. 'Got it at Oxfam for less than a pound,' she said with an air of surprise. 'Can you believe it?'

'Um?' I said, stifling a laugh.

Movie night had become our thing. Neither of us owned a TV but we made do with my laptop. The week before, she'd come past with *Fried Green Tomatoes*, and we'd cried like idiots, shouting 'Towanda!' as we downed our drinks.

The week before that, she'd appeared with a plate of suspicious-looking brownies and we'd laughed most of the night. She was the bad friend I'd never had, only she was a good thirty years my senior.

Over the past few years I hadn't had the pleasure of this – friends dropping by unannounced. To be fair, in London, if it's not booked into your calendar, it doesn't happen at all.

The truth was that most of my friends were at very different stages of their lives. Meg, my dear friend from uni, had three children and could barely find the time to brush her own hair, let alone meet up for lunch. And with my busy schedule over the past few years, I'd lost touch with most of my other friends, apart from the occasional, obligatory lunch or supper. Now that Mark and I had split up, there would be even fewer of those.

Sue, Angie and Adam were the first real friends I'd made in years.

Angie was like that naughty aunt who gave you your first fake ID, or snuck in the booze – you know, the best one?

She looked at me from the gangway. 'The woman said it should still play, but if not…' She held up her other hand, in which there was a bottle of wine. 'There's this?'

I laughed. 'Hopefully not also from Oxfam?'

For someone who lived on a very cramped houseboat, Angie had a bit of a problem with trawling charity shops. When

things got too much she just took a load back though she admitted there had been a few times she'd bought something
she'd donated by mistake – 'That's when I know I should have
kept it, you know.'

'Bargain bin,' she said now, referring to the wine. 'But looks,
you know, what's the word?'

'Potable?' I tried.

'That,' she said with a grin.

'Come on in.'

I poured us each a glass of wine and we watched a young
Kevin Costner tackle the seas and swim like a merman.

'You know, this is alright,' I said, taking another sip.

'Not bad,' she agreed.

'I'd forgotten how good-looking Costner was.'

'Vintage,' she agreed. 'Brownie?'

'Angie, you're a bad influence, you know that?'

She laughed. 'Yeah, I mean, look what I just made you do
there,' she said as I rewound to the part where Costner takes his
shirt off, which, to be fair, had been my idea.

'You know,' she said, giving me a sly look. 'McAdam has a bit
of that going on…'

'What?' I said, spilling wine on my shirt. I had been trying
and failing to forget our walk on the beach earlier.

She grinned. 'You know, that dark blond, blue-eyed sort of
thing…'

'Has he?' I said, all too innocently.

She laughed when my face started to colour. 'You're blushing,' she said in delight.

'It's the wine,' I said, shaking my head at her.

'Oh yes, the *wine*,' she said, rewinding the film again. 'So
when are you seeing him again? Breakfast, is it?'

'It's not like that. Anyway, it's only lunch.'

Her mouth fell open and she started to laugh. 'Oh yes, only lunch.'

'Shut up,' I said, stifling a laugh.

CHAPTER TWENTY-THREE

I convinced Fen that it would be best if we met away from the farms, and our meeting place became the little river where I'd first seen him and Arthur all those months ago. Fen didn't argue. I think he knew, perhaps even more than me, our friendship was something we had to safeguard.

As winter gave way to spring, Fen and I began work on the abandoned fishing boat that he'd found. Using tar that he'd bought down at the village tackle and boat shop, we repaired the hole, and then waited for it to dry before we took it for its maiden voyage. We had one paddle and one large branch, and our agreement was that we'd take turns with each. Arthur came with us for our maiden trip, though he preferred to stay on Fen's shoulder rather than in the somewhat damp hull.

Water seeped into the toes of my boots and filled my stockings. There were slick patches of mildew and nowhere to sit that didn't result in a wet bottom, but I'm not sure that I'd ever smiled quite as much as I did on that day when we took the boat out.

The sun made a surprise visit, and lemon-coloured sunlight flickered against my eyelids. I discovered that I preferred to be at the tiller, and that I was surprisingly good at it, especially compared to Fen, who liked to steer us into branches and trees along the riverbank.

After that first voyage, I went to bed dreaming of the gentle swirl of the river, following the waterway until it reached the open ocean.

I'd taken Fen's advice and found more sensible clothing. In the rag bag in the kitchen was an old, plain blue dress that used to be one of the uniforms for one of the downstairs maids. The dress was for an older girl, and was thus several sizes too big, but this meant I could simply wear it as a protective smock over my clothing. It had a white cuff and collar that I had unpicked to make sure it didn't look too much like a uniform. But if it did, at least from afar, no one would think much of Fen being seen with someone in service. I kept it rolled up and hidden in a satchel in a groove in the trunk of Old Tom, the wild pear tree, and would slip it on just before I met up with him.

It was only later that I would realise how much worse this small addition would make things. But right then it was a good compromise, one that left Celine no room to complain about the state of my clothing. What the eye cannot see, I reasoned, Celine could have no cause to make grief over.

For the first time in my life, I was having adventures that didn't come within the pages of books.

'I wish, in a way, that summer wasn't coming,' said Fen one day, as we sat in the boat.

Arthur had taken up residence on my lap, while Fen drew a lazy paddle towards shore.

'Why?' I asked in surprise. 'Think of how much more fun we'll have when the weather warms.'

'You, maybe. But me da will need my help more than ever with the new season. He's already said that it might be time for me to quit school.'

'Quit school?' I said in shock. 'But you're still a child.'

He looked offended. 'I'm twelve – 'tis time.'

Fen was three years older than me, but still I was horrified that he would think that. 'No, it's not! They can't do that.'

'Why not?'

'No one finishes school at twelve!'

'Your lot, maybe. Mine, well, I'd be one of the few that went that far, since the laws changed.'

I blinked. It was one of the first times we'd ever really spoken about our differences. Still, I knew Fen. I'd heard the way he spoke about the books I'd lent him. We'd spent hours re-enacting *The Lady of the Lake*. I saw his passion for learning new things. How could that be over at the age of twelve?

'Can't you tell him that you want to go all the way – finish school properly? Wouldn't he understand?'

'And who would pay for that? He needs me, needs my help – especially now that he's getting wor—'

'Getting what?'

'Nothing, he just needs me now.'

'Why?'

'He just does.'

But I didn't like the idea of change, not now that I had found Fen. I couldn't go back to the way it was before. With me hiding out in the library, not knowing what it was like to have a friend of my own, someone who made every day richer, more fun, simply by being part of it.

'Will I still see you?' I asked, knowing I was being selfish. The choice – or rather, lack of choice – he'd been presented with was far more serious than my own childish needs. His father needed him, but I couldn't face the idea of giving up my friend.

'Don't be a goose. Course you will.'

CHAPTER TWENTY-FOUR

'Are you cheating on Gerald?'

Adam was standing in the kitchen, heroically ignoring the soup-related crime scene that surrounded him, and looking at the geranium on the windowsill, which had had to make room for a pretty new one with yellow petals in a blue pot.

I laughed. 'That's Harriet,' I said.

'Oh well in that case, good for Gerald.'

I grinned. 'Anyway, try this, and tell me if it's any good,' I said, dipping a spoon into the thick butternut and orange soup that was bubbling away merrily on the stove and handing it to him to test.

He blew on it, and then tasted it. His eyes closed in apparent bliss. 'Amazing.'

'You're kidding!'

He popped an eye open. 'Why are you surprised? It's so good.'

I frowned, needing a possibly unbiased second opinion. I took the spoon out of his hand, dipped it into the soup and tried it myself. Despite half scalding my mouth and needing to fan it with my hand, the sensation on my tongue, beyond pain, was… pleasant. More than pleasant, actually. 'It's good!'

I felt as if I'd just been handed an award, one of those big blue ones that said '*First Prize*'.

At his confused look, I explained. 'Adam, my dear friend, I am many things. I can navigate the Underground as if the map were printed on the inside of my eyeballs. I find it surprisingly okay to stand up in front of a crowd and make a speech without first getting sick on someone else's shoes. I can say the twenty-two times table backwards—'

'What? Really?'

I waved my hand. 'Of course. I could do all the times tables backwards by the age of seven.'

He was staring at me as if I were an alien.

'That's besides the point. My point is that I can do those things. Yet, I have never, and I mean that literally, as in *never ever*, been able to cook something that didn't taste like a boiled sock.'

Adam looked at the recipe on the counter. Next to it, I had crossed things out and added things in so many times that it now resembled more of a scientific formula than a recipe. I had also phoned my brother exactly twenty times to describe the problems I was having and have him run interference as if he was talking me through disarming a bomb. At one point I'd even hung up, saying, 'I can't handle this! I'm going to bloody Tesco!'

But he had phoned back and said, 'Okay, breathe, Smudge.'

'Not cinnamon?' I would ask.

'God no, awful! Try some more orange zest. Phone me back.'

'Right, better. Still, something vaguely sock-like. Maybe it was the turmeric – bad idea?'

'Are you crazy?' exclaimed Stuart. 'Do you want to poison everyone?'

'Really, it's poisonous?' I asked in horror.

'No – just a terrible combination for that soup.'

'Ah.'

The tiny houseboat kitchen looked as if something had exploded inside it – something like all my other attempts at Sue's 'Tried and Tested No-Fail Butternut Soup'.

That is, honest to God, what Sue had called her soup when I asked her for an idiot-proof recipe so that I too could take part in the annual spring drive for the Tremenara community allotment. It had seemed such a lovely idea at the time. Relaxing, almost. I had pictured myself sitting in the tent that they would be putting up, looking at all the spring flowers and vegetables, chatting to my neighbours, avoiding the Bishop's homemade beer. My mildy deranged neighbour had recently offered to come past the cottage and perform an exorcism on my house after news reached him that I had bought Seafall Cottage.

All I can say is that Sue failed to take into account the level of idiocy I can apply to cooking.

'You know, you could have bought soup from Waitrose and sold that,' said Adam.

'You know who does that?' I asked.

'Who?' he asked, taking another spoonful, to my surprise and delight. I could have kissed him right then.

'Smart people.'

He laughed. 'I thought you were gonna say quitters.'

'Yeah, well…' I put on a very bad American accent. 'It's true, my momma didn't raise no quitters here.'

At the allotment, to my complete surprise, my soup went down a treat. When Sue came past to thank me, I just shrugged. 'Oh, it was nothing, happy to help.'

When she said that it didn't taste much like the recipe, I gave her a puzzled look. 'Oh well, different kitchens, you know.'

'Well, I think it's wonderful.'

'Thanks,' I said.

Behind her, I could see Adam trying not to laugh.

When she left, he shook his head. 'Women!'

'What about us delightful creatures?' I asked.

He laughed. 'You're all mad. I mean, that right there – instead of telling her how difficult it was, you're just so gracious and she has no idea at all how hard you worked.'

I patted him on the back. 'Adam, Adam,' I said, shaking my head, 'let me explain something to you. All those sisters and you still don't get it.'

'Get what?'

'Women, Adam, do not communicate by mere words.'

'They don't?'

'No. You see, I didn't need to tell Sue that I had trouble with her recipe – she *knew*.'

'She *did*?' He looked thoroughly confused.

'There was the look, didn't you see it?'

'What look?'

I shook my head. 'And she said it tasted different.'

'Yes – so?'

'She knew.'

'She knew you made her soup seven times and had to call in for reinforcements?' he said, grinning.

'No! God no. What, do you think women are psychic? She just knew that I was the idiot that proved her idiot-proof "no-fail recipe" wrong.'

He threw back his head, roared with laughter and gave me a hug. 'You're fun, you know that?'

I blinked. Was I? I hadn't been called that in a long time.

When Adam left to go sample the Bishop's beer, Angie sidled over, wearing a mustard-coloured smock and round, rose-tinted sunglasses.

'Hello, John Lennon,' I said.

'Haha,' she said sarcastically. 'Anyway, I saw that…' She pointed towards Adam. 'That hug.'

'Where's Yoko when you need her?' I said, narrowing my eyes.

'What about Yoko?' asked Adam, coming back with a plastic cup of beer for me.

'Nothing,' I said.

'Gary's beer is something else,' he said as I took a sip.

'Gary?' I asked.

'Gary Bishop.'

My mouth fell open in surprise. I looked over to the stall where the Bishop was standing with his Russian beaver hat, his bare arms covered in a wealth of tattoos, many of which were crosses. 'That's why they call him the Bishop?'

Adam looked at Angie. 'You know, you wouldn't think that this was someone who could say the twenty-two times table backwards.'

Angie looked at Adam and shrugged. 'Who can't?'

His eyes popped open. 'Really?'

She took a sip of beer. 'No, man,' she laughed. Then she looked at me. 'Prove it, what's twenty-two times twelve?'

'It's 264,' I said automatically.

'Okay, what's twenty-two times fifty-two?'

'That's not really part of the times table, but it's 1,144.'

Angie looked at Adam. 'Is that right?'

He looked at me, and then said, 'I'll google it.'

CHAPTER TWENTY-FIVE

Calais, 1915

Dearest Fen,

Thank you for the beautiful diary. I love it. I don't know how you got it – or the beautiful ribbons. Aquamarine, of course.

I've decided that I'll write our story – from the start – using our little code from when we were children. You know I can do it by heart now?

Don't wish the dreams away. That's how I find you.

Yours always,

T

CHAPTER TWENTY-SIX

Present day

I was aboard *The Floating Bookstore*, lounging on a beanbag and defrosting by the wood burner, turning the pages of a surprisingly riveting novel by Louis L'Amour, which I'd found due to Angie's madcap filing system. I was lost in the Wild West with a lone cowboy on a mission, someone I pictured with rather blue eyes and a lazy smile, when Angie refilled my cup of coffee and interrupted my reverie.

'So,' she said, giving me a meaningful look.

'Shall I read aloud?' I asked.

'No – just wanted to ask how you were doing?'

I set the book down. 'Ah, the divorce?'

She nodded.

'Well, he finally agreed to it – we've had a few back and forth emails from the lawyers but it looks like it'll be finalised within the next month.'

'How do you feel?' she asked.

'I'm okay. I thought I'd be worse, but I think the truth is that we've been circling it for years. Now, well, I can finally move on.'

'I'm glad,' she said.

'Me too.'

'The first one is always the hardest,' she said, taking a sip of coffee.

'The first what?'

'Divorce.'

My eyes went wide. 'Have you been divorced?'

'Of course.' She shrugged. 'Who hasn't?'

'Really?'

'No,' she laughed.

My mouth fell open. 'You have to stop doing that!'

She grinned. 'Why? It's so fun. Anyway, I was almost married once.'

'You were?'

'Yes, to the previous owner of your houseboat actually.'

'What happened?' I asked.

'Life, I think. To be honest, I'm just not the marrying kind.'

'I'm surprised,' I said. 'I mean you're always trying to pair me up with Adam…'

'That's different,' said Angie, laughing.

'How's that?'

'Cos it's fun.'

I threw one of her beaded cushions at her.

'Okay, okay, enough. Go back to your Western, please, this is a respectable place,' she said before offering me another suspicious-looking brownie.

The next morning, I got an early start on the cottage. The kitchen was starting to resemble a kitchen, finally. The blue and white tiles I'd chosen totally transformed the walls, making my dream of having a farmhouse kitchen something of a reality. I'd been trawling the local shops for more blue and white Cornish pottery and I couldn't wait to put my finds on display once the pale grey wooden counters were in place, along with my pride and joy, a sparkling new duck-egg blue Aga. After the success of my soup, I was sure I could (eventually, after much error) become someone who cooked.

More importantly, the cottage was now, finally, rot-free. Even the window had been repaired, so now it was possible to stand in the living room and not freeze half to death.

I was sweeping the floors, my iPod on high while I swept along to the sound of the Beatles, when I caught sight of the old man standing in the doorway. I jumped with fright when I saw him.

He was still wearing that same jacket, the one with the patches on the elbows, and his eyes were startlingly blue. He stared at me for some time, then tipped his hat at me, an old-fashioned fedora. He put something on the counter, turned on his heel and left.

I watched him go, then, after half a beat I raced after him, deciding that it was high time we had a discussion about what he was doing here. And why he was never here when the builders were, or Adam. But, as usual, as soon as I got into the garden he was gone.

He was certainly sprightly for his age – and bold as brass too.

I went back inside and saw, on the old counter, a letter. Only, of course, it wasn't addressed to me.

CHAPTER TWENTY-SEVEN

The first time I got into trouble was after we'd decided to visit the pirate cove.

'You can get there from the house – did you know that?' said Fen.

'You told me once, but I haven't been. How do you get down?'

'There's little steps cut away in the rocks, right by the cliffs. Want to see?'

'Yes!'

We trekked past Idyllwild, the barren fields dry after harvest, noting how the leaves on the ground near the stream had turned shades of burnt amber and bronze as we made our way towards the cottage.

For a heart-stopping moment I thought he would lead me inside, but Fen led me away, past the cliff walls. I stopped when we saw someone in the distance.

'It's just me da,' said Fen. 'It's okay, let's go this way instead.'

I was disappointed that Mr Waters had chosen this moment to come home, but I followed after Fen as we retraced our way past the secret entrance to the very edge of the wall, where the ground fell away in a terrace.

'From the house there's a slightly easier way down, but we can do it this way as well. The paths sort of meet up – you'll see.'

Below, the waves crashed and churned. I could smell the briny scent of the ocean; the wind was cold and crisp as we walked. The pathway was slight, a squeeze even for our small frames.

We wound down and around, to where the rocks gave way to a winding, chalky road amongst the silvery seagrass and an abundance of purple wildflowers. The closer we neared the cove, the quieter it got. Here, the water was limpid, gentle.

We stepped onto the small sandy beach and sat down.

'Have you ever been here before?'

'Yes, but not this way. Tim, my cousin, took Rose and me to explore a few years ago, from the farm road. Father doesn't like us to come here.'

I didn't mention that I was forbidden to come to the south part of the estate at all.

Fen looked at me now. 'Why not – why doesn't he like coming here?'

'Doesn't like the water – doesn't trust it.'

He nodded. 'There's something in that, I suppose. It's beautiful, but it's wild, and if you forget that, well, it could be dangerous.'

'I suppose so.'

'It's strange, because it's the one thing that calms my father down – the sea. Since we moved here, it's really helped him.'

'Helped him, how?'

Fen hesitated. 'Well, before, he used to have so many more episodes. That's what me mam calls them.'

'Episodes?' I asked in surprise.

'He gets sick, I suppose.'

'Sick? What happens?'

He picked up a rock and threw it in the water. But he didn't say anything. I saw him absently touch his boot – the one on the foot that was twisted somewhat – and give me a sideways look. 'I'm… We're not really supposed to talk about it.'

'Why not?'

'They don't want anyone to know.'

'Is it bad?'

'Aye, sometimes.'

'You can tell me, Fen. It's not like I'd ever tell anyone.'

He nodded, looked out to sea. 'It's like a fit. He shakes, cries. It's hard to speak to him, he gets…'

'What?'

'Violent.' He touched his foot again.

'Violent,' I repeated. I looked at his foot. He'd said it was an accident, but I couldn't help wondering…

I hesitated. 'Is that what happened to your foot?'

His face look pained. 'It wasn't his fault – he was sick, I knew that.'

I gasped.

He looked at my wide, horrified eyes, and said, quickly, 'He didn't hit me or nothing like that. It was an accident. He was starting to… He shakes, and screams, but the only person he hurts is himself. We just try to calm him down. When it happens we know to get him to his bed, out of harm's way. It's the only way to help. I was trying to do that, to get him to follow me, but he started shaking, hitting himself. I tried to get him to stop, there was a struggle, and I fell down some stairs. It wasn't like he could help it,' he said, his eyes sad.

I put my hand on his shoulder.

'But he blames himself. Though he shouldn't, I was the one who didn't want to go to a doctor. Da wanted to take me straight away, but I was worried, you know, of what would happen to him? In case they took him from us.'

'Oh, Fen.'

He looked at me. 'Yeah, by the time I did see a doctor it was too late, because it had healed the wrong way. They tried breaking it again to set it right, but it's never been the same. It's one of the reasons we moved, you know. Da didn't want to stay where that had happened. Anyway, now he doesn't get them as much – his episodes. It's worse in the winter, when it gets dark. In summer, he's better. Even he's surprised at how much better he's been. A few weeks ago we were worried they'd come back when the long hours at the farm started, but it hasn't been as bad. Now when he gets them, he just sits in the living room ands stares at the sea. It really helps.

'He's a good man, me da – been through a lot. Wouldn't hurt no one. He taught me how to charm foxes, did I tell you that?'

I shook my head.

'That's how I got Arthur. It's all about patience. It's how I tamed you too, Tilly Asprey.'

'Really?' I said with a laugh.

'Oh yes,' he said, picking up my hand, and giving it a kiss.

I looked away from his gaze, felt my heart start to pound, and a crazy grin spread across my face.

'See, you wouldn't have let me do that before…'

I sneaked a look up at him, shaking my head. 'I wouldn't say that,' I said, then blushed furiously.

CHAPTER TWENTY-EIGHT

'PTSD, do you think?' I asked, the most recent diary pages scattered in front of me, where Tilly had described Mr Waters' episodes.

Adam nodded. 'Jeez, poor guy! Back then they didn't understand it.'

'God, that's sad. It explains the cottage then, perhaps.'

He looked at me in surprise. 'What do you mean?'

'Well, if he needed a place away from prying eyes while he had these outbursts.'

He whistled. 'That makes sense.'

It was late, but it was hard to call it a night. Adam and I had swapped our pages as we decoded Tilly's diary, until well past 3 a.m.

He poured me another cup of coffee. His blue eyes had dark shadows beneath them, and his hair was sticking up from where he'd been leaning back in the egg chair.

'Thanks,' I said, reaching out for the cup. One of Angie's charity shop finds, a ceramic unicorn with a rainbow horn, it was so kitsch it was cute. 'I see you used my super-cool mug,' I noted with a grin.

'Only the best for you,' he replied, sitting back down in the egg chair. 'You know, not that I'd heard too much of you before…'

'What?' I protested. 'I'm really big in… Finland. Okay, parts of Finland. More like one small village.'

'No, but seriously. Somehow, I didn't expect you to be like this,' he said, indicating the mug and my Minion slippers.

I nodded. 'It's true. So very few can envision such coolness, I admit.'

'Well,' he laughed. 'I think you're cool.'

'Thanks. It's all Ray Bradbury, you know?'

He gave me a puzzled look. 'The science fiction author?'

I nodded. 'Well, a reader sent him a letter asking for life advice on how Ray had turned out the way he had, overcoming obstacles and becoming so successful, and Ray's response was: "Be your own self. Love what YOU love."'

'Love what you love?'

'Yup, it's simple but profound – basically you need to be true to who you are.'

'Is that why you wear all those funny T-shirts?'

'Yup.'

'See, you're cool.'

I laughed. 'You're probably the only person on this planet who thinks so, but thanks.'

'Didn't your ex?'

There was a moment's silence, in which the presence of Mark had been invited in, and I tried to push him out again.

'Sorry, I shouldn't have…' began Adam.

I shrugged. 'No, it's fine. Um, Mark had a picture of the way things should have been, I think, and it didn't always work out that way. To be fair, perhaps I wasn't the sort of woman he should have been with.' I pictured the glamorous form of Jess. 'I think, with Mark, there should have been high heels and stockings and slips. Not, you know, rainbow unicorns and Spider-Man tees, probably.'

Adam raised a brow. 'Slips?'

'You know, those sexy satin things.' I waggled my eyebrows. 'You wear them at night, set the mood…'

His eyes widened. 'Well, okay now, I am a guy so I ain't gonna pretend that *that's* not like the male equivalent of rainbows and unicorns.'

I giggled. 'Okay, fair enough.'

'You said *love* what you love…'

I laughed.

He winked, and I felt my stomach flip. Winking should *not* be allowed.

Then he said, 'I mean, look at you. It's not like you'd need a slip to look sexy.'

I blinked.

There was a pause. 'I just meant…'

I was thirty-two years old, it was ridiculous to be blushing, but that's what was happening. I put my hands on my warm cheeks and said, 'You find the Minions sexy? Well, that's fine… I mean, maybe it's a little disturbing, but there are worse things, I'm sure…'

He smiled and looked at me for a long moment – while I tried not to suggest anything stupid, like that I could probably find a slip somewhere. Then he said, 'Yeah, how about we go back to this before I get myself into any more trouble?'

'Oh no, I want to hear more about your fondness for little yellow men,' I said, waving a slipper at him.

'Shut up,' he said, grabbing my arm and pulling me towards him, so that I stumbled and fell on top of him.

His arms came round me and I found myself, somehow, on his lap. Before I could stand up, he was moving my hair away from my eyes, giving me that languid smile of his, and I was lost. I didn't know who made the first move; I didn't care.

My head swam as I sunk into his kiss. I forgot my name, desire flamed inside me and I didn't know if hours passed or minutes. My hands were in his hair, not letting him go.

CHAPTER TWENTY-NINE

Cornwall, 1907

Tilly

The first time I saw the house was by accident. We hadn't planned on going, but when Fen saw something from the boat one afternoon, he said, 'Lie down – quick.'

'What?'

'Just do it, trust me.'

I grumbled, but did as instructed. 'I'm going to get wet.'

'Wetter, you mean.'

I shrugged, and peered up at him from where I lay. Even Arthur seemed amused to see me huddled at the bottom.

'Why exactly am I lying down here?'

'Me mam just went by the road.'

'Your mam?' I asked in surprise and interest. My head popped up quickly in my haste to look.

'Stay down,' he ordered.

I huffed, hunching down, and peered over the rim of the boat. In the distance I could see a dusky dress walking away down the dirt path.

'Didn't you want her to see me with you?' I asked, wondering why it bothered me, when I knew he was simply being cautious. I wasn't the only one who would get in trouble if they saw us together.

'If she saw you then there'd be questions. And,' he said, eyes mischievous, 'you'd miss your chance, Tilly Asprey.'

'For what?'

'Well, I thought that you wanted to see the cottage. Don't you ask me at least once a week?'

I sat up quickly and the boat rocked precariously, sending up a heavy splash of water that sprayed both Fen and Arthur, who shot me a very disgruntled look.

'The cottage!' I whooped. 'I can see it, finally? Today?' I took hold of the oar and started making rapid strokes towards the shore.

Fen laughed. 'You're such a goose.'

'I can't believe you live here,' I said, when a little while later we walked into the garden around the cottage.

It was like something out of a fairy story. The stone cottage, set above the rock face, looked almost like it was about to fall off the edge of the cliffs into the sea below.

'Seafall,' I said.

'Pardon?'

'That's what I'd call it, if it was mine.'

He grinned. 'I like that.'

Spring had come early to the cliff-top garden; I could see wildflowers, tulips and purple irises in bloom. My mouth opened in surprise at the unexpected sight. 'It's lovely,' I said.

'It will be, got plans to create more of a garden here. Da wanted to grow daffodils here as well. He's mad about them, thanks to your father,' he laughed.

We'd been hearing about their latest hybrid for weeks. There had even been someone from the papers round to write an article on the new variety that Father said would change the face of daffodil farming, as it was so much hardier. Rose and I had even been summoned to the farm to have our pictures taken; it had been very exciting.

'Before we came here, that's all he spoke about when he was sick – the daffodils. He wanted to see the fields full of them. Your da had told him all about them, you see. Then he got the offer to come work here...'

'Michael Fenwick Waters,' said a cold, hard voice from behind. Fen straightened up and his face went pale. He turned around with a fixed smile on his face. 'Hello, Ma.'

'Hello, Ma?' said a short, stout woman standing behind him. 'Hello, Ma, is it!' She had broad shoulders and a face that looked like a crab apple – red and streaked with white. 'Don't be talking about your da with anyone, do you hear me?' she said, hands on her hips.

Fen smiled. 'But Ma, this isn't everyone. This is Tilly.'

Mrs Waters crossed her arms. '*Lady* Matilda,' she said with a pointed look at Fen. ''Tis nice to meet you. Though I am surprised to find you here.' She made a poor attempt at a smile.

'I'm not a lady,' I corrected her. She was giving me a hard stare so I continued, in a rush of explanation, 'What I mean is that my father's a baron, um, so you would address my mother as Lady Asprey, but not me, or my sister, officially, um, I'm just Miss Matilda, but everyone calls me Tilly.'

Mrs Waters' face had closed. 'Thank you, *Miss* Matilda.'

I swallowed. Somehow, I had made it worse.

'Mam...' began Fen.

She crossed her arms. 'We spoke about this already. Your father won't be impressed. Bid La— Miss Matilda good day.'

He just stared at her.

She turned to me. 'Thank you for your visit, Miss Matilda,' she said, dismissing me. In that moment, I despised my own name.

I knew Fen would be in trouble as soon as I left. I was sorry I'd insisted on coming now. 'Mrs Waters, it was my fault. I asked Fen if he'd show me the house.'

Mrs Waters' rigid smile faded. 'Well, it's not my place to say, but your father wouldn't like it. He's assured us that no one from the big house is to come down here. I think it's best if you don't come again.'

'But why?' It was out of my mouth before I could take it back, even if I'd wanted to.

'It's no place for you, Miss Matilda. I'll say goodbye now. I've dinner on the table and Mr Waters is resting,' she said, waiting for me to leave. I had no choice but to turn around and head on home.

As I made my way up the stone steps, I heard her raised voice. 'Don't let me catch you talking about yer da to anyone, ever again, do you hear?'

I never heard Fen's response.

Later that day, I was to regret going there even more. Celine tried to prepare me in her own way. She hovered in the doorway, 'I did warn you, child,' she admonished, as my mother flew into my bedroom, purple with rage.

'Is it true?' she asked, her hand clutching her chest as if she was manually attempting to slow her racing heart. Her eyes bulged in unconcealed rage.

'What?' I answered, though, of course, I knew.

'Is it *true* that you have spent your time in the company of some…' She paused, gathering herself. 'That you have been roaming around your father's estate with some boy in your father's employ?'

'He isn't employed by Father, he's my friend.'

'Your *friend*? You cannot be friends with the children of the parents your father employs.'

'Why not? Father is friends with Fen's father, that's why he built him a house.'

Mother's face grew pale. 'They are not friends, Matilda. And he built his new employee a house, that is different.'

'No, it's not! Father said they were friends – he told me so himself. If Father still treats Mr Waters as a friend, even though he works with him, why can't I do the same with Fen?'

'Because you can be friendly with someone who works for you, Matilda, without being friends. Your father may like this boy's father, but they do not socialise together, and they both understand that distinction.'

'Does it really matter who his family is?'

'Yes, I am afraid that it does matter a great deal who his family is. You're young, but I had thought you understood your position. Our people cannot be friends with those who work for us – it blurs the lines. We can't have them thinking it is acceptable to be so familiar,' she said, appalled.

I stared at her. 'You are a snob.'

I expected her to slap me, or worse, but she simply shrugged. 'Perhaps, but it's a reality nonetheless. And one that I think you do understand, even if you pretend otherwise.'

I saw then that she had been holding something behind her skirts. She brought it forward now. It was a bundle of blue cloth, one that I recognised.

'Why else would you have gone to all the trouble of masquerading as a maid?'

I blinked. 'That's not what I was doing! I wasn't pretending to be anyone else – I used that dress simply to protect my clothes.'

Mother shook her head in exasperation. 'Really, Matilda! I know that is what you told Celine – and kind-hearted soul that she is, she believed you until today's events – that's why she came forward with this dress. She has been thoroughly reprimanded for not coming to me earlier.'

'I didn't need to pretend anything. I'm sorry Celine feels that way, the dress wasn't about anything except keeping my clothes tidy. Fen is my friend, I don't care if he's a farmer's son and I'm a lord's daughter. What difference does it make, really?'

'A great deal, actually. What happens if his father's employment doesn't work out and your father has to let him go?'

'Then that is their business – it's not between us.'

'Now you are just being naive. We are not friends with these people for a reason. They are employed by us and we cannot be showing favouritism.'

'I don't think anyone would see it that way.'

Mother scoffed. 'Really? So that's why Mrs Waters came up here, desperately upset about the whole situation? You've put them all in a terrible predicament. She can't very well order you away, and if her boy is caught with you, they'll be the ones who pay the price. If it makes you feel any better, she was just as horrified as I that the two of you have been sneaking off together. Thankfully, she wasn't aware of this,' she said, holding up the rotten dress. Mother straightened. 'It stops this minute. You will be kept inside the nursery every day. Celine has been given the key and the responsibility – I had expected that she would keep a better eye on you. Know this,' she warned, 'if you are caught again, her dismissal will be because of you.'

My mouth fell open in surprise. I wasn't overly fond of Celine's constant attention, or her tireless attempts at getting me to master French, but I was fond of her.

Mother continued, 'You will be permitted outdoors as usual in the afternoon, however this will only occur with Celine or another member of the family present to supervise. You will not stray far from the house. This will be your life, from now on, until you are made to understand. Are we clear?'

I was furious. 'No, I don't understand why you are punishing me like this – you can't keep me locked up!'

'Yes, I can.'

'For how long?' I asked.

'For as long as necessary.'

CHAPTER THIRTY

'Adam?' I called. It was the morning after the kiss when I came knocking on his door. I hadn't wanted him to leave the night before, but after I'd fallen asleep, he'd gone home for the night. When I woke up, I missed him. Every day for the last week we'd had breakfast together. Since I'd moved into the houseboat community, spending time with Adam almost every day had become one of the easiest things in the world. I was finding that my first cup of morning coffee didn't taste as good unless he was having one with me.

Usually, it was him at my kitchen door, so this was a change. I was looking at his collection of potted herbs with a grin, thinking of how much Gerald had grown since I'd given him his name.

I heard footsteps then the door opened a crack. A woman with long red hair was looking at me with a curious expression.

'Can I help you?' she asked. She had a silky, American drawl.

I looked at her in shock, and frowned. 'Um, yes, I came to see Adam,' I said, wondering if I'd gotten onto the wrong houseboat, though I knew I hadn't.

She raised a pale red brow. 'Oh, well, I'm afraid he's not home right now.'

I nodded and took a step back.

'Shall I tell him you came past?'

'Er, yes, can you tell him Victoria came by?'

The door opened wider. 'Oh – you're the biographer, right?'

I nodded.

'Yeah, he mentioned you,' she said with a smile. Her teeth were very white and even. She was tall, and willowy. Her skin was flawless. I saw her eye my T-shirt with some amusement. 'He said you were so funny with all your T-shirts. I thought he'd made that up, actually,' she smirked.

I wished I wasn't wearing the Supergirl one.

'He did?' I said, not sure if she was trying to be offensive. Wondering what he'd said about them. Wondering if for once I should start listening to my mother about my wardrobe.

'I'm Jenna, by the way, Adam's fiancée.'

I felt my stomach drop. 'I, er, thought that you and he…' I cleared my throat as she shook her head.

'Oh *that*? God, cold feet, you know how it goes, right?'

My eyes widened. 'Do I?' I said in surprise. 'Um, it was quite definitive from what I heard. I mean you… left him, for someone else.'

She nodded. 'Right, well… like I said, we're sorting it all out now.' She said it as if it were some small misunderstanding at the grocery store, instead of an affair with her boss that had gone on for years.

'Is there something you wanted from him?'

'Yes. Well, I just wanted to speak to him.'

She cocked her head to the side, looking me over. 'There wasn't anything between you guys, was there? Adam didn't say there was – I mean, he said you were friends, but that's it. I hope he didn't give you the wrong idea.' She gave a little laugh. 'I'd hate to have to beat up his new little friend,' she added with a wink.

I was fairly sure I could take her, but still, my mouth flew open in surprise. I didn't give her the satisfaction of telling her

Adam and I were just friends. 'Um, just tell him I need to speak with him.'

'Okay, sure,' she said.

I backed away.

'Nice meeting you,' she called.

'Er, yeah,' I said, hightailing it out of there.

I made a beeline for Angie's bookshop, and when I got inside, I closed the door and put the little closed sign up in the window.

'What is it?' she asked in surprise.

'Sorry, but my need is great. There's no one here anyway.'

She shrugged. 'Okay. Do you want to talk about it?'

I leant against the door. 'Have you got any more of that bargain-bin wine – you know, the one that got us pissed in under ten minutes?'

'The one that made you feel hungover for two days?'

'Yes.'

'Of course, bought ten bottles.'

I gave a short laugh. 'Good, I need it.'

What I loved about Angie was that she didn't say things like, 'But it's still morning.'

Ten minutes later, I'd filled her in about Jenna.

'Aha! I knew you had the hots for him.'

'No,' I denied. 'I'm barely divorced,' I added with dignity. I had some more wine, and then squinted at her. 'Of course I have the bloody hots for him! Have you seen him?'

'McBlondeshell? Course I have.'

'Exactly.' I pulled a sad face. He was more than that. We were friends; he made me laugh, he thought I was fun. 'Also… there was this kiss…'

'A kiss?'

I nodded, topping up my cup of wine as I thought of it.

'Just a kiss?' she asked, as if it were nothing. 'You haven't slept together yet?'

I shook my head. 'You don't understand, Ang. It was more than that. It was one of those rock-your-world, weak-at-the-knees, forget-your-own-name kind of kisses.'

Her eyes widened. 'Shit.'

I felt like crying. 'I *know*.'

She cut me an enormous slice of orange polenta cake. Angie seemed to think she could solve the world's problems with sweet treats.

'And she was funny about my clothes,' I said, stabbing at the cake with my fork.

'WHAT?'

'Yeah.'

'What did she say?'

'Nothing bad exactly,' I admitted. 'But there was a look.'

'A look?'

'A *look*. You know the one.' I sighed. 'He just can't take her back. She's mean. A mean, mean girl,' I said, slurring slightly already.

'O-kay,' said Angie, taking the bottle of wine out of my hands. 'No more wine for you.' I sighed, and she patted me on the arm. 'Did *he* say they're back together?'

I shook my head. 'No, she did. Then she made a little joke about how she was going to beat me up.'

Angie looked at me. 'I could take care of that for you, you know. I know a guy.'

I laughed. 'What?'

'Well, I do.'

'Someone who offs people, Angie?'

'No… Well, never mind. Do you want to go back to your place and watch *Waterworld*?'

'No,' I said glumly.

She shrugged. 'How about *Back to the Future?*'

'No, I just want to stay here and feel sorry for myself.'

'I have a better idea,'

'What?'

Ten minutes later, we were in the Tremenara community allotments, playing poker with Gary – aka the Bishop – Jason, Derron and Dave, Sue's husband, who ran the allotment gardens.

'So this is what the Tremenara men do in the day,' I said, looking at my hand of cards. 'And Angie.'

Dave lit a cigar. 'Only on Thursdays,' he said.

'Yeah, on Friday it's bingo,' said the Bishop, and we all laughed. 'By the way, you're sure you don't want me to go to your cottage and perform a cleansing ritual?' he added, his dark eyes serious. 'I think it would be a good idea. Help get rid of any negative energy. I did it for *The Endeavour* and it worked well, didn't it, Dave?'

'What's a cleansing ritual?' asked Derron, shuffling the pack of cards.

'Waving around a bunch of burning sage?' said Jason, shaking his head.

'*No,*' said the Bishop haughtily. 'There's candles too.'

I snorted. 'It's fine, thank you.'

'I know Gaz is a bit…' Dave searched for a word while every one of us tried not to shout out suggestions like mad, crazy, off his head. 'Alternative,' he supplied.

'Good one,' said Angie.

'Thanks,' said Dave, while the Bishop shot her an offended look. 'But there may be something to it. Our barge used to give us endless problems. We went through three different motors, there were always these random leaks – cost us a fortune. Till, when we were at the end of our rope, Gaz came by and did one of his cleansing rituals, and it's been perfect ever since.'

'Was your own fault,' Jason told Dave.

'How's that?' I asked.

'He renamed the boat,' said Derron, almost in a whisper.

I shrugged. 'Yeah?'

Everyone gasped, even Angie.

''Tis the worst luck ever,' explained Jason.

'If you're going to rename it, you have to take it out of the water... bad juju,' said Angie.

'Juju?' I said with a laugh.

'It's not funny,' said the Bishop. 'I had to go through eight bunches of sage before it was cleansed.'

I wasn't the only one whose mouth twitched.

Jason gave me a look. 'So you don't believe in any of that stuff? Is that why you bought the cottage?'

I shrugged. 'Sort of. It's not that I don't believe in bad energy...'

'So you haven't seen any ghosts, then?' asked Derron.

I shook my head. 'Nope, not one.'

'Just lost fifty pounds,' he said sadly. 'Had a bet going.'

'So you think it was all bollocks then, the rumours about your cottage?' asked Jason.

I shrugged, thinking of Tilly and of Fen. 'Not completely,' I admitted. 'Just not what everyone thinks.'

CHAPTER THIRTY-ONE

Cornwall, 1908

Tilly

The calluses on my palms went away, my French improved, and I was more miserable than I'd ever been in the whole of my short life.

Celine took her role as my jailer seriously. Except in my prison, my keeper kept up a running commentary about why I couldn't be a friend to a boy like Fen.

'What did you think was going to happen?' she asked me one day, while I was staring pensively out of the window. 'You're young now, which is the only reason it is forgivable. But if you'd been older, well…'

I looked away. It was typical of adults to think that only they had the right or the capacity to feel. I was tired of being told that something was wrong for no other reason than we had more money than they did. As if that made any sense at all. I'd never thought of myself as radical. Until I met Fen, I'm not sure I really thought about things like that at all.

'It's better this way – for you to forget about him. It's kinder. I hope you can see that someday.'

How was forgetting your best friend a form of kindness?

Still, in her own way, she meant well. I could not say the same for Rose, who, as usual, only seemed to think of herself.

'It's tiresome being around you, Tilly. Lately even more so than usual.'

I didn't answer her. But she continued, losing all patience. 'You can't tell me that you are this surprised at how they reacted. I mean, what on earth were you thinking? Did you even think about how it would look – running around with that boy? I heard he's a cripple too. Honestly, you would think you could have aimed a little higher when you took leave of your senses.'

My world turned red.

Something wild and deep and shocking took charge. I flew at her with my fists and my teeth and my feet, each part of my anatomy at war with hers. My throat grew hoarse from the screeches I was making. It took all of Celine's strength to pull me off.

'What is the meaning of this?' roared my mother, tearing into the room.

I was unable to speak beyond my sobs and over Rose's hysterical wails.

'She's an animal! You god-awful little savage! This is what happens from letting her run wild,' Rose flung herself at Mother, as I gasped for breath. When my vision cleared, I saw the blood welts I'd left behind on her face.

My mother's voice was barely a whisper, but I could hear her as if she was shouting. Her voice was high and cold and I felt a sudden prickle of fear at what I'd done. 'How dare you attack your sister like this!'

I looked at her, tears making steady tracks down my face. 'She called him a cripple,' I said, trying to get her to understand.

My mother looked at Rose for a second, then back at me. I waited for her to say something, for some sort of emotion to be revealed behind her cold eyes, something that would let me know that she understood. But there was nothing there. They only narrowed further as she said, 'But isn't he?'

* * *

It wasn't long afterwards that I planned my first escape. I waited until Celine was in her bed before I snuck in and stole the key. I knew there would be trouble when I got back, but I didn't care. If I could at least explain to Fen what had happened, why I'd disappeared without a trace, it would be worth it.

I carried my boots and tiptoed out the silent nursery in the chill of the night and ran towards the river. I didn't know how I would sneak into the cottage, or which room was Fen's, but I had to try. I slipped through the concealed entrance and made my way silently into the garden.

I hesitated when I saw a light on in the potting shed. I could only imagine how much trouble Fen would get into if his father caught me sneaking around here. I took slow steps and held my breath, but just as I was about to make it past the shed unseen, en route to the stone cottage, my foot bumped an overturned flowerpot, and made a dull thudding sound.

A figure peered out of the shed and my heart began to race. 'Goose?'

I was halfway back towards the wall when I turned.

'Fen?'

'What are you doing here?' he whispered.

I swallowed. 'I just wanted to, well, to come and say sorry.'

'Why are you sorry?'

'For getting you in trouble… for everything.'

'You didn't break the window.'

I stepped forward to see him better. His hair was still as wild as ever, though he seemed slightly taller. He was wearing an old knitted jumper; it was blue like his eyes.

'What?' I asked.

'The window – didn't you know? I thought someone told you.'

At my blank look, he continued, with a throaty laugh. 'Well, I wasn't going to say goodbye without a fight, so I tried to visit you the other night.'

'What? You didn't! When?'

'A few nights ago. Me mam told me that she'd gone to your mother to tell her that you'd been here, but I kept looking out for you… I never realised that they'd actually lock you up for it. So as the weeks went by, I thought well, enough, you know? I asked one of the maids which one was your bedroom—'

'You didn't!'

'Oh yes, I did,' he laughed. 'Thought it was right romantic too, I must say. Very Shakespeare.'

I laughed.

'Yes, well, you should laugh. It was your sister's room, and instead of a soft tapping on the glass, I broke the whole pane.'

I gasped. 'Why didn't anyone tell me?'

'I'm sure they thought you'd do, well… this,' he pointed out.

'I would have.'

We shared a grin. 'Come inside,' he said, beckoning me to the potting shed. 'Come see all the seedlings.'

I followed him into the shed, breathing in the scent of potting soil, honeysuckle and wild lavender.

'What happened after you broke the window? Did you make a run for it?'

'Ah, yeah…'

His face was close to the lantern light, and that's when I saw the greenish bruise that covered most of his eye socket.

I gasped. 'What happened?'

He shrugged. 'Me da.'

'Oh my God, because of me?'

He frowned. 'No, because I was an idiot who broke your da's window. Doesn't matter.'

'It *does* matter!'

'No, it doesn't. At least now your da knows that I've been punished, so all is well.'

I let out a heavy sigh. 'No, it's not. It's my fault.'

'It's no one's fault,' he said, squeezing my shoulder. 'And I'd do it again.'

'You would?'

'Of course.'

'So what did you want to tell me?'

'Tell you?'

'Yes, if you'd got the right window, and hadn't broken it, what did you want to say?'

'That I'll always be your friend, Tilly Asprey, even when you can't be mine.'

CHAPTER THIRTY-TWO

Present day

The next day began with a hangover that would last until midnight the following evening.

I made some coffee, fed the ducks outside my window and got dressed. When I left, I passed Adam's houseboat and felt my shoulders slump – I didn't want to think of him with Jenna.

I hadn't gotten back until late, after playing poker with the guys and Angie until well into the evening, when we took the party back to the Bishop's boat and finished off the rest of his homemade beer.

I felt like death warmed up.

At the cottage, I lost myself in work, the manual labour helping to combat my fatigue and hangover. Today was a momentous day as, after weeks of work, which had involved laying down cables and drilling holes into walls and beneath the floors, for the first time in its over one-hundred-year history, there was now electricity at the cottage, along with a brand-new front door. Alas, my old brass key would be only an ornament.

I unpacked my new kettle. There were no floors just yet, but at least I could have a cup of tea on the premises. I made the vow then to avoid alcohol for as long as possible. 'Forgive me, liver,' I said. 'For I have sinned.'

So far I had one cup and no sugar but still, it didn't matter.

I took my tea into the garden and stood by the shed, wondering if it was the same one where Tilly had found Fen that night. It would be incredible if it were. I opened the door and for a second I could imagine the scent of wild lavender.

I was excited to bring the cottage back to life, and to learn a little about the people who had been there before.

Before I'd left the Bishop's boat, I'd somehow managed to agree to one of his 'cleansing rituals' for the cottage. In my drunken stupor I'd said to Ange, 'It's only sage, right? What harm can it do?'

None, I supposed. But still, I wasn't too crazy about my new pal Gaz running amok through my soon-to-be-restored cottage with his Russian hat and a pile of burning herbs, even if I *had* finished all his beer.

My mobile beeped and I dug it out of my pocket. It was a message from Adam.

'*Where have you been, stranger?*'

For a while I stared at it in shock, unsure what to respond. Another text came through.

'*I came past the cottage yesterday but you weren't there. I've got some new pages for you.*'

I stared at the message for some time. How could he just act as if nothing had happened?

'*I thought you were busy?*' I texted back.

His reply came almost immediately. '*Busy? Never too busy for you. Want to meet up? How about lunch? Got something I want to tell you.*'

I could just imagine what it was. I suspected it had something to do with a long-legged, redheaded ex-fiancée.

'*Sorry, can't today. I'm off to London tomorrow, but we can meet up when I'm back on Tuesday,*' I replied, thinking I'd deal with the damages then. I went back to working on the cottage, trying and failing to ignore the knot in my chest.

On my way home, I popped into the Harbour Cafe ordering a cappuccino from Sue and taking a seat at the counter.

'You're looking a little worse for wear.'

'Thanks,' I said.

She shrugged. 'Dave told me you joined their poker game.'

I smiled, pushing my hair behind my ears. 'Yeah. Remind me never to do that again.'

She shook her head. 'I know you're on a sabbatical, but I can tell you right now, that's no way to spend your time.'

I laughed. 'You don't have to tell me – or my liver. We're both paying the price today.'

She grinned. 'Can I get you something to eat?'

I nodded. 'What do you recommend?'

'The sea bass. It's pretty great with the new potatoes and rocket from the allotment gardens.'

'Great,' I said, taking a sip of my coffee, just as the door swung wide, letting in a blast of crisp air.

Just then an American voice drawled, 'Ah! Finally, someplace warm. I thought I was gonna die of cold.'

I looked up and felt my stomach drop.

The speaker had long red hair and looked like she'd just stepped out of the pages of a catalogue for fashionable winter attire. She was wearing a stylish cream coat, with her long slim legs encased in leggings and expensive-looking leather boots. She took off her cream knitted hat and shook out her hair, her eyes scanning the room for an available chair. Unfortunately, they also found me, even though I did my best to sink into the floor.

'Victoria?' she said, in her loud, carrying voice. Half the room turned to stare. I hunched my shoulders and silently prayed for her to go away.

'Do you know her?' asked Sue, as Jenna made her way towards me.

'That's Adam's fiancée, or ex-fiancée, I'm not sure which,' I said, still desperately hoping that he hadn't fallen for this awful woman's lies again.

Sue's brown eyes popped. 'His *what*?'

'Jenna,' I said, as she came to stand in front of me. 'You're still here. How…?' I couldn't bring myself to say anything more. 'How?' I repeated.

'I'll be in town for a while,' she said, her tone implying that I was foolish for thinking anything less, while giving me a mega-watt smile.

'Oh. Great,' I said, feeling anything but great as I cleared my throat. 'So you're staying with Adam?'

'Oh… no. I mean, he wanted me to,' she said, giving me a very fake smile. 'He practically insisted, poor thing, but have you seen the size of that little boat of his? I mean, you can hardly swing a cat in there. You might not realise this, as you're British, but where we come from the houses are, well, a lot bigger.'

I managed to bite my tongue, somehow, though I wanted to give her perfect long legs a swift kick.

When I saw Sue's shocked face, I could tell I wasn't the only one.

'So I'm staying at this little inn, just up the road,' she continued, blithely ignorant of how obnoxious she was being.

'The Black Horse Inn?' I asked, feeling a mild sense of poetic justice.

'Yeah, there,' she said, giving a little shudder. 'Absolutely vile, as you can imagine. No heating to speak of, but it's a small price to pay for love.'

'I'm sure,' I said, wanting to stab her with my cappuccino spoon. I got up before I could carry out that thought and cleared my throat. 'Ah, Sue, it'll just be the coffee, thanks. Got to run.'

Sue nodded. 'Yeah, you've got that thing,' she said, playing along. As someone who had been steering me towards Adam since I'd arrived, she understood that I needed to be anywhere that his beautiful fiancée wasn't.

CHAPTER THIRTY-THREE

Cornwall, 1908

Tilly

Every day I waited for midnight so that I could sneak out and see Fen. I was careful during the day to follow all of Celine's instructions, and I took a conscious interest in my lessons, especially botany. I felt mildly guilty at Celine's enthusiasm, as she thought I'd finally given up on Fen and as a result was really trying her best to encourage it.

She sourced books and took me along to meet Terry, one of the gardeners, who showed me around the greenhouses and spoke to me about what grew when and how, all while I held a secret smile in my heart, one that got me through Rose's insufferable scorn and my mother's smug belief that her plan had worked.

Dark circles formed beneath my eyes and every day was a constant battle with fatigue, but I was happier than I'd been in weeks.

As night fell, I counted the hours till the household went to sleep. As time passed and I seemed less resistant to my incarceration, Celine began to keep the key in the same, careless spot on her bureau. It was easy to convince myself that this was ample justification for my theft.

In the still hum of the darkness, I tiptoed out like I had that first night and made my way to the cottage, to the shed and what had become our midnight garden. Together we'd plant seeds that I'd got from Terry during the day, and Fen and I would work out a plan for the kitchen garden. Sometimes Arthur came to find us and would curl up at Fen's feet, like a cat.

Here, away from the roar of the ocean, we were safe. 'Mam sleeps like the dead, and da, well, he doesn't like to come out at night,' Fen told me.

'Why not?'

'Just doesn't like the dark.'

Every night he'd show me the seedlings that had come to life. We planted whatever we could find: hollyhocks, tulips, dahlias, feverfew.

I'd tell Fen about what I'd learned from my books. Show him the pages that I'd turned down just for him.

We became fascinated with the language of flowers, and the early Victorians.

'Apparently, almost all the flowers stand for something. And when you're sent something like this,' I said, pointing to an illustration of datura, 'you were really telling someone that they had deceitful charms.'

'What about these?' he said, pointing to meadowsweet.

I opened up a book with old-fashioned writing, scanned the contents, and then snickered, 'Uselessness.'

He laughed aloud. 'The only problem is that everyone would know what you were saying.'

'How's that?'

'Well, most of the Victorians knew about this, didn't they?'

I nodded. 'I suppose so.'

'Well, if it were me, I'd prefer that it was more of a secret code. I mean, what's the point of sending datura to someone when, say, your great-aunt knew what you were saying as well?'

I laughed. 'Good point! You know, if it were me, and this were my garden...'

'It *is* your garden – it's *our* garden,' said Fen.

'You know what I mean. Well, if it were truly mine, I'd only plant the most unusual plants and flowers. And I'd use that to create a secret code.'

He nodded. 'Not the usual hothouse flowers.'

'Exactly.'

CHAPTER THIRTY-FOUR

Present day

The London sky was the colour of pewter, and from the open kitchen came the scent of caramelised onions and green peppers. I breathed it in, along with my surroundings. I loved Cornwall, but there was something about London too, something that couldn't help but make me feel alive.

The crowds were another story. I hadn't missed those.

'Cooking? *You?*' said my editor, James Marsons, with no attempt to hide his scepticism as he took a seat opposite me. We were in a cafe around the corner from his offices, near King's Cross, where we'd decided to meet while I was in town finalising the paperwork for the sale of my former marital home.

James had grown a moustache, but he still looked like he was only barely out of his twenties. He was tall, thin and pale, with large green eyes that never missed a thing.

'You look tired, James,' I said, noticing the shadows under his eyes, like dark bruises.

He waved a slim hand. 'Course I'm tired – and pale. Haven't been outside in six months. You used to look like this too, you know. Except, my God, look at you! You've actually got a tan. How? Also, are you really wearing a skirt?'

I shrugged. 'I walk, I go outside, sit in the sun, do some gardening…'

He looked at me as if I had suddenly switched over to Japanese.

'The skirt, well, that's only because I'm staying with my mother at the moment and she stole my suitcase and bought me this to wear instead.'

He shook his head and gave me an amused look. 'You do look nice, though. More importantly, are you really living on a houseboat?'

I nodded, and couldn't help but smile. 'Oh, it's lovely. It's tiny, of course, but I'll actually be really sad to leave it once the cottage is ready. There's this little family of ducks who come visit me every morning, and I wake up every day to the sound of the water lapping.'

He shook his head at me in mock disgust. 'And you're cooking for other people who are still alive to tell the tale?' James was clearly not ready to let that one go.

As my editor for over ten years, he'd sampled more than one failed dinner experiment, after which we'd had to resort to takeout instead, so he had reason for his scepticism.

'I know, I know, but things have changed. *I've* changed.'

'I can see that. You look great – really. I was hoping when you called that you were ready to talk about a new project.'

I smiled. 'You know me too well. I have something, I think… but it's early days yet.'

'Can I hear a little bit about it?'

I hesitated. 'Not yet. But soon, I promise.'

'I can't wait,' he said. 'Okay, tell me about this cottage of yours.' So I did.

'When it's ready you should come down, have a break, it'll do you good,' I told him.

'You know, after seeing you and how great you look, I think I will.'

* * *

Walking the familiar streets around London, it was hard to believe that I wouldn't be calling it home ever again. Earlier in the day, I'd met Mark at the lawyer's office as we finalised the last bits of paperwork for the sale.

The house in Chelsea had sold for more than we'd expected and I was finally closing the last chapter between Mark and me.

We were both overly polite to one another. Though it didn't last too long on Mark's part. Suzie, a clerk with a too-tight bun and even tighter pencil skirt, had looked at me and remarked, 'It's always a bit sad to sell your first home, isn't it?' And Mark had given me a cold look and said, 'Not that we needed to.'

I'd closed my eyes and counted to three. A few months ago all I would have been able to do was retaliate with hurt and anger. Perhaps I really had changed, in more ways than one.

Before we left, I gave Mark a smile, and said, 'Look after yourself.'

He nodded. 'You too, Smudge.'

Back at my parents' place in Knightsbridge that evening, my mother poured me a glass of wine, and said, 'So, your father and I have been talking…'

I looked at my father. We shared a look that said, '*Your mother spoke, and I agreed.*' He nodded along, but his big brown eyes were amused. They were the same eyes as mine. He was wearing his navy bathrobe, and the little tufts of dark hair on his balding head were standing up.

'And we've decided,' Mum continued, 'to buy a cottage in Cornwall too.'

'Ah,' I said, fixing a smile in place. I cleared my throat. 'That's great.'

'Just for holidays, you know,' she said.

I exhaled.

She snorted. 'Don't be like that. It'll be lovely.'

'Yes, it will,' I said, taking a sip of wine. 'Have you decided where you'll buy?'

'No, not really.'

'Well, I think with your granddaughter to think of, it just makes sense that you consider Cloudsea, you know, so you're closer to her.'

She nodded. 'Yes, well now you mention it, that does make sense.'

I buried a smile. Stuart was going to kill me, but it would be worth it.

To be honest though, having my parents around a bit more wouldn't be the worst thing in the world.

Until… 'What's that?' I asked, pointing at the pile of plastic bags in the corner of the kitchen.

'Oh, *that?*' Mum said, dismissively. 'Just some stuff for charity.'

Out of the top of one bag I could just make out what looked like a shoe. I stood up to take a closer look.

'I think I'll call it a night,' said my father, exiting fast.

'Is that what I think it is?' I said, pointing at the bag, where it looked like one of my Converse trainers was poking out.

She shrugged. 'I've been through your suitcase and made three piles for charity. Thought we could go shopping tomorrow, what do you say?'

I gave her a look. 'No! Stop going through my suitcase, or from now on I'll book myself into a hotel whenever I'm in London.'

Part of me hoped she'd say, 'Fine, book a hotel.' There I'd have peace and quiet – and access to the full extent of my wardrobe, judgement-free.

But she just sighed. 'Okay, fine, you win. But please consider giving up just one of the bags.'

'Half a bag,' I conceded. 'And we visit one shop tomorrow, that's it.'

God help me, but I liked my new skirt.

When I climbed into the spare bed that night, I thought of what James had said about how much I'd changed. The truth was that so much had had to happen before I could actually live a simpler life – but it was simpler now, at last. All I needed now to feel perfectly content was a slice of Angie's lemon cake, a good book, and perhaps the company of my favourite blue-eyed American.

I tried not to think of Adam, but it was hard. I couldn't deny that my feelings for him had grown. The kiss had just pushed it all to the surface.

Why did Jenna have to turn up now?

CHAPTER THIRTY-FIVE

Cornwall, 1908

Tilly

There was a solitary flower lying on my dressing table. It was the first thing I noticed when I entered my bedroom to change before dinner.

It looked like an ordinary daisy, with thin, pale, spiky petals and a bright yellow stamen, but I knew who it was from.

Wrapped around the stem was a thin piece of paper. I unravelled it, saw Fen's messy handwriting and began to laugh.

Goose flower.

Soon, Fen and I were taking other inspirations from the Victorians. One night, while we worked at the wooden table that he had pulled into the shed, measuring soil into the waiting pots in the early April light, we decided to create a coded alphabet as well.

'Celine told me that the Victorians used to send secret letters, often written in code. The place where you put your stamp, for instance, had a hidden meaning. We could do that – you know, if you want to send messages in the day.'

Fen agreed. 'Da told me that during the war they used coded messages too.'

Taking a pen and pencil, we worked out our own cipher text.
I copied it out for both of us. 'Keep it safe.'

He nodded. 'I'll keep it here,' he said, burying it in a small
blue pot. 'So no one will find it.'

He took a green flowerpot from the shelf. 'We'll use this one
for the messages. I'll put it next to the big pear tree by the brook
– Old Tom, it'll be our mailing box.'

So our secret communication began. Old Tom proved to be a
good aid. As I appeared more docile at home, and reports of my
new studious side gained traction, I was allowed to venture out alone
again. Though someone from the house was never too far away.

'Celine tells me you've progressed quite well,' my mother had
said. 'I'm glad to hear it, glad to see you've put that foolishness
behind you.'

I had given her a tight smile and ignored Rose's disbelieving
scoff – something I was later to regret.

Most days, I would sit underneath the branches of the pear
tree and read, and when I was sure that whoever had been appointed to follow me wasn't looking, I would slip my fingers
beneath the pot and quickly place my latest message inside, or
take one out and slip it between the pages of my book. Later, at
home, I'd read it in private.

In time, our made-up code became as easy to read as if it had
been written in plain text. Yet, with the aid of the cipher, we told
each other things that we couldn't have face-to-face.

I learned sometimes he worried that his father's black turns
would drown them all, and I discovered that it was one of the
reasons he was always outdoors.

I told him how I dreaded the idea of living like Rose, and
how disappointed they were when I hadn't been the boy they so
longed for. How my name was meant to have been Mathew, and
how they had to call me Matilda instead.

Our letters kept me sane on those endless days of monotonous lessons and Rose's endless tirades against Father's refusal to allow us to dress in the season's latest fashions.

With the arrival of spring, the fields became a golden horizon, with daffodils as far as the eye could see. My favourite place to view them was from Old Tom; it was like being surrounded by a sea of sunshine.

With the promise of summer came the first storms. Fen opened the door to the shed one night and found me shivering.

'You're soaked to the skin, goose,' he said in sympathy. 'Come in.' He hustled me inside, shrugging out of his coat and wrapping it around me.

My teeth chattered as I tried to speak. 'D-didn't think it would come down so hard.'

Fen was exhausted from the long hours at the farm, but he wanted to hear everything that had happened since my last message to him. We waited for the storm to subside, but it only intensified. Well after when I would usually leave, we were still trapped in the shed. We sat against the wall and there in the quiet, with the rain beating a steady tattoo outside, he slipped his hand in mine, and I smiled under cover of night.

In the morning, they found us fast asleep, curled around each other like spoons. When I opened my eyes there was a clatter and a shout and the first thing I saw was Rose's smug, scornful smile and the look of horror on my mother's face as she snatched my hand away from Fen's.

CHAPTER THIRTY-SIX

Present day

'Did you hear about Graham Waters?' asked Angie, as I took a seat at the little table with the potted fern, which also held one of the illicitly created and curated piles that subverted her anarchic filing system. This one I'd started myself, with a selection of novels set in the Wild West.

Her long grey hair was loose, and today she had on a T-shirt that said, '*Save the Rhinos*'.

The store was busier than usual, and I'd taken refuge with my cappuccino – a first for *The Floating Bookstore*. Before Angie and I had become friends she'd only believed in plain, percolated coffee, but it seems things had changed in my brief absence.

'What happened?' I asked, fearing the worst.

'Adam took him to Truro yesterday, and it looks like the new treatment is working. They're running some more tests and keeping him down there for a few days, but Adam said that it's looking good.'

'I'm so glad,' I said. 'I know how worried Adam has been.'

She nodded. 'Have you seen him yet?'

I shook my head. 'Not yet.'

'You must have passed each other?'

Before she could start asking me about him, or his possible fiancée, I changed the subject. 'Did you get a new coffee machine?'

She shrugged, trying and failing to look innocent.

I looked at her. 'Is this your way of saying you missed me?'

She snorted. 'Don't be so soft.' But she couldn't quite hide her smile.

'So… I met Jenna,' said Angie.

'Oh?' I said. It was my turn to feign innocence.

'Yes, seems like she's driving Gilly bonkers down at the Black Horse Inn. Apparently she's written several complaints and even demanded that she get in someone from London to look at the heating system. Gilly was apoplectic.'

'I'll bet,' I sighed. So Jenna was still here. I'd hoped that while I'd been in London, she would have just disappeared, but it looked like I was out of luck.

'Well, the one good thing is that at least she's not staying with Adam.'

That was true. Though I remembered how she'd told me he'd begged her to stay.

'So you haven't spoken to him at all?' Angie persisted.

'No, but I will. I'd rather hoped to today, but he's in Truro, and I don't want to do it over the phone.'

She cut me a rather large slice of chocolate pecan cake.

I shook my head. 'You're bad for my waistline,' I said, though I ate it anyway.

There was the telltale scent of burnt sage lingering in the cottage. I suspected the Bishop had let himself in to perform the cleansing ritual.

The tangy scent of herbs mixed fragrantly with that of fresh paint. I was covered in paint splatters, and my shoulders ached, but I was satisfied.

For the first time in decades the walls in the sea room were freshly painted and free of damage, not a vine or a leaf in sight. I stood and looked at my progress, gazing upon the blue-green ocean through the large, round window with a contented sigh. We were still far from finished, but it was starting to look more like a home every day.

Jack and Will had left earlier but I carried on, wanting to see the room completed. It was close to 10 p.m. when I finished.

My neck and shoulders were stiff and sore, but still I cleaned the brushes I'd used, along with the roller, with turpentine, then went to the kitchen to wash my hands. I was surprised when I heard a knock at the door, so late at night.

'Adam?' I said in surprise.

'Hi,' he greeted me. He was wearing that blue jumper I loved, the one that made his eyes look almost electric. 'What are doing here?' I asked.

'I – well, I came to see you,' he said. 'Um, obviously.'

'Right. Come in,' I said, opening the door. 'Coffee?'

'Love a cup,' he said, his eyes taking in the room. 'Can't believe how different it looks. It's amazing.'

'Thanks,' I said, switching on the kettle. 'So Angie told me about your uncle. I meant to call, it's great news.'

He nodded. 'Yeah, it's made such a difference,' he said, coming to stand behind me.

I swallowed as his hands traced the splodges of paint on my arms, a gentle caress. I stepped away quickly and he frowned while I levelled ground coffee into the cafetière and filled it with boiling water.

'So I met Jenna,' I said, not looking at him.

'I see,' he said, folding his arms. 'I thought that might be the case.'

I looked up at him.

'Well, after the other night I didn't hear from you for days, even though I kept trying to call and text, and I had to wonder what happened.'

'I ran into your fiancée is what happened.'

'*Ex*-fiancée,' he said. 'Why didn't you just call me?'

I looked at him in disbelief. 'I find your fiancée in your boat, first thing in the morning, and she tells me that you guys are going to work things out, that it was all a little misunderstanding between you – but *I'm* the one who should have called *you*?'

'Yes, actually. Because if you had, then you would have known that I told her to take a short walk to hell. Instead you did what you do best, right? You decided to avoid me, and my calls, and run off to London for a week.'

My mouth fell open. *He* was angry. I couldn't believe it.

'Well, it's true, isn't it? I mean, I told you how my ex had an affair with her boss, skipped out on our wedding and left me to try and sell the house we'd just bought together, and you think that just because she showed up here I'd go running into her arms. Christ, I mean, after all this time we've spent together, I thought you *knew* me.'

'And I thought you knew *me*! I mean, I moved to Cornwall after my husband had an *affair*, and I'm supposed to just think the best when I find another woman in your home? Especially one you've got a history with?'

'Yes – especially when you knew what I had gone through. If Mark had showed up here, my first thought wouldn't be that you'd got back together,' he said, turning on his heel.

'Even if he told you that we had?'

'Yes, even then!'

'Then you're lying to yourself!' I shouted, but he'd already left.

CHAPTER THIRTY-SEVEN

Cornwall, 1908

Tilly

For the first time in my life, the whispers I heard in my secret refuge behind the library curtains were about me.

I heard, 'Imagine if she wasn't still a child?' whispered more than once, and it wasn't only Martha who pointed out that thirteen wasn't quite as young as all that. 'Girls that young get into trouble all the time. What if something happened?'

I'd lived in the countryside long enough to know what they meant.

Aside from that scandalous speculation, the question everyone kept asking, while I became a ghost in my own house, was what would be done with me. Mother wouldn't look me in the eye and Rose gloated as if she'd won some great victory, not realising that her own life would change, too, as my parents were forced to consider their options.

Mother insisted that the Waters family be removed. Father, thankfully, refused.

But that didn't stop Mother, or Mr Waters, apparently, as I heard later that Fen had been sent to live with his aunt in Yorkshire the next day.

I was devastated, and I wasn't the only one. Mrs Price took it the hardest. From my perch behind the curtain in the library, I heard Edmund tell Martha, 'And why shouldn't Mrs Price be upset? She has every right. Fen's her nephew, isn't he? She was that glad to think they'd come to live here. And now this? I don't think it's right that they sent him away like that.'

'I know,' whispered Martha. 'If you ask me, it's the young miss who should have paid the price. It was she who was found at their cottage, she who was sneaking about at night.'

'Aye, but he was sneaking too, they're both to blame,' said Edmund.

'Yes, but it's not like she's getting punished, is she?'

Later that day, I approached the kitchen in trepidation. 'Mrs Price?'

She looked up, her face folded into a frown. 'Oh, 'tis you, is it?'

I noted her tone. We'd been friends of a kind before, when she used to pack me lunches that I would take on my adventures with Fen, but perhaps all that had changed now.

Her manner became brusque. 'I don't know nothing about it, so don't ask. What you two did…' She shook her head. 'Well, I thought you had more sense.'

'Please, Mrs Price. No one will tell me anything. I haven't had a chance to say goodbye, even. If you could just give me his address, maybe I could write—'

'And risk my *job*?' she cried, horrified. 'No disrespect, miss, but I'm not daft. You can't ask me to take that kind of a chance for you.'

I hadn't thought of it that way. Mrs Price sighed. 'Now, look, lass, I don't wish to be cruel, I really don't, but haven't you done enough?'

I blinked back tears, while she continued, 'That family has been holding on by a feather. A feather. You don't know the half of it. And sending Fen away now? Well, I just don't know what will happen. She won't forgive them this, I can tell you.'

'Who? What do you mean?'

She put her hands in her hair and gave a vigorous shake of her head. 'Never mind that, I shouldn't have said anything about it. Only it seems unfair, is all. It's he who will suffer most. Your lot never suffer, do they? Not when it comes to this sort of thing. I told him that, right from the start.'

Mrs Price's words, 'your lot never suffer', would prove false soon enough, though it brought little consolation. A few days later, I was sent to the Amelia Laurens School for Young Ladies.

What was worse, and it was hard to imagine anything worse than having Fen torn out of my life and the pair of us being sent away from our homes, was that in the crossfire, Celine became our casualty. She was summarily dismissed without any references, though I had railed and cried and tried to get my parents to understand that it wasn't her fault.

'I did warn you, Matilda,' said Mother coldly, 'that if you persisted, Celine would pay the price. You made your choice.'

I'd made my choice and in the process Rose had got her revenge. She'd been the one who betrayed me, biding her time until she could ensure that I was well and truly caught, even if it meant that she too had to lose her governess. 'You can say what you like, Tilly, it all comes down to the fact that you did it. Perhaps next time you'll think twice about attacking me,' she said on the day of my departure.

'I will,' I agreed. 'Next time I won't let you recover.'

Father took me to the school himself. He seethed with suppressed anger during the train journey, his jaw clenched; the scar on his hand glowed white as he balled his fist.

I was to understand later that I'd done something that to him was even more unforgivable than sneaking out against their wishes: I had risked Idyllwild.

'You don't even realise what could have happened, what you put in danger,' he said at last, as we arrived that cold morning at the school gates. 'And now you get to have what you have always desired,' he added, referring to my wish to receive a proper education, 'while I must go home and attempt to deal with the damage.'

It would be two years before I saw him again, and many more before I truly understood what he meant, and that actually it had very little to do with the fact that I had dared to fall in love with a boy who no one thought I should.

My time at the Amelia Laurens School for Young Ladies got off to an ominous start when I was assigned a room with a girl who made Rose seem sweet. Her name was Katie Thorpe, and her face looked as if it had been permanently set into a scowl, at odds with her wispy blonde hair and syrupy-sweet voice.

When Miss Laurens showed me into my room, Katie magnanimously welcomed me by announcing that she had readied my side of the room.

The headmistress beamed at her. 'That's what you'll find here, Miss Matilda – great friends, willing spirits and an appetite for learning.'

My smile was thin. All I could see was that the girl had ensured that my part of the room appeared to be a rather barren cell in comparison to hers. There was even a thin white ribbon tacked down the centre of the carpet, which clearly marked where her space ended and mine began. I noticed that mine did not include the small sofa or the chest of drawers.

Miss Laurens took my case from me and put it on the bed. The finality of it made me want to howl. 'It's alright to be a little homesick,' she said kindly.

If this was what homesick was, I didn't know how anyone recovered.

When Miss Laurens left, Katie fixed me with an appraising look and dropped the helpful demeanour; whatever she saw, she seemed to find me wanting. 'I don't like wet, whiny girls. So if you're going to cry, I suggest you take yourself off someplace else.'

'I'm *not* going to cry,' I said, though I had been on the verge. My chin began to wobble in a way that mortified me.

She shot me a look of revulsion, while I clamped my Judas chin with my hand and quickly looked down.

'See that you don't. Furthermore,' she said, with a smirk, 'we aren't going to be "chums", just so you know. Not after what I heard about why you're really here, what you *did*. Miss Laurens might make an exception based on the amount of money your father gave her, but the Thorpes will not.'

The one advantage of having Katie Thorpe as my roommate was that the enemies she'd boiled with her burnt-sugar voice had formed an outsiders' club that welcomed me as one of their own from the start. This mainly consisted of one, Alice McKibbon. She was shy, kind and had a stutter that made any sort of speech painfully difficult to witness. As a result, she was the person Katie Thorpe despised the most.

What I discovered upon meeting Alice was that it was terribly difficult to keep feeling sorry for yourself when someone so clearly had it much worse that you did.

Alice was short and pudgy and had hair that on a good day liked to frizz. But she was smart and funny and quick to stand up for others. 'Ignore K-Katie. We all do,' she said.

Later, I discovered that she had cousins who could easily rival Rose in their vapidity, and were every bit the type of girl Mother wished I'd been. The Hammond twins – Rebecca and Emily – were, I discovered, one of the reasons Mother had agreed to send me away to this particular school when they were searching for a solution for what to do with me.

The Hammond family were exactly the sort of people that my mother wished to be associated with: rich, connected, highly regarded by the monarchy and one of the oldest families in the south. Mother particularly liked the idea of the twins' brother, the future Earl of Monthesay, Charles Hammond, as a match for Rose.

Their father, Arnold Hammond, had been a general in the South African war, and as such, shared some common ground with Father. Unfortunately, it proved difficult to get my father to act in any way upon this connection.

I should have realised that sending me here was not solely as a consequence of my friendship with Fen. Rather, it was a calculated decision to bring our family closer to the Hammonds. And, unknowingly, when I befriended their cousin, poor Alice, I played my own part in my mother's scheme.

The Hammond twins' room was two doors down from mine, and only the very lucky were invited in. They both had chestnut curls and bright green eyes, but they weren't identical. Emily's features were more delicate, and they matched her mild, soft-spoken manner. Rebecca, though not as classically beautiful, was the one who captured your attention. There was something about her, a kind of charisma that made her hard to deny, like a force of nature.

The first night she invited me into their room, she ushered me in with Alice, and we took a seat on a plush velvet chaise before the fireplace. It was easily one of the biggest rooms in the estate, furnished extravagantly.

'So,' said Rebecca, looking at me. 'You're Rose's little sister?'

'Yes,' I said.

'I'm Rebecca. This is Emily.'

SUMMER AT SEAFALL COTTAGE

Emily, dressed in pink, smiled in welcome from her seat on the bed.

Rose had met the Hammonds on several occasions, due in no small part to Mother's schemes, but this was the first time I had been formally introduced to them.

'You don't look anything like her,' Rebecca pointed out, her eyes narrowing.

I didn't know if she thought this was a good thing or a bad thing – I suspected the latter.

'I take after my father.'

Emily peered at me from the bed, her face cocked to the side. 'I think when you're older, you'll be prettier, don't you, Becca?' She was holding a box of Turkish delight, which she offered round.

Rebecca shrugged. 'We haven't met your father. Doesn't he spend all his time on some flower farm?'

I nodded. 'Idyllwild – they grow daffodils there. He breeds different types.'

Emily's eyes widened. 'That sounds dreamy.'

Rebecca's eyebrows shot into her hairline.

Emily shrugged. 'Well, it does,' she insisted. 'I love the name...'

'Thank you,' I said, though I had had no part in its creation. I missed it terribly.

'Speaking of what happened on your father's farm,' said Rebecca, somewhat crudely, and with a naughty grin. 'Is it true?'

'What?' I asked.

'D-don't!' stammered Alice. It was the first time she'd spoken.

'D-d-don't worry, cousin,' mocked Rebecca with a catty smile, and in a pretty good imitation of Alice's stutter, much to her mortification. Alice's cheeks had gone scarlet. I set my teeth, and Rebecca continued sweetly, 'I just want to hear the truth – set the record straight.'

'Well, it's got to be better than the rumours, surely,' agreed Emily, fishing out another Turkish delight and popping it into her mouth.

'So,' Rebecca prodded, 'what happened? Why were you sent here? Did you really try and sabotage his farm? That's what Katie told us.'

'I did not.'

'What then?'

'I was friends with someone they didn't approve of.'

'Is that all?' said Alice, shaking her head.

Rebecca narrowed her eyes. 'I bet it was a boy.'

I shrugged.

'Who was it?' asked Rebecca.

I didn't know why I answered. 'The son of the head gardener at Idyllwild.'

Their eyes popped.

'You mean a commoner?' said Emily. 'This *is* going to be interesting.'

CHAPTER THIRTY-EIGHT

Present day

Someone was gardening at night at Seafall Cottage.

One morning, I discovered that the leaves had been cleared and the weeds had vanished. And now, as the wintry chill gave way to spring, the first bloom appeared, a solitary, blue velveteen stalk, in a mound of clear, turned earth.

The only person it could have been was the old man. Perhaps it was his way of apologising for taking the letters, or was meant to be a kind of payment for sleeping in the shed.

I'd found an old tin mug and a gas cooker hidden behind the door in the old, potting shed, which explained how he was able to survive when there wasn't electricity or heating. I hadn't, however, seen him again. My guess was that he came at night, well after I had left.

I'd have to speak to him eventually, find some other solution, but the few times I'd come past or stayed later into the evening, in the hopes that I would see him, he hadn't come past. I suspected he simply stayed away. I couldn't help wondering how he knew when I was there or not.

There had been so much activity here lately, what with the builders and my daily, small efforts over the past months. I began to think I'd scared him off. I wished I could find him and ask him what he knew and why he'd taken the letters from the chest.

He never came when Jack or Will was here, and the last time I'd seen him was when he was standing in my kitchen. The day he tipped his hat at me.

I still hadn't told anyone about him. But he was harmless, I was sure of that. I left bread and bottles of water in the shed, but he never took them. Instead, I'd find new packets of seed, and notice that the earth had been freshly turned. He couldn't have much, so why not take the bread and water? Did he want me to know that he wasn't destitute? Pride can be a hard thing, I figured. But still, what was with the letters? It seemed like he wanted me to have them, and the diary too. So why not just come out and speak to me about it all, if he knew something I didn't?

There was only one person that I wanted to discuss it with, and that was Adam. But we hadn't spoken in days. Not since our fight.

While we watched *Divine Secrets of the Ya-Ya Sisterhood* – another one of Angie's one-pound charity finds – I filled her in on what had happened, how angry he'd been.

'I mean, how can he honestly think that I would just know that he hadn't taken her back?'

Angie popped some microwave popcorn in her mouth and frowned. 'But he didn't, did he? I mean, she's still hanging about, but I haven't seen them together.'

'Yes, I know.'

She shook her head and pressed pause. 'Do you want to know what I think?'

'Probably not, but go ahead.'

'You're both idiots,' she said. 'Does it really matter who's right, when really you both just want the same thing?'

As she pressed play and the film flickered back into life, I thought that perhaps she had a point.

CHAPTER THIRTY-NINE

Surrey, 1909–12

Tilly

Gone were the days of idle stimulation, lazy French lessons by the river, gardening by the light of the moon and paddling in the little boat with my best friend. The person I had to try not to think of at all.

Now my life centred on rules and routine. There were set times for everything. From the time I woke up, to when I got dressed, ate my first meal, took my first break – everything had a dedicated, reliable schedule. My grief found a certain comfort in it.

Like some of the girls who came from families similar to mine, my prior education had been decidedly uneven, and Katie Thorpe loved nothing better than to make my life a living hell as a result. I didn't know why she despised me. Alice had a theory that it had something to do with a scandal in her own family's past, and she resented the implication that we were similarly tarnished.

One evening, things came to a head after dinner when I entered our room and she flew at me in a rage. Her pale eyes popped as she looked from her bureau to me. 'I've spoken to you about keeping to your side of the room. How dare you leave these disgusting weeds on my desk? I suspected that you were a sentimental little fool, but honestly this is ridiculous. Take them away at once,' she told me, shoving a clutch of half-dead plants at my chest.

In my confusion, my hands came up and grasped them. Katie gave me one last look of derision. 'Did you think you'd leave that there and afterwards we'd be friends? No wonder you had to slum it to find people who want to be with you,' she said in her cold, high voice.

I blinked. Rebecca had obviously been talking. 'The only slumming I've ever done has been to share a room with you,' I told her.

'Well, lucky for you, it won't be for long.'

She stormed out before I had a chance to ask her what she meant.

As I peered down at the flowers in my hands, I felt the colour drain from my face. I sank down on the nearest bed and I didn't care then if Katie came back in and saw me crying. I didn't think I could care about anything else ever again. Because they weren't weeds at all, they were a bunch of wildflowers tied with a string. Each one was different and unique, except for a small clump of daisies, also known as goose flowers.

I never found out how Fen sent those flowers. There was no one to ask, and as the days passed, no new message arrived. But I never stopped thinking about where he was or what he was doing.

In September, I was to receive another shock when Rose joined the school herself. There had been no letter to prepare me for her arrival and no one in my family or the school's administration had taken it upon themselves to let me know that she'd be joining me.

'Surprise, little sister!' she said with a smirk when I found her sitting on my bed one evening after dinner. 'You didn't think I was about to let you have all the fun, did you?'

I looked around and to my horror saw familiar objects from Rose's old room littering the surfaces, creeping past the sanctity of Katie's thin white line.

Finding that I had somehow, miraculously, got myself rid of Katie, only to have gained my sister instead, was like swapping a rash for an infection. There was little comfort in the fact that I would finally get to say goodbye to Katie's dark scowls if it meant that I would have to share a room with the person responsible for sending me here in the first place.

'You're coming here?' I said in shock.

'Well, I don't see why you're that surprised, really. I had to finish up some things over the summer, which is why I was delayed, but after Celine left, what choice had I left? I mean, it's not like they could send you away to school and hire me another governess.'

'When Celine was fired, you mean.'

'Well, whose fault was that?'

'Yours! You're the one who told them to follow me.'

'You stole a key and snuck out at night – I didn't force you to run around with that dirty little—'

'Stop it! Don't speak of him that way!'

'Fine. Anyway, Tilly, I did you a favour.' She looked around. 'This is much better than being at home. There are the Hammonds to think about, for one. Mother says we'll probably be spending most of our holidays there. We've already made a date for the summer at Monthesay, after that there's the home in Italy – Rebecca said it is simply glorious in winter.'

'You speak as if we'll never go home again,' I said with a frown.

'Oh, well, I might, but *you* definitely won't, not for a long while at least. Mother's prepared to send you as far as Switzerland if need be. There's some school for hopeless cases there.'

'What?'

'Well, that was the compromise, wasn't it? The one father made with the head gardener – your little boyfriend's father. They had to send you away, you see, so that he could bring his son home.'

CHAPTER FORTY

Present day

The sun was doing its last call with a cocktail mix of salmon and magenta swirls when I approached the office of Waters Solicitors, with more than a touch of anxiety in my chest.

Adam opened the door after I knocked, then leant against the doorjamb, giving me that lazy smile of his that crinkled the corners of his eyes.

His tie was loose, and he'd folded up the sleeves of his white shirt.

'Hi,' I said.

'Hi,' he replied.

'I just wanted to tell you that I don't run away when things get tough. I know you think that – based on the short time you've known me – but believe me, I stuck out my marriage for years even though I probably should have called it a day a long time ago—'

'I know,' he said.

'You do?'

He picked up my hand. 'Yes. I shouldn't have said that.'

I nodded. 'Thanks.'

'I mean it. I regret it. Look, I'm sorry about Jenna too. I know how it must have looked, but honestly… the only person I want to be with is you. But if you need more time, I can wait.'

'I don't need more time,' I said, my arms circling his waist.

He moved aside my curtain of hair. 'You don't, huh?' he said, his eyes growing dark.

I shook my head. When we kissed, I forgot to breathe. My knees turned weak and my head began to spin.

'How do you do that?' I asked, when I finally came up for air.

'What?'

'That. You're bad for me,' I said.

His arms circled me. 'I don't think so.'

I smiled and looked down. 'No, me neither.'

'So…' he said, his hand trailing down my arm. 'How about the next time one of our crazy exes shows up, we phone the other and let them know that we are not, in fact, getting back together with them?'

I nodded. 'So we communicate.'

'Yes,' he winked. 'You wouldn't think that would be so difficult for a *writer*.'

'No, you wouldn't, but then again, there's a reason we are writers, not talkers…'

He laughed. 'Good point.'

Later we went back to the *Somersby* and I attempted to make something from the first cookbook I'd ever had – a recent purchase, using fresh vegetables from Sue's allotment and fresh salmon that we'd picked up at the deli in the village.

'You don't need help?' Adam asked for the third time.

'I've got this. Stuart and Sue said that I overcomplicate things.'

He kept a straight face. 'You? Never.'

I flicked a dishtowel at him. 'Shut up.'

The salmon was mildly burnt in the lemon butter sauce, but the braised cucumbers and garlicky potatoes were not.

I dished up with a grin. 'Voilà!'

Adam eyed the kitchen, and I saw him take in the little char mark on the countertop from when the fresh lemon juice had hit the-too hot butter sauce and the whole thing had gone up in flames, before I quickly put a lid on it. But he didn't say anything, just gave me a wink.

'Looks fantastic,' he said. 'I think you've certainly improved.'

CHAPTER FORTY-ONE

I was sixteen the year I saw Fen again. It was the first year since I'd left home that I could count the nights I'd slept in my own bed on more than one hand.

With Mother's attention wrapped up in Rose and her burgeoning relationship with Charles, I was granted a taste of freedom before we prepared to host the Hammonds that summer.

What I discovered were all the changes to Idyllwild. The farm had doubled in size, and everywhere you looked you could see a bright, yellow sea of flowers that stretched far and wide.

Walking along the river, there were times when a snap of a twig would make me turn, and I was sure I'd see a little boy with curly hair and the bluest eyes, but I never did.

Old Tom's branches were covered in ivy, and the little green flowerpot was still there, though no hastily scribbled note awaited me beneath the terracotta rim, just as no young boy came haring past with an impish grin and a fox named Arthur perched on his shoulder.

I was haunted by the memories of us. Of rich chocolate soil crumbling beneath my fingers as we gardened in the moonlight, of paddling down the river in our rundown boat, of the taste of sweet pears, bursting with juices that trickled down our chins as we grinned at each other underneath a perfect Cornish sky.

I walked along the cliffs to the walls that concealed the cottage behind, but that was as far as I dared go.

That summer, Mother was in her element, as it was the first time we would be having the Hammonds to stay.

The twins, along with their brother, Charles, and one of his school chums, Stephen Clapham-Stiles, would be coming for the better part of August. It was hoped that by the end of the month, an engagement would be set between Charles and Rose.

Every inch of the house had been given a thorough clean, new curtains had been ordered and the spare rooms given a fresh application of wallpaper. It was the only time I'd ever seen my mother so quick to smile in all my years. Even Father had been persuaded to take time off to get up a shooting party with the boys.

Rebecca arrived later that week, like a brisk summer breeze, declaring herself 'in love with daffodils' and this 'wild, thoroughly romantic part of the world'. Perhaps Mother, for the first time, saw the colour of the grass on her own soil, though I was glad she never heard the twins' snickers when they were shown their 'sweet, parochial rooms'.

While Rebecca turned everyone's heads, it was Alice who I was the most glad to see. Her hair was frizzier than ever, and she hadn't yet lost her stutter, but she was without a doubt one of the most welcome sights to be seen or heard. 'G-G-Granny wanted me to go with her to New York for the summer, b-b-but I was afraid you wouldn't survive the month with those three,' she said. I still wondered how she was related to them. I'd been thanking my stars for sending me Alice McKibbon since I met her.

Knowing that Father was unlikely to play the part of the gentleman farmer for more than a few days, my cousin Tim had been called upon to pick up the post, and a venerable host he was too.

'What are you doing, Spriggy?' he said, while we were picnicking on the lawn. I was lying down on my front, writing a passionate editorial about the women's movement for the little newsletter Alice and I had founded at school.

'Hmm? Just writing,' I said, looking up. 'Isn't it funny that we live in a country where throwing a rock at the prime minister's house is considered more outrageous than giving women basic rights?'

'Not this again,' sighed Rose. She darted a nervous look at Charles. 'You promised.'

Charles had his hat over his head, and we could hear faint snoring.

'It's just an observation,' I said with a shrug.

Rebecca plucked the last petal from the daisy in her hands and said, 'I find the whole concept of the suffragettes tiresome, truly.'

I was about to launch into a heated diatribe when Alice intervened. 'Why do you call her S-S-Spriggy?'

Tim laughed. 'Well, when she was little, Tilly was just this little sprig of a girl – thin and tall, all elbows and knees.

I laughed. 'Not much has changed.'

'I disagree,' said Stephen Clapham-Stiles, who was sitting with his back against a tree, eyes closed and looking like he was about to join his friend in an afternoon nap.

I blushed, attempting to get back to my letter.

'Rose,' he continued, 'don't you think your sister should put away her books for once in her life? I mean, we've come all this way and all I've seen of her is the top of her forehead. It is a rather nice forehead, but still.'

They all laughed. Rose said, 'I'm not my sister's keeper.'

'Oh ho, Rebecca, looks like you've got some competition!' said Charles, who had wakened at the sound of our laughter. He roused himself into a sitting position and gave her a surprised look. It wasn't often that someone in the male persuasion looked elsewhere when she was around.

Rebecca gave him a thin smile. 'Stephen just likes the chase.'

'And you've been giving him one for years,' guffawed Charles.

'Hilarious,' she said. 'Anyway, I shouldn't worry, we all know what Tilly's type is.'

'What is that?' asked Stephen. 'Blond and tall?'

'Well, that depends… I mean, he might have been, for all I know.'

I looked at Rebecca, puzzled. Then realisation dawned. I gave her a hard look. But she ignored me. 'Haven't you heard about how and why Tilly came to school with us? It's a fascinating story.'

'Something about you making friends with someone you shouldn't have, that's what I heard,' said Charles.

'Oh, it wasn't as innocent as all that. It was a romance, after all,' said Rebecca.

'What?' exclaimed Stephen, his eyes popping. 'You're joking!'

'If only,' said Rose.

'I'm going inside,' I said, sitting up.

Tim shook his head. 'They were just children. Stay, Spriggy.'

'How sweet, who was it?' asked Stephen.

'The gardener's son, wasn't it?' said Rebecca.

'*No!*' said Stephen, amazed. 'Tilly, I never pictured you slumming it.'

I gritted my teeth. 'I wasn't slumming anything.'

He raised a brow.

Rebecca smiled. 'So, Stephen, I shouldn't worry. I should think you'd be a vast improvement on her usual conquests.'

I stood up and gathered my things. '*You* would think that.'

Later, after dinner, Alice said to me, 'You shouldn't bait Rebecca. She'll be out for blood now.'

It was good advice. Pity it came too late.

The next day I sought refuge in the library. Stephen had risen to Rebecca's challenge and I was finding my patience wearing thin. The door burst open just as I was going past and something solid and human-shaped slammed into me. I spun backwards, rubbing my left shoulder, which had borne the impact. I looked up in shock to see a pair of blue eyes, staring at me in equal surprise.

'Tilly?'

I blinked. It felt like the world fell away then rushed at me all at once. 'Fen?'

A dimple appeared at the corner of his mouth and his eyes lit up. It was the same smile. The same curly brown hair. He was taller than me now, and more handsome than I'd ever realised. I felt myself swallow.

'I wondered if I'd see you,' he said, and right then it felt as if I were still thirteen and no time had passed at all.

'Michael?' came a voice from behind the door.

Fen turned around and I saw behind him a man in a brown suit with a gold monocle in his left eye.

Michael?

'My apologies. May I introduce my tutor, Mr Neil Canavan. This is Miss Matilda Asprey.'

It was strange to hear Fen so formal.

Mr Canavan bowed slightly. 'Miss.'

'Your tutor?' I asked.

'Yes,' answered Mr Canavan. 'Michael is one of the best students I've ever had. I used to teach your – well, speak of the Devil,' he said, just as Tim walked into the room, followed by Rebecca and Charles Hammond.

I don't believe it,' cried Tim. 'Can it really be old Canavan?'

The laughter lines around Mr Canavan's eyes creased. 'Now this is a pleasant surprise. As I was saying, miss, I was once the tutor to your cousin here.'

'A million years ago now,' said Tim. 'But how wonderful to see you again. My uncle said that he wanted someone for the job of training up his new agent.'

'New agent?' I said, looking from Tim to Fen.

'Not yet,' said Fen.

'But that's the plan, eventually,' said Father, coming in from behind and clapping him on the shoulder. 'As we expand Idyllwild – we've got the best man, coming fully on board in the new, expanded role.'

Rebecca was staring at Fen with interest. At some point I felt her look at me, saw her eyes widen in realisation, and a slow grin spread across her face.

There had been a time when I could tell what Fen was thinking just by reading his face. Now, he didn't even call himself Fen any more. I didn't know what to do with that.

I had thought of him every day for three years. I'd missed him more than I could bear. I had driven myself crazy wondering what had happened to him, what he'd been doing. But I had never considered this. That somehow, with me gone, my father would have welcomed him in and taken him under his wing.

I didn't know what I felt about it. Anger, possibly. Confusion. Something else too.

There was only one person who would give me an answer, and I sought her out. 'How long has he been tutored here?' I asked Mother, when I got her alone.

She, at least, could be relied upon to show her displeasure. 'Excuse me?'

'Why didn't anyone tell me?'

'Why should we tell you?'

I blinked. 'You sent me away just because we were friends, and yet Father welcomes him into the house?' I recalled how he'd even gone so far as to pat him on the back. It was so strange and confusing.

'He has not welcomed Waters into the house. And it's not the same thing – you were sneaking out at all hours to see him as a child. Your father is simply ensuring that his future agent receives a proper education.'

I blinked: Waters.

'I don't need to explain anything to you, Tilly. Your father takes care of his own, and you should know that.'

'The way he took care of me?'

'What do you mean?'

'Well, I think it's patently obvious what's more important to him, what's always been the most important thing to him.'

'And that is…?'

'Idyllwild. Even if he has to get rid of his youngest daughter in the process, his farm always comes first.'

She pursed her lips but she didn't deny it.

I had never imagined that, when I finally got to see him again, I'd ever find myself avoiding Fen. But that's what I did those first few days. We hadn't had a chance to speak privately, and while I knew it wasn't his fault that my own father had, in his own way, chosen him over me, there was a part of me that felt a sense of betrayal nonetheless.

Rebecca didn't help. She seemed to find any excuse to venture around the library during Fen's lessons. I tried my best not to let her see that it bothered me, especially when once I came downstairs to see her laughing with Fen, her hand on his sleeve.

'She's just doing it to get a reaction out of you,' whispered Alice.

At the sound of our footsteps Fen looked at me.

'Tilly?' he said. Rebecca's eyebrows rose at his informal tone.

'Waters,' I said, striding off.

Fen found me by Old Tom. I had shimmied up the tree and was sitting with my back against its trunk, my head against my knees.

'I thought I'd find you here.'

I looked down. 'Did you?' I said, my voice colder than I intended.

'I did,' he said, swinging himself up and taking a seat next to me.

I looked away. 'I never expected to find you here,' I said.

'I gathered that. I thought they'd told you.'

'They had not.'

I picked at the bark; Fen touched my hand. 'I thought – maybe – you'd be happy to see me.'

I looked up. 'Happy?' A fat tear slid down my face. 'Fen, I thought you said that you'd always be my friend, even if I couldn't always be yours.'

'I said that,' he agreed.

'And?'

'We were children then.'

'So it was just a lie?' I felt the air leave my lungs.

'Yes.'

I pushed past him, jumped off the branch.

'Stop, Tilly!'

'Leave me alone!'

'Tilly, I was never your friend.'

I stopped; I felt suddenly sick. The tears came fast and fresh. 'What?'

He grabbed hold of my arms. 'What I mean is, you were never *just* my friend, Tilly Asprey. I fell in love with you the first day I met you.'

'You loved me?'

'I never stopped.'

I gasped, the sobs starting. 'But you did stop, I never heard from you.'

'Didn't you get my letters?'

I blinked. 'There were no letters.'

He kissed me, hard, and I gasped. 'I wrote so many,' he said.

'What?'

'Whenever I could, I sent you a letter – sometimes twice a day when I was missing you like mad. You didn't get them?'

I shook my head, biting my lip.

'I caught the train, when I hadn't heard from you. I paid some woman from the kitchens to leave flowers in your room. I thought you would know that they were from me.'

I closed my eyes. 'I did.'

He brushed away my tears and held me tight.

'Oh, Fen, it's always been you.'

We sat beneath Old Tom, and he told me about how my father had gone to Yorkshire after I was sent away to school and personally fetched him back.

'None of us knew why. I think, but I'm not sure, that maybe Mam had something to do with it.'

'What do you mean?'

'It's just a hunch. I know your father felt badly when I was sent away, after they found us together that night. But when I found out that you were gone too, it felt so unfair.'

'Oh, Fen,' I sighed, leaning against him, 'none of this has been fair. But I'm glad it was this way. At least you got to be with your family.'

'But not with you.'

'We should have known that it would never be easy.'

'Yeah, and now with Da ill, it'll be even harder.'

I looked at him. 'What?'

'Yeah, it's… He hasn't been well for a while. It's one of the reasons that I agreed to it all. I mean, someone has to look after the farm.'

'Does it have to be you?'

'Well, what would happen to my family if I didn't?'

When we parted we made a pact to meet at dawn the following morning – it seemed safer that way, with less chance of us being caught. Once again, Fen and I were back to keeping secret hours just so that we could be together.

In the darkness, we snuck down to the cove and watched the sunrise bathe the sky in swirls of magenta and mauve.

'You always pick up the sea glass,' Fen noted.

My hair was loose, and it whipped around in the wind. I nodded, bending down to pick up a blue-green pebble. 'It's my favourite colour,' I said.

He moved a rogue strand of hair away from my face.

'One day, when I have a house of my own,' I said, 'I'll put them in bottles everywhere, and the only colour I'll wear will be aquamarine.'

He laughed. 'And the only animals you'll keep will be foxes?'

'Quite right. And I'll only have round windows, and the biggest window seat you can find.'

'Aquamarine, of course?'

'Naturally.'

'Is that what you'd have on your fingers too?'

I looked at him. 'What do you mean?'

'The ring you wear, when you get married.'

I bit my lip. 'Perhaps.'

He moved closer. 'And in this home, who would you share it with?'

'Apart from my foxes?'

'Yes.'

'I'd quite like a sea turtle.'

He laughed. 'Really? Is that all – just you and the foxes and a sea turtle?'

'Maybe. As you know, I am a suffragette now.'

He leant in and kissed me, and I felt my stomach swoop. My breath caught, and the world fell away. I looked up into the bluest eyes. 'I could always do with a fox charmer.'

He grinned and held me close.

CHAPTER FORTY-TWO

Present day

The daffodil farm was breathtaking in spring. The yellow flowers stretched on for miles, creating an incredible lemon wash against the sea and sky.

The farm was open to visitors, and Adam and I walked for what seemed like miles. But when we got peckish we decided to visit the teashop near the entrance. It was rather sweet, with vintage menus that looked like old botanical prints, glass domes housing an assorted array of mouthwatering cakes, alongside steel garden furniture and green shrubs in French-style wooden boxes.

'Hello, Adam,' greeted a woman with short blonde hair, wearing a red apron sprinkled with flowers, when we took a seat.

'Nora, hi,' he said, and then introduced us.

'Victoria, this is Nora, one of the owners of the farm. She runs the teashop.'

She held out a hand and winked at me. 'I know you, of course – you beat me to the cottage.'

I frowned. 'Oh yes, that's right – I'm sorry.' I pulled a face.

She laughed. 'No, it's fine. It's probably better this way. It would have been cruel to demolish the old place for a bigger tea garden. I heard that you're renovating it, is that true?'

I nodded. 'Yes. It's a big job, but I'm getting there – I have electricity now,' I confided.

'Yay,' she said, with a wide smile. 'To tell you the truth though, just between us,' she said, giving Adam a wink, 'I'm not sure I would have been able to go through with it. I mean, they already say it's haunted, and I wouldn't want some ancestor of mine harassing us because we disturbed their remains or something.'

I frowned. 'Your ancestor?' I asked.

'Oh yes, very distantly. My great-grandmother used to live here. Gosh, it was such a long time ago now.'

'When – um, how long ago?'

'Oh, a hundred years or more, at least.'

My mouth fell open, and I saw that Adam's did as well.

'You're related to the Aspreys?' I asked.

'Distantly. We were cousins. Found out a few years ago, can you imagine?'

CHAPTER FORTY-THREE

1913, Cornwall

Tilly

At last, the moment arrived for which my mother had prayed: Charles proposed to Rose.

The party that was held in what was optimistically called the Great Hall was the largest that had ever been thrown at the estate. The champagne flowed like water and no one was happier than Mother.

People came in from far and wide. There were so many guests that we had to seek accommodation at inns and hotels around the county, ferrying them to the party through the daffodil fields.

I heard Father say that it was some of the best advertising he could ever have had. In a fit of magnanimity, he'd invited half the household staff to attend and celebrate their joy.

For the family, new dresses had been ordered in the latest styles. There were silks and suits and a band that serenaded the young happy couple. The doors stood open, welcoming in the cool night air, and in the garden a cascade of lanterns flickered under the moonlight.

It was the first real party I'd ever attended. There were uniformed waiters serving cocktails, laughter braying in every corner and, later, there would be music and dancing till dawn.

My hair had been curled and pinned up. I wore a dress with sheer, pale blue voile and a black lace overlay with a scalloped edge, and I was doing my best to avoid Stephen Clapham-Stiles, who kept asking me to dance.

I slipped behind a marble column during the speeches, and came face-to-face with Fen. He looked young and impossibly handsome in his tails. His hair was tamed, and his eyes searched mine. I looked away.

'Aren't you going to call me Waters again?' he whispered in my ear.

My mouth curled into a grin, which I tried to hide.

I heard his laugh, while I faced the front to hear the speeches. I kept my hand behind me and his fingers found mine. I lifted my glass as my father asked us to toast to Rose and Charles's happiness.

'At least your mother's happy – now.'

I looked at him. It wasn't like Fen to sound bitter.

The musicians started to play again and Stephen came forward, seizing my shoulder. 'Excuse us, dear chap. This lady promised me a dance,' he said, pulling me towards him.

I stumbled along. 'Stephen, perhaps later,' I said, but he was strong.

'Oh no, we're going to dance,' he said. I noticed that he was barely able to stand straight.

'Stop it.'

He stumbled. His words were slurred. 'You smell like peaches, did you know that? That's all I think about now – peaches. Maybe I should take a bite?' he sniggered.

I looked at him in disgust. 'You're drunk.'

'You're not?'

'No.'

'Ssso,' he said, coming too close, breathing into my hair while I attempted to twist away. 'Was that him?'

'Who?'

'You know, the boy – the one they found you with,' he said, squinting at me. 'I has – haven't – been able to stop thinking about you since I heard… picturing you, so naughty…'

'You're disgusting.' I tried to pull away, but he was too strong, his hands clamped around me like a vice. His breath was rank from too much whisky and tobacco.

'Come on,' he said, pulling me towards the gardens. He was strong, and he marched me further and further away from the party.

'I want to go back inside, please.'

'No, you don't,' he laughed. 'Stop teasing…'

'No, Stephen,' I hissed. Next thing I knew his fleshy mouth was descending on mine. My arms were flailing as he locked me in an embrace. I pushed him away as hard as I could. 'Stop it!' I yelled.

But he wouldn't listen. 'Oh, come on, be kind to me.'

Suddenly he was pulled away from me.

I staggered to the side, gasping for air, staring in horror as Fen and Stephen launched themselves at each other's throats. Fen wrestled him to the floor, but despite Stephen's drunkenness, he was lashing out violently.

'Stop it!' I yelled, just as Fen landed a blow to Stephen's face. I wasn't the only one to gasp, or hear the crack of bones.

'WHAT IS THE MEANING OF THIS?' roared Father. 'How dare you get into a brawl here. This is a disgrace, Waters!'

'No, Father, it wasn't Fen's fault,' I yelped.

He turned to me, eyes popping. Then he looked from me to Fen, mouth open. 'This was over you?' he hissed. He looked disgusted.

'Oh yes,' came a smooth voice. I looked up and saw Rebecca leaning against a pillar, a glass of champagne in her hand. She gave a small smile and her chestnut curls caught the glow of the lanterns. Her bright green eyes showed mock concern. 'I saw it all. Seems young Waters there just can't let your daughter go.'

I closed my eyes.

'Rebecca, stop lying!'

It wasn't me who said it, but Alice McKibbon. We all turned towards her.

'I saw Stephen pull Tilly into the bushes and try to man-handle her. Look at him, he's drunk.'

We all looked. Despite the blood gushing from his nose, Stephen grinned.

'Is that true, Stephen?' asked Rose, who was standing behind Father.

'Just a little kiss,' he said, holding up his thumb and index finger. 'Thought she'd like that… I know how she likes her little secret flings.'

Fen clenched his jaw. I could see the scar on Father's hand glow white.

'Mr Waters heard her yelling – I'm sure he was only trying to help,' said Alice.

Fen stood up.

'Is that true?' asked Father.

He inclined his head once.

Father looked at us again and gave a stiff nod. He ordered one of the footmen to take Stephen to his room then turned to leave.

I looked at Alice as she came to stand next to me. 'You know you never stutter when you're sticking up for someone?'

'D-Don't I?'

I shook my head. 'I think you should give that old tongue of yours a talking to – let it start speaking up for itself.'

She grinned. 'She's not wrong, you know.'

'Who?'

'Rebecca. I d-don't think it was just him coming to your defence. I doubt your father does either.'

I sighed. 'I know.'

I found the first note under the flowerpot by Old Tom.

I gave a half-smile. It had been almost four years since I'd received one. It was just one coded word, though I doubt anyone would have understood it anyway.

Mantua.

In *Romeo and Juliet*, it's the place that Romeo is banished to after the death of Juliet's cousin, Tybalt.

Fen no longer had his lessons at the house, nor was he invited to any of the other parties. I think it was Father's way of trying to avoid the inevitable. If Mother could have had her way, the entire Waters family would have left on the morning train the following day.

After the Hammonds left, I heard my parents arguing late one night. I crept out of my room and edged closer to their door.

'He stays, Helena. That's final.'

'No, John – you can't, not now. She's finishing up at school, then what? You heard Rebecca, it could so easily happen again, and this time—'

'It won't.'

'How can you be so sure?'

Then, unbelievably, I heard my father say words I'd wished he'd say a thousand times before. 'Would it be the worst thing in the world. I mean, really?'

'You can't be serious! Of course it would. For one, she's far too young.'

'And later – when they're older?'

'I will *not* accept this! You're speaking like it's inevitable. It's an infatuation, and a dangerous one – one that she doesn't need to ruin her life over.'

'Perhaps she's been too sheltered here,' pointed out Father.

'She hasn't been *here* in years, thanks to you.'

'Don't pretend that you didn't send her and Rose to that school for a reason.'

'I don't – I did that deliberately, and I'm proud of the outcome. But Tilly hasn't been here almost at all. Her own home,' she added.

'So what's your solution – throw her at every male you can find?'

'No, but perhaps it's time for something else.'

A few days later, I discovered their solution. It was to become a debutante, spending the season in London and being officially declared of marriageable age to society.

'Don't pout, Tilly. I think it's wonderful that your aunt Cassie has agreed to sponsor you.'

I didn't.

Rose was livid. 'I can't believe you get to do this and I didn't – I mean, it's utterly wasted on you.'

I couldn't help but agree. I had no intention of marrying anyone, and now that Fen was back in my life I had no intention of letting him go again.

I also didn't want to quit in my final year of school. 'I have responsibilities – I can't just leave.'

'Why?' scoffed my mother. 'Now that Rose is engaged, why would you possibly go back?'

'Well, to carry on, of course.'

'Carry on?'

'Yes, to finish my final year and perhaps try for a place at St Hilda's at Oxford.'

Her eyebrows rose. 'Your father would never pay for that. Good Lord, sometimes I just don't know where you come from!'

I looked at her and frowned. 'You know, neither do I.'

PART THREE

CHAPTER FORTY-FOUR

Present day

'Are you sure he's up to visitors?' I asked Adam for the third time, as we parked the car and headed up to his uncle's house by the harbour.

'Yes, don't worry. And he's curious to meet the person who bought the cottage.'

I nodded. 'Okay.' I was nervous about meeting him, because I knew that Graham Waters had mixed feelings about the cottage. Also, I didn't want to disturb a sick man with my questions.

The Waters' home was a sweet terraced house near Tregollan harbour. It had neat flowerboxes and a clipped drive. As soon as we appeared, the door opened.

'Aunt Maggie,' said Adam, giving an older woman with salt-and-pepper hair a hug. She was thin and tired-looking, with dark circles under her eyes, but her smile was warm.

'This is Victoria,' he said, introducing us.

'Mrs Waters,' I said.

'Oh no, love, just call me Maggie, everyone does. Come in, dinner's almost ready. Did a roast…'

'Oh, wow, thanks – that's so much trouble,' I said.

She raised her hands. 'It's no trouble,' she laughed, 'been doing this every Sunday for thirty years, could do it in my sleep now.'

We laughed and she led us into the living room, where a man with silver hair was lying on the sofa and shouting at the television, where a football match was causing him some distress. 'No, bloody offside – you tosser!'

'Hello, Uncle Graham,' greeted Adam with a laugh.

He looked up and grinned. 'Adam, my boy!' he said with enthusiasm.

Adam leant over and gave him a hug. 'Hello, old man.'

'Old man, ha!'

'This is Victoria,' said Adam, introducing us.

'Ah yes – the mysterious cottage buyer,' he said, hitting the pause button. 'TV record – been saving marriages since 2007,' he said with a wink.

I laughed. 'Really?'

'Well, no – not sure when it was invented, but ever since, probably. Now, sit, sit,' he said, and Adam and I took a seat on the other vacant sofa.

'Shall I give you a hand, Mrs – Maggie?' I asked.

'Oh no, don't worry, make yourself welcome.'

'How're you feeling, Uncle?' asked Adam.

'Ah, I'm grand, Adam, just grand.'

Seeing the expression on Adam's face, he smiled. 'We're through with the chemo now, it's a good thing, trust me,' he winked. Then he looked at me. 'Couldn't find a better nephew. These past few months, he's been a godsend with the business – though you're meant to be closing it down, not ramping up production,' he said, turning back to him.

Adam ran a hand through his hair. 'You try explaining that to some of the villagers. Every week they keep bringing me new work.'

Graham shrugged. 'Not the end of the world. Anyway, you may have reason to stay... put down some roots, take over instead of shutting it down,' he looked from Adam to me. 'Know what I mean?'

'Yeah, Uncle, I think people on Mars know what you mean. I'm pretty sure they're out there now, going a darker shade of green on my behalf.'

I bit down a laugh. I couldn't deny that the idea of Adam staying longer was something worth celebrating. Though I did wish that Jenna would leave. She'd found herself a job at a local PR firm and was keeping herself busy, getting on everyone's nerves as she tried to turn Tregollan into the next St Ives. And in her spare time, she kept trying to win Adam back.

I'd run into her at the Harbour Cafe again, and she'd mentioned that she'd drummed up some interest from a five-star hotel chain who were going to make an offer on the Black Horse Inn. 'Can you just imagine what that'll do to this town?' she asked with glee.

'Yes,' I said, 'and I'm not sure it would be a good thing at all.' Hating the idea of turning this unspoilt part of the country into something it wasn't, I frowned. 'Aren't you staying there now?' I asked, wondering at her incredible lack of tact.

She simply shrugged. 'Exactly – I'll be doing everyone a service. Just wait.'

Before I left, she called out, 'So I hear that you and Adam are an item now, even after my little warning the other day?' She gave a fake laugh. 'I'm only joking. Look, to be honest, I'm grateful to you.'

'Grateful?' I asked in surprise.

'Yes,' she said with a wide smile, tucking her long, sleek red hair back with a manicured hand. 'He needs to get it out of his system – all that anger and rage. You're the rebound. I don't blame him for that. He's just doing what he needs to do. So, in the meantime, I'll be here, waiting, until he comes to his senses.'

My mouth fell open. 'He already came to his senses – that's why he's with me and not you.'

She gave me a casual smile. 'Like I said, I'm grateful.'

I shook my head. 'You should be, he's happy now.'

It was the first time I saw her smile falter.

I'd spent the next few days trying not to let her words get to me. She had the sort of insane confidence that could make a saint second-guess himself. Adam wasn't on the rebound, I decided, firmly. Or was he?

After lunch, which included roast beef, Yorkshire pudding, and the best apple pie I'd ever had, Graham turned to me and said, 'Adam said there were some things you wanted to ask me – about the cottage?'

I hesitated.

'Go on, I won't bite – been ordered not to,' he said with a grin.

I laughed. 'Well, Adam told me that the reason the cottage was abandoned was because of the rumours—'

'That's not why it was abandoned.'

'But Uncle Graham, you told me about the rumours, the curse – said it gave you the heebie-jeebies.'

'And it does,' he said, shivering. 'No offence, Victoria, but that's not why the family abandoned it.'

'Was it because of what happened to your grandfather?' I asked.

'You mean when he was a baby?'

'A baby?'

'Yes, well, my great-grandmother was pregnant with my grandfather when she came to live with her sister. Her husband had just died, around the same time the Aspreys left. It was all very unexpected. My great-grandmother never spoke about what happened at that cottage, but by then there were enough rumours in the village, so as my grandfather grew up, she told him they'd had nothing to do with the place. Most people thought it was cursed because of all the noises they used to hear down there. Then one day, when my grandfather was about fifty at least, she told him that actually he was the owner of the old, abandoned cottage. The deed said it was to go to Michael Waters' heir. By then he wouldn't touch the place if you paid him. I have to say, we've all sort of felt the same way.'

I blinked. Adam and I shared a look. 'You know, I was so sure that your great grandfather was Fen,' I said. 'I never realised that they had another child afterwards and that's where you come from.'

He shook his head. 'Neither did I.'

'Fen?' asked Graham.

'Michael Fenwick Waters – I suppose he was your great grandfather's older brother.'

He looked at us like we were mad. 'Alfie never had a brother.'

CHAPTER FORTY-FIVE

Cornwall, 1914

On 4 August 1914, one word turned all our plans to ashes: we were at war.

At first we went about our lives as if nothing had happened. Mother was surprised when my aunt Cassie wrote to her and said that under the circumstances my coming out would have to be postponed, so at least I was able to go back to school.

Rose would be staying at home. She'd gotten what she wanted – which was the bejewelled engagement band on her finger. She would spend the next few months plumping up her trousseau. Her first words after she heard of the pronouncement of war were, 'But what about my wedding?'

Father snapped at her. 'Is that your only concern, truly?'

'Shouldn't it be?' she'd asked.

'What happens if they call Charles to service?' he asked, his voice hard.

'Why on earth would they do that?' she said in real surprise.

Father looked at her in disbelief.

Fen and I didn't get a lot of time together before I had to leave for school, but we snatched every moment we could. Midnight had been our time as children, and now as we verged into adulthood, dawn took its place – at the cove.

It was where we spilled all our secrets. Fen told me that, over the past few years his father had gotten worse.

'Mam had to call in for a doctor the other day – after we got the news. It's the first time she's ever done that.'

War was the only news anyone spoke about these days. In the beginning, people were stockpiling supplies and snatching at newspapers, as if there would be a shortage of paper overnight.

'But I thought he was doing better here?'

I remembered how we'd spoken about it here, years before. About his father's episodes, how the fear would make him senseless. It explained why sometimes, now, he had to be taken home from Idyllwild, and why Fen had to fill his place, and perhaps why Father had ensured that they would have a future agent in him.

'It's his old troubles really. The doctor prescribed some sedatives and at least that's calmed him down a little. Me mam hates it – says people are beginning to talk.'

I thought of the rumours that had surrounded the Waters family since they'd first arrived. 'I think they always have, Fen.'

'Yeah, but now it's not like he can work. And with the war coming it just makes it worse.'

'Why? I mean, it's not like they would call him up, would they? I mean, not when he's ill?'

He shook his head. 'No, but I might go.'

I sat up, leaning back to look at him. Felt the cold on my side from where I'd been lying warm against him along the rock wall.

'What? No, you won't.'

He nodded. 'It's my duty, Tilly,' he said seriously.

My mouth fell open. 'You can't be serious – not after what it's done to your father.'

He shook his head. 'That's what it means to serve – to fight for King and country.'

I blinked; I couldn't believe what I was hearing. 'But Fen…' I tried to be rational, calm. 'Even so, I don't think they'll let you fight anyway.'

He gave me a hurt look. 'Because of my foot, you mean?'

I bit my lip. 'Yes, but not just that. They aren't heartless. You're your parents' only son, and if they need you at Idyllwild, I'm sure you won't have to go.'

He stood up. 'I think the war is about more important things than a flower farm. I mean, my father fought for something he wasn't so keen on, with imperialism, but this is different, Tilly. This is our home and it's being threatened, we can't ignore that. You can't ask me to.'

I stood up. 'Oh yes, I can.'

'Tilly,' he said, kissing me hard, holding my face between his hands.

My head swam, and when I came up for air, I said, 'You can kiss me as long as you like, Fenwick Waters, but I'm not changing my mind about this. I haven't gone for years without seeing you to risk losing you again.'

He looked at me, gave me a small smile, and said, 'Alright then.' Then he kissed me again. 'I'll just keep trying.'

Most of the young men were like Fen, jumped-up and proud and excited to serve. The footman, Edmund, had been one of the first to volunteer, and he was cheered on by everyone in the household – except Father.

Mother summoned Edmund into the drawing room to receive her congratulations. I don't think I was the only one who saw Father's stilted speech, heard how empty his words sounded.

'Really, John,' she admonished. 'You could have tried to sound a bit more sincere.'

'Sincere? He's a fool, Helena. They all are. The only thing that young man has volunteered for is to get himself killed. Why should any of us be proud of that?'

'Oh, don't be ridiculous, Father. It'll be over by Christmas, anyway,' said Rose.

He scoffed. 'If you believe that, my dear, you'll believe anything.'

Father's words proved a correct presentiment. Christmas came and went, and the war continued.

I delayed my return to school, and in the meantime sought out our general practitioner, Dr Collins, on the pretext of a series of headaches. While he examined me and prescribed plenty of rest and fluids, I asked him about whether or not they could afford to take all types of soldiers to the war.

'Every fit and able boy will be welcomed,' he said. 'It's remarkable – Edmund was the first from Idyllwild, that should do everyone proud. In the village, the Harvey brothers signed up at the same time.'

'What I mean is, will they accept just anyone? Where do they stop?'

'Why? Are you wishing to volunteer?' he teased.

I pursed my lips. 'No, what I mean is I have a… cousin,' I lied. 'And there is a problem with one of his feet, you see, and I think he wonders—'

'Oh yes, I see. Well, I'm afraid that if the condition is serious, he may very well not be able to go, as there is plenty of marching to be done.'

'So if it was a visible malady it would be unlikely?'

'Oh yes. I mean, they aren't as cruel as all that. No, they wouldn't take him, definitely not.'

'And the boys around here – they would be signed off by you?'

'Oh yes, and I can assure you I will do a thorough examination. We want to make sure that those we send off have the best chance of being able to come home.'

I breathed a sigh of relief. 'That makes me feel much better.'

I went back to school with a somewhat lighter heart, confident in the knowledge that Fen would be safe. And we'd made up, of a kind, and had said goodbye at the cove.

'I wish you didn't have to go,' he told me.

'Me too. But it won't be long now, just another year.'

He nodded. 'I might be gone as well, if I join the fight.'

I kissed him so I didn't have to speak, so I didn't have to contradict him. I knew that Dr Collins would never sign him off, and I was desperately relieved.

On a midnight search, I discovered the pile of letters that Fen had sent me, hidden in the office, confiscated no doubt by the staff, who had been instructed to do so by my parents and I read them till the candle burnt out.

Now that I was volunteering in the school office, I had no fear that my letters would be confiscated again, and for the first time since I started school, I was receiving regular mail. A few weeks later, a letter from Fen confirmed that the good doctor had been true to his word.

'I should have realised he'd be like this – far too soft, that's what everyone says about him. When he treated my father he prescribed bed rest and a vacation, as if they could saunter off somewhere. He doesn't live in the real world...'

I breathed a sigh of relief.

Though I should have known it wasn't to be. Fen had set his heart on the idea, and a few weeks later he wrote to tell me that he'd gone as far as Plymouth and had finally found a doctor willing to sign him up.

I was horrified when he wrote to tell me that he'd be leaving in a week's time. I made up an excuse to Miss Laurens, about being needed at home, and took the next-morning train back to see him before he left.

Rose took one look at me and scoffed. 'You're too late, he's already gone.'

No one was more furious than Mrs Waters. She stormed into the house with a letter in her hand. Mathew, the new acting footman, who'd taken over Edmund's post now that he had been called up, could barely restrain her. She had on an old bonnet and her boots were covered in dirt, which she tracked all over the floor.

Mother, Rose and I came down when we heard her scream.

'Fetch him to me now! Fetch that bastard! I want to look 'im in the eye!' she roared.

'What is the meaning of this?' demanded my mother. 'How dare you come in here and address the staff in this manner?'

She looked at Mother, her eyes flashing scorn. 'How dare I?' Her eyes found mine, and fairly snapped. 'Course you're here – you're probably the first 'e told! Did you encourage him, eh? Tell him to be a man? When you were writing him in your little secret letters?'

At my look of shock, she continued, 'Oh, aye, you didn't think I knew about that, eh? Your little coded messages – been going on fer years. They've even got their own language, can you believe it. He promised me, after the last time, that it would stop. But it never has. They just like to fool you. And now he's gone, thanks to you.'

I took a deep breath, and said, 'Mrs Waters, I understand how upset you are about Fen. I am too, please believe me. Fen wanted this – I tried to talk him out of it. And my father had nothing to do with it—'

She took a flying step forward. 'OH YES, HE DID!' she roared, brandishing the letter in her red hand. 'My boy may have been the idiot that went to that quack to get it signed off, but they only accepted him because of this!' she said, waving a piece of paper around.

Father came rushing in – obviously someone had summoned him to the scene – but when he saw her, his face went pale. 'Mrs Waters…'

'You've done it now,' she said. 'You really have. I stopped myself all those years before because it wasn't what Michael wanted. He loved you, you know? Said you were the best friend he'd ever had. He said now is the first time he's ever felt betrayed.'

Father's eyes filled with tears.

We all looked from Mrs Waters to him in shock. 'It was the boy,' said Father. 'He insisted. It's what he wanted – he wanted to go, he begged.'

'Aye. So you helped.'

'Yes.'

She dashed away an angry tear. 'Well, I'll help too. I have documents of my own – in your own hand.'

Father looked pale. 'Please, understand it was for him—'

'Was it? Or was it something else – perhaps to do with this daughter of yours?'

Father turned, blinking confusedly at me. It was like he hadn't registered that I was there till now.

'While you get rid of him at war,' continued Mrs Waters, 'she gets to come home.'

'No, it's not like that.'

'So, what? After this war, they'll simply get married? You'll allow that?'

'My daughter marry your cripple son? Over my dead body!' hissed Mother.

'Helena!' Father roared.

But Mrs Waters just stood there, a cold smile on her face. She was filled with righteousness, a calm in her rage, like the eye of the storm. She folded the piece of paper, in which Father had agreed to send her son to war, neatly in two, and said, 'That's what I thought.'

Meanwhile, Father looked at Mother as if she'd just signed his death warrant.

CHAPTER FORTY-SIX

Present day

Graham Waters' statement that his grandfather didn't have a brother – that he had no idea that Fen existed – shocked me.

Adam and I each took turns, babbling as we tried to convince him otherwise.

Finally, I pulled out the diary and told him what we'd found, what we'd uncovered about his family.

He was flabbergasted. 'This whole time no one ever said anything. My great-grandmother just pretended like Alfred was her only son. She died when I was about ten,' he explained. 'But why, though? Why would she have done that?'

I shook my head. 'I have no idea.' I couldn't imagine what would drive a mother to deny that she'd had a son. From Tilly's diary it was clear that Mrs Waters loved Fen. It had to be something else. Perhaps she felt betrayed when he wanted to be with Tilly? But still, was it enough for her to cut him out of their history?

He got up and shuffled over to the television set. Next to it was a large shelf on which some old photographs were displayed. 'I mean, I remember them showing me my great-grandfather. She used to tell us all about what happened to him.'

'What do you mean?' I asked, as he took an album off the shelf and brought it over to us.

He sat down with a sigh, rearranging his joggers. 'Well, it was legendary stuff, you know. About the woman who married this strong ox of a man who went off to war, and when he came back, he was completely changed. It was just so sad. But I suppose so many of them were like that, really.'

He opened the album and started flicking through the old photographs.

After a couple of minutes he said, 'Ah here, here's my great-grandfather. And that must be Alfie,' he said, pointing to a young boy, standing next to a tall, very thin man with solemn eyes.

'Gosh, I haven't looked at these for ages,' he said, pulling the picture out of the sleeve. We leant over to have a look. The boy was about eight years old, had very large eyes and was smiling. He looked, ever so slightly, like Adam.

'You can see the family resemblance,' I said.

'You can,' agreed Graham, turning the picture over to look at the date. There was a small intake of breath. 'Well, I'll be…'

He handed it to Adam, who passed it on to me, whistling. On the back, it said, '*Michael and son, 1903*'.

I looked at it. 'What?'

'Look at the year. It couldn't have been my grandfather, could it? Alfie was born the year the war broke out, in 1914. It must be him – Fen.'

My mouth fell open. 'You're right.' I couldn't believe I was looking at a picture of him.

My hands traced over the picture, thinking of the young boy, Tilly's fox charmer, with his wild, unruly curls and blue eyes.

I reached for Adam's hand and squeezed it.

'Is he what you pictured?' he asked.

I looked up at Adam, wondering if Fen's eyes had been the same shade of blue. 'I think so. It's weird. He's a stranger to me, of course, but I feel like I know him. I almost feel like I recognise him.'

Adam tucked a loose curl behind my ear. 'I don't think it's that strange – not really. I mean we've heard so much about him. I feel the same way.'

'This whole time,' said Graham, 'I had no idea.'

I looked at him. 'We can tell you about him, if you'd like.'

He looked at me, his eyes a little moist. 'You know, I'd like that very much. When I first heard that you bought the cottage, I thought you must be mad. I'm sorry – I did.'

I shrugged. 'You wouldn't be the first.'

'But now, well, I'm beginning to think that maybe everyone else was.'

'Well, it's like a lot of things in life – that cottage has known real heartache, but some incredible things too.'

'Like what?'

'Well, at one point it used to belong to a fox charmer,' I said.

'A what?' said Graham

And so I explained about Fen's talent, learned from his father, of training foxes.

'He liked you,' said Adam, during the drive back to the marina.

'Do you think so?' I asked.

'Definitely.'

When we got to my little houseboat, he lit the wood burner and took a seat in the egg chair, while I poured us each a glass of wine.

'He wanted you to have this,' he said, holding out the picture of Fen.

My mouth fell open in surprise. 'I couldn't! That's your family history, not mine. It belongs to you.'

'You found them, I think it belongs to you just as much.'

I took the photo, biting my lip. 'I'll make a copy and give him back the original.'

'If you want,' he said, giving me his lazy smile.

'No,' I said. 'That smile is dangerous.'

'What?' he replied, the picture of innocence. 'Come here.' And he pulled me onto his lap.

'You know, this is where the trouble started with us the last time.'

He wrapped his arms around me. 'I'm not sure I'd call it trouble, exactly…'

'You know I have a perfectly good sofa?'

He shrugged. 'I like this chair.'

I snuggled against him. 'Me too.'

CHAPTER FORTY-SEVEN

Cornwall, 1914

Tilly

The letter that came from Fen was full of apology, but I wasn't ready to forgive.

'I had to sign up, Tilly. We're at war, and I need to do this. I'm sorry that I went behind your back. I hope you can understand that I couldn't stand by and not do everything I could to join the fight. I hope you can forgive me. Or at least understand. After everything my father did, all his sacrifices, how would it be if I didn't at least try to be half the man he was?'

But I didn't understand, and I didn't forgive him for risking his life.

I had gone back to school with the household in chaos, my family reeling from their encounter with Mrs Waters. Father didn't explain, and none of us could understand why it affected him so. But after that day, it was like the heart went out of him, I suppose.

I'd been at the school for a few weeks when I realised that I couldn't do it either. I was barely able to concentrate. Every day we heard about the casualties, how many people were lost. It got so that you dreaded getting the mail. You could see it on the faces of the students and the teachers combined. We were all living under the weight of the war, waiting for its shadow to fall on us.

I couldn't sit around and bide my time – especially knowing that Fen was out there.

I hated him for risking his life. Dr Collins' words echoed in my head. Someone like him may not have the best chance of getting back. I wished that he didn't feel he had something to prove.

CHAPTER FORTY-EIGHT

Present day

'So I found out something interesting about your cottage,' came Angie's voice down the line.

'Well, hello to you too,' I said.

She laughed. 'Hello.'

'What did you find out?'

'Well, it's more like *who* I found, really.'

'What do you mean?'

'I was chatting to one of my customers, Fran – she used to run the bakery down by the harbour, made the best cakes this side of West Cornwall. I can't tell you how many times me and Stevie used to go down there just for her apple pies, she served them with clotted—'

'Angie!'

'Yes, sorry, well, she came into the shop today and spotted your books and we started chatting and reminiscing, and you won't believe it but she's actually related to Adam – well, the Waters. Her granny used to work for the Aspreys.'

'You're kidding?'

'No, she was the cook, apparently.'

I gasped. 'Mrs Price?'

She gave a surprised laugh. 'How on earth did you know her name?'

'It was, um, written down in some of the stuff that I got in the house.'

'Really?'

'Yeah.' It wasn't exactly a lie.

'Well, anyway, she knows you're interested in what happened to the Aspreys and she said she'd be happy to talk to you if you want. Seems her grandmother told her a lot about it. Fran's a bit of a history nut. She had her grandmother write down her life story apparently. It's a good idea – so many things go missing when people die. I wish I'd asked my own… Anyway, you free to see her tomorrow?'

'Definitely.'

The next afternoon, I went with Angie to Fran's house, which was along the estuary, not far from the marina.

'Pretty part of the world,' I said as we walked.

'Yeah, wait till you see her cottage. It's lovely – real traditional fisherman's cottage.'

It was pretty, with whitewashed walls, a slate roof and roses along the little stone wall. I smiled at the name etched in the wooden plaque: Sandcastles.

Fran opened the door on the first knock. She was in her early seventies with a neat brown-grey bob and kind eyes.

'Oh, you look just like you do in your picture,' she said, tapping the back of a hardback on which my publisher had slapped an old black and white photograph of me. 'Come in, I made some pie.'

Angie's face lit up.

Fran showed us into a small living room with whitewashed stone walls and a blue and white striped sofa. Fresh pink peonies sat on top of the coffee table, next to a plate of biscuits.

'I love your cottage,' I said.

'Thank you, dear. It's around two hundred years old. My husband, Frank, and I restored it some years ago. But you'll know all about that, with your new place. Angie said it's quite a project.'

We sat down, and I nodded. 'Project is definitely the word. When I bought it there wasn't even electricity.'

'Us too. It takes time, but you'll get there.'

I looked at the clean white walls, the cosy room, the fireplace, 'I hope so.'

Fran poured us some tea, then offered round the biscuits. Angie piled her saucer with three.

'What?' she said with a grin, noting my expression. 'You'll see when you try them. My life has been incomplete since Fran left the bakery.'

Fran guffawed. 'My daughter still runs it, and with the same recipes I used for forty years.'

Angie shook her head. 'Nope, not the same. Don't get me wrong, Beth is good, but she's not you,' she said, stuffing a lemon cream into her mouth.

I laughed. 'Anyway, Angie tells me that your grandmother used to work for the Aspreys?'

Fran nodded. 'Oh yes, she started when she was only seventeen.'

'She was the cook, right?'

I'd read about Bertha Price in the diary, of course – and her ominous start in the culinary arts. It was nice to know that the family talent had been perfected over the generations.

'She was quite young to be a cook. I thought you had to work your way up in those old houses?' said Angie.

'You did,' agreed Fran. 'She worked for another family up in Plymouth, apparently, though not for very long. She didn't have that much experience.'

I remember reading Tilly's descriptions about boiled chicken and kept my mouth shut.

'Then she was placed as the cook for the Aspreys, though she wasn't all that qualified. That was on account of her family connections.'

'She didn't happen to be related to Michael Waters, did she?'

'Yes,' said Fran, looking at me as if to ask how I knew that. 'Bertha's sister was Michael Waters' wife. I believe Jean Waters managed to secure Bertha Price's job with the Aspreys because her husband had fought with John Asprey in the war.'

I nodded. I'd gathered that the connection between the men was why Bertha Price was given the cook's job – I hadn't realised that *Mrs Waters* had arranged it though. 'Are you sure she was the one who secured Bertha's post – not her husband?'

She nodded. 'Yes, I believe so. It was certainly her way.'

'What do you mean?'

'Well, that was one of the reasons I wanted to talk to you. Put your mind at rest a bit. I mean, about all those silly rumours.'

'Oh yes? I've heard a few people seem to think that John Asprey locked up Mr Waters in the cottage.'

She nodded. 'I know, and it isn't right.'

'What isn't?'

'That the Aspreys took all the blame.'

'Why do you say that?'

'Well, because if it hadn't been for Jean Waters, and what she did, well, maybe the Aspreys would still be there now.'

I sat back in surprise. 'What do you mean?'

'She set out to ruin them – and she succeeded.'

'Ruin them?' I repeated. 'The Aspreys?'

She nodded. 'Oh yes. Look, there are parts of it that I can understand – to a point, you know. I mean, she had cause in a way, but she took it too far – far too far – in the end. And it didn't just ruin their lives, but everyone else's too, hers included. No one was the same after that.'

Fran stood up and fetched a box from the kitchen. 'A few years ago, I was working on the history of Tregollan. It's a project that's so close to my heart. I got my grandmother to put down her account of living here during the First World War. There's all these stories that go untold when people die and I didn't want our piece of history to go with her.'

Angie sat back and got herself comfortable. Evidently Fran was a bit of a storyteller.

'Well, after the war broke out it changed everything, as you can imagine. But I think to really understand what happened, you have to go back to before the Great War, to a war that only ended twelve years before. You see, for the lives of the Aspreys and the Waters, these two wars were like bookends. There was the one that pulled them together, and the one that pulled them apart. The Boer War was the start.'

I nodded. 'Yes, I believe John Asprey and Michael Waters met during that time.'

Fran nodded. 'Yes, they did. It was this connection that would bind them together, whether they wanted it or not, for the rest of their lives. So, from Jean Waters' perspective, she married a tall, strapping bear of a man in Michael Waters. He was confident, and strong—'

'The sort of bloke who could open a jar with his bicep?' suggested Angie.

Fran laughed. 'Exactly. Well, anyway, she loved him. Apparently he was quite a catch, and they were happy for a while. They had several children and their lives were pretty good. Then Michael was called off to fight in South Africa. When he came back afterwards and she fetched him from the station, she could barely recognise him.'

'What do you mean?'

'He was so thin and frail. In time, he became quite unstable mentally. He used to have these fits, and had to be removed.'

'It was post-traumatic stress disorder,' I said. Adam and I had already guessed as much.

She nodded. 'But of course no one knew about that then. After the First World War, people started to realise what had happened to some of these soldiers, but back then...'

'How terrible.'

She nodded. 'So she cared for him, and he trusted her and told her about what had happened to him. He was a prisoner of war, and had been beaten and tortured for months.'

I gasped.

'That's not the worst of it.'

'There's worse?'

'Oh yes.'

'He was captured because he'd been protecting John Asprey.'

'During battle?'

'No.' Her eyes were huge. 'He was a deserter.'

'No!' I said in shock.

'He left the war. Michael Waters went after him to make him come back, and they were captured. When they were finally released he lied for him. He'd been through so much, had been brutally tortured, but he kept that secret. They became friends in the camp, I think.

'Then, when they got back from the war, Jean had moved to Yorkshire, to be back with her parents. And he grew ill, and they lost children to consumption – TB. Jean blamed John Asprey for everything. If he hadn't gone after John, he wouldn't have been a prisoner of war for two years and wouldn't have come back so damaged. Well, anyway, she wrote to John Asprey a few years later, telling him about Michael's fits, how ill he was, how

consumed with fear, and how he needed a place away from prying eyes. How he spoke every day about the daffodils…'

'*She* wrote to John Asprey,' I said in realisation.

'Oh yes. She was letting him know, you see, that she *knew.*
It's why they built that house – she made him do it, and later it
would be the reason she always seemed to get her way. I mean,
even my grandmother got her post as the cook as a result.'

'What did Michael Waters say about her blackmailing them?'

'I couldn't say. I should imagine he felt badly about it, but
they still moved there. Then when things started to unfold between her son and John Asprey's daughter—'

'It was like having a gun over his head – he wanted to protect
his friend but he also had the one son left and now he was in
danger.'

She nodded. 'Knowing this, it's easy to see Jean finally pulling that trigger.'

'What do you mean?'

'Well, she'd lost two boys and a girl to consumption, her husband had come back a broken man from the war, and now war
had come into their lives again and her only son wanted to fight
too, like his father. She thought he'd be safe, as there'd been an
accident when he was young and he was permanently injured,
but he was declared fit to go to battle anyway – because John
Asprey signed a letter confirming it.'

'What? Why would he do that when he'd been a deserter
himself?' asked Angie.

'Exactly,' I agreed. ' He was working on the farm at this point
and I think they were friendly. But perhaps there were more
incendiary reasons too.'

'To get him out of the way?' guessed Angie.

'Yes,' said Fran. 'Well, I'm sure that's what Jean must have
thought. It solved the problem about what to do regarding the

blossoming romance between Matilda Asprey and young Waters. If he went to war and didn't come back…'

'So she told the War Office about John being a deserter,' said Angie. 'But couldn't he have simply denied it?' I asked.

Fran shook her head. 'Apparently John had admitted as much in a letter to her husband, so she had proof. And at that time, when people were being handed white feathers left and right for not enlisting, it would have caused quite a scandal, as you can imagine. Before anyone could lay the claim, the Aspreys disappeared.'

'But how come no one knows about this?' I asked.

'Well, it was hushed up. I think it was decided it was best to keep it quiet, and by then Mr Waters had passed away. Young Michael was at war, and Mrs Waters was living in the village with the Prices. She was the reason that Bertha now didn't have a job, and it was decided it would be best not to tell anyone why this had happened. Especially as she had a surprise herself, with a new child to look after. I don't think she wanted that child to have to bear the mark of what she'd done, so she kept it to herself. As time passed, people filled in their own blanks about the story, and what they knew about Mr Waters' fits in the cottage – his "episodes" got coloured with that of John Asprey and his rather austere reputation. People thought he'd used that cottage to keep someone locked up there, instead of what it was – a safe place for a friend.'

I shook my head. 'But what happened to them, the Aspreys?'

Fran sighed sadly. 'The rumour was that they fled to Switzerland, I believe. Though I'm not sure if that was confirmed, I just don't know.'

CHAPTER FORTY-NINE

Cornwall and Dunkirk, 1914–15

Tilly

Two things happened that year that were to mark the turning point from bad to worse in my mother's limited affection for me. The first was that I decided to become a volunteer nurse, joining the Red Cross as a VAD (Voluntary Aid Detachment), and lying about my age in the process, as they only accepted girls of twenty-three or older.

I received my training and certificates several months later from a military hospital in Torquay, along with my friend, Alice McKibbon. We learned, amongst other things, basic first aid, how to properly roll up a bandage, make a medical bed and clean out bedpans. Most of all, we learned that real nurses saw us as something rather nasty that they had stepped on with their shoes.

The second incident to frustrate Mother was that I immediately volunteered to be stationed in Dunkirk, at a field hospital run by the Duchess of Sutherland, Millicent St Clair-Erskine – or 'Meddlesome Millie', as she was dubbed, for her interference in matters of bureaucracy and for daring to care enough to put her money, her time and her social conscience to good use.

'You'll make us a laughing stock by associating with her. We need you at home – there's so much to do with the wedding. Now that Charles has volunteered, we're going to have to move it forward,' wrote Mother, in the week before I was dispatched.

When I told Alice, she sighed, straightening her starched white cap. 'They're all like that. They don't hear what we hear, see what we see. For them, despite the rations, and the inches it takes up in their newspapers, it's something happening someplace else.'

Not for me, and not for much longer. Not when we joined the No. 9 Red Cross Hospital, the tented unit at Bourbourg, in July 1915. Later it would become known as the 'camp in the oatfield'.

On my first day, I was told to report to Nurse Hedgemond. 'She's sort of a dragon, I must warn you,' said Susan, one of the other VADs. She was a girl with short brown hair, who managed to smile despite looking dead on her feet. 'She's French, bit of a stickler for the rules, but at least she won't have you dusting the shelves or trying to make yourself useful someplace else. Here, if you've got a pair of hands, they're going to be used. Hope you're not squeamish. And that you got enough rest on the boat, because there'll be little of that here. Anyway, we're happy to have you, especially with your French – apparently it's excellent.'

There was a dry laugh from behind. 'Excellent French – I wouldn't go that far.'

I turned around and my mouth fell open. 'Celine?'

Susan looked from me to Celine. 'Do you two know each other?'

Celine smiled.

'Yes, from another life,' I said with amazement.

It turned out that while Celine had been a rather mediocre teacher, she was a first-class nurse, and in time would become a first-class friend as well.

For us, the war wasn't against bombs or gas or even the Germans, it was against the cold and the dirt and the spread of disease. During those first few weeks I learned that on days when I thought I was so tired I might faint, I could carry on. I learned that after the initial shock of seeing an open wound, touching a dead body or having to hear the screams of someone being operated upon, you can almost get used to anything.

Except death. It was the one thing that I never got used to. Each one felt like a personal affront.

I learned important truths, like the value of laughter. How vital it was to say a little joke. To put on your pearls and dress up at midnight and dance beneath the stars while a phonograph played just so the soldiers could for a second think that they were somewhere, anywhere else.

I learned how to lie, how to school my face so that I didn't give anything away. How to smile and laugh even though the bottom had just fallen out of the sky.

I'd joined as a VAD in an attempt not to think of Fen, but all I did, every minute of the day, as I administered to an endless stream of wounded men, was think of him.

CHAPTER FIFTY

Dearest Tilly,

You'd think that you couldn't sleep in a trench with the sound of the men and the guns, not to mention the smell. It's so bad it could detach itself and form into its own assailant, I swear. You'd think that you'd want to keep your eyes open just to keep them on the rats – they're enormous, Goose, you wouldn't believe, like cats, and I hate to think what makes them so big.

But despite all this, I can sleep.

It's a mixed blessing, because when I do, I see you. Sometimes you're collecting sea glass, or you're climbing Old Tom. Sometimes we're children again in my da's potting shed. But it's always you and me, and when I wake up, sometimes it hurts enough that I have to check that I haven't been an idiot and stood up.

Yours,

Fen

CHAPTER FIFTY-ONE

Present day

'John Asprey was a deserter? Are you serious?' asked Adam, taking a seat opposite me in the Harbour Cafe where we'd decided to meet after he finished work.

I filled him in on the details.

'Oh man, I'm so bummed I had to work. I'd suspected there might be blackmail involved, but I never thought it was Mrs Waters.'

'Me neither.'

We'd taken one of the tables outside on the cobbled street, which gave us the best view of the leisure boats in the harbour. People were walking past in shorts and sleeveless vests, with the kind of smiles that said 'Summer's here!'

'I mean, I knew there had to be some big secret, but I never suspected that,' I said. 'Can you imagine?'

Adam shook his head and took a sip of his beer. 'No – I mean the way Tilly described her father, I would never have imagined that.'

I nodded.

'But still, you don't know how you'll react until you're in these situations yourself,' said Adam. 'I have a friend who joined the army, fought in the war in Afghanistan and went AWOL. One of their assignments went wrong, civilians were killed, and he just lost it, he said. When his teammates were heading back, he stayed behind in some broken-down apartment. Took him a full day before he walked back into camp. He quit after that. You'd think, in today's age, people would be more understanding, but you'd be surprised. His dad still won't talk to him.'

I shook my head. 'That's rough.'

'Yeah. He's good though; did therapy, think it helped a lot. It's not as bad now as it was back then. Honour was everything in those days.'

I nodded. 'It's so sad. I mean, as a result, John Asprey lost the thing he loved the most anyway – his farm.'

Adam's mobile started to beep, and he looked at it and grinned.

When he saw me looking, he just shrugged. 'Nothing important,' he said, putting it on the table. 'I'll just settle up.'

When he was gone, his phoned beeped again, the message lighting up the screen.

'*Speak soon*,' it said. Followed by several little X's.

It was from Jenna.

I tried to forget about it. Trust was important in a new relationship. There could be a hundred reasons why she was texting him. Though I was trying very hard to see why he'd smile like that.

When he came back, I decided, with a heroic effort, to push it out of my mind.

He winked, and gave my hand a squeeze. 'We gonna go?'

I nodded. We'd promised Jason and Derron we'd go past the pub tonight and hear them play. It was the first time I'd see The Piston Rings perform a gig that wasn't on their houseboat.

Angie had already secured us a table, along with Dave and the Bishop, who was, as usual, wearing his Russian hat, despite the heat.

I sat back against Adam while the boys launched into their set, soothed by Derron's haunting voice.

We'd just ordered our second round of drinks when I saw Jenna in the doorway, looking every bit as beautiful as she had the first time I'd seen her. I tensed slightly as Adam moved, but it was just to raise an arm.

She waved, looked at us for some time, and then left.

He whispered in my ear, 'She's going home tonight.'

I turned around and looked at him. 'She is?'

He nodded. 'Yeah.'

'Why now?' I whispered. 'She told me that you were just on the rebound. Said she wasn't going to give up on you, she was going to wait me out.'

He nodded. 'She told me the same thing.'

'She did?' I might have known.

'Yeah, but I told her that she'd have to wait for a very long time.'

'Why's that?' I said, his voice sending shivers down my spine.

'Because I've been falling for you since the first day I saw you, and every day it just gets worse.'

I bit my lip and looked into his eyes. 'Really?'

He nodded. 'I love you.'

I closed my eyes, and in front of everyone, kissed him. There were cheers and whoops all round.

'I love you too,' I said, blushing like mad.

CHAPTER FIFTY-TWO

Dearest Fen,

I dreamt of our garden last night. How we said we'd plant only the most unusual blooms, not the usual hothouse flowers.

They were beautiful and strange. Especially the blue thistles and larkspurs; I remember them most of all. They seemed almost to glow in the moonlight. Because, of course, it was night-time in my dream. Perhaps, because when we were still children, that's when we made that pact.

I've been thinking that, when the war's over, that's where I'd like us to meet. Promise me that's where we'll meet? We'll start with the garden. That's where you'll find me.

Yours always,

T

CHAPTER FIFTY-THREE

Present day

I found the next letter in the garden, propped up amongst the hollyhocks.

And then I found one against the newly installed window frame in the kitchen.

A new letter found me every day; each time I visited the cottage.

I didn't know why he chose to do it this way, as if it was all some kind of game. I should have minded, but I didn't. I went along, finding each one, like I was taking part in some mad Easter egg hunt, each prize a small gem into the past.

I didn't give up without a fight though; I laid traps of my own. Tried to hare him out.

I came at midnight and at dawn. When the weather permitted I camped outside, and when it didn't, I took my sleeping bag into the potting shed. But each time he outwitted me.

Once, on a particularly grim Tuesday, I rolled over in my tent and groaned. It wasn't the fact that I now had a cold and a headache and was in desperate need of a bumper pack of pills, but there right on top of me was a new letter.

Adam had a rather more practical solution.

'I think it's time you called the police,' he told me, when I ventured back to the marina in search of an ear I could bend and some strong coffee. 'Also, I can't believe you never told me about him before.'

I shrugged. 'It's because he's harmless,' I said. 'If he'd wanted to hurt me or anything like that it would have happened by now. I mean, I've been there for months.'

'Well, that makes me feel so much better,' he said.

I laughed. 'You know what I mean.'

'Well, if you're not going to call the cops on his ass,' he said, as I choked on my coffee and giggled, 'then how about a partner for your next stakeout? I was a Boy Scout, so I know a thing or two about camouflage.'

'You weren't!'

'Was too! I have a Swiss army knife and everything.'

I laughed. 'So you could, what, whittle us something while we wait?'

'Er, no… My whittling skills are pretty bad. They kicked me out because of that.'

'They kicked you out?'

'Scout's honour.'

I laughed.

Later that evening, we set up camp in the house. 'I don't understand why you would sleep in the shed instead of the house?'

I shrugged. 'I was hoping I'd catch him. You know, where he normally ventures.'

'Which is everywhere. Otherwise you wouldn't have found that letter in the stove.'

'It was on the windowsill, but yes, good point.'

The advantage of having a Boy Scout for company was that he came prepared. There was a camping stove, and later, fresh coffee, baked beans and noodles.

'Were the beans a good idea? I mean, really? Are we ready to take our relationship to the next level?' I jibed.

He laughed. 'Er, there's doors here, you know.'

I suppressed a giggle. 'Okay.'

'Anyway,' he said, noting my pile of used tissues. 'If I still think you're cute surrounded by these…'

'What!' I said, blowing my nose again. 'You think I'm cute with this?'

'Well…' He waggled his hand. I punched his shoulder. 'Come here,' he said, and I curled up into him in our sleeping bag.

Even with Adam and I taking turns to patrol the grounds, there was no sign of the old man. In the morning there was no letter either, not in the house, anyway.

'Maybe he doesn't like me,' said Adam. I was glad that his first thought wasn't that I was going mad. 'Though are you sure you're not just coming across them instead of him putting them places for you to find?'

'Of course he's putting them places for me to find – the whole house has been ripped apart. I didn't even have a windowsill for him to put it on until the other day. And when I woke up yesterday, there was a letter on top of me!'

'You sure it's not the builders. Maybe they're leaving them out as they find them?'

I shook my head. 'It's not them. They've been down in Truro for the past few days, working on another job.'

When we got to the car, Adam stopped in his tracks. There, on the dashboard, was a letter. I made to open the door but it was locked.

'Now that is weird,' said Adam

'You see!'

CHAPTER FIFTY-FOUR

Calais, 1915

Tilly

I had been in Calais for six months when I got the news that my parents had left Idyllwild. During a time when I felt that nothing could shock me further, my mother's letter still managed to do so.

> 'I regret to inform you that it is your father's decision to leave Idyllwild until the war is over. We are leaving for Switzerland this week. You may hear some things; I am afraid there is some unfortunate business with your father's war record, which will no doubt be cleared up soon. In the meantime, it was thought prudent to leave. Rest assured that it is all a grave misunderstanding. Unfortunately, the wedding between Rose and Charles has been postponed until matters are sorted out as well.

I would find out later that the true cause of their departure came as a result of Mrs Waters, who had been true to her threat to make Father pay for what he'd done. Though I believe she must later have regretted the missile she fired, as it helped to cause the heart attack that killed her husband and altered forever the love between her and her son, and led to her leaving her home not long afterwards.

After she found out that Father had signed a letter that enabled Fen to join the war, she sent her own to the War Office, supplying an account of Father's conduct in the Boer War.

Rose would never marry Charles. To Charles's credit, this was not as a result of the conflict between our fathers, but because he died at the Battle of the Somme in July 1916.

My parents would never see Idyllwild again.

Fen went home for his father's funeral. He tried to get his mother to reverse what she'd done but there was no going back. Not when she'd sent proof.

Fen said that when she found out that Father had built them the house, and that he'd put it in their names, it was the only time he'd seen her cry.

CHAPTER FIFTY-FIVE

Present day

The front gate no longer hung off its hinges, though I hadn't had the heart to clear it of ivy. It would always be the secret cottage to me.

In the dusky light, the stone walls were the perfect shade of old parchment. Dust-pink roses trailed over the sign, which read '*Seafall Cottage*'.

So much had changed since the first time I'd seen it. Not least the fact that there was now a door, painted the colour of sea glass.

I stood in the terraced garden, where I'd first found myself many months before, and simply stared. There were still seagulls on the roof, but the garden had been cleared of the debris. Gone were the old, rusted-out car and the mountain of beer bottles and pizza boxes.

I stepped inside, through the blue and white kitchen with its brand-new duck-egg Aga and French grey counters, through to the living room, where fresh paint and plaster had replaced the cracks and vines that had once held the walls in their embrace.

Now there were two new white sofas and a soft grey coffee table made of driftwood. The understated decor allowed the room's best feature – the large, round window with its petal-shaped panes and its view of the blue-green ocean crashing amidst the rocks – to stand out. It still remained a sea room.

The turreted staircase with its pattern of sea-glass spirals had been restored. And, according to the builders, the upstairs would be finished in a week.

I couldn't believe that I was finally about to call it home. Though I knew I'd miss my little narrowboat.

Angie had taken the news the hardest.

'You can't move,' she'd said, when I told her that the cottage was almost ready.

'I'm only ten minutes away. It's not like I'm moving to London.'

'But what about our movie nights?'

'We'll still do them!' I'd told her, squeezing her hand to reassure her.

Adam came in now, with some of the boxes for the kitchen, and found me staring out the round window.

'That will never get old,' he said.

I turned around and gave him a hug. 'Or this,' I said.

He nodded. 'Have you seen him?' he asked, referring to the old man.

'Not for a while,' I admitted.

'He's probably gotten the hint, finally, what with all the furniture being moved in. He's probably moved on.'

I looked at him and frowned. 'Maybe.'

I couldn't explain why it made me feel sad, but it did.

CHAPTER FIFTY-SIX

Rouen, 1916

Tilly

I'd been transferred to a hospital in Rouen, and on the second of the month, long before dawn, we received our first convoy of wounded soldiers from the Battle of the Somme. Four more convoys would appear over the next forty-eight hours, each carrying over a hundred soldiers.

I forgot what a full night of sleep was – we all did. We kept going until we thought we'd fall over, but there was no rest, not for the next two weeks.

I told myself that personal letters had ceased because of the battle. It made sense, didn't it? Though I couldn't stop myself from going around each ward looking at the faces of the men in search of Fen, my heart full of fear. His last letter said he hadn't been stationed far from here. Each wound that I cleansed, each arm that I touched, each voice I heard could have belonged to him.

I was restocking supplies when I heard someone say, 'Hello, Goose.'

I dropped the tray I was holding, the surgical equipment that I'd just cleaned falling to the ground in a deafening clatter, but I didn't care.

'Fen!'

His arm was in a bandage and his face was covered in bruises. 'Someone said you were here,' he told me.

I rushed over and hugged him tight. His eyes closed. I looked up and saw him wince.

I jumped back. 'What's wrong?'

'Nothing,' he said. 'Some ribs have cracked.'

My eyes widened. 'Have you been checked by a doctor? Let me fetch someone.'

'I'm fine, don't worry. Just let me enjoy this for a while. Come here.'

'Okay,' I said, helping him to a chair and sitting down next to him.

'Am I really here, seeing your face? I can't believe it,' he breathed.

I shook my head, tears clouding my eyes. 'Me neither.'

He picked up my hand and held it. 'I didn't know if I'd ever be able to do this again,' he admitted. 'It's been…' He blew out his cheeks. 'It's been hell, there's just no other word for it.'

I swallowed. 'I'm so sorry, Fen.'

He shook his head; his eyes were full of pain. 'You know, I understand now what happened to my father.'

I nodded. 'Me too. I've seen a few people who have what he did. It's just too much to witness. I sometimes wonder how anyone can go back to normal life after this.'

'With this,' he said, squeezing my hand.

I closed my eyes. 'Yes. I was so sorry that you had to bury him alone.'

'I knew you couldn't get away, and anyway, I thought maybe you wouldn't want to be there after everything.'

I shook my head. 'No, Fen. Wouldn't that be the worst thing imaginable? That when we finally get to be together, we let our families come between us? Anyway, I don't think your father would have wanted that.'

'No, he wouldn't,' he agreed.

He took something out of his pocket, wrapped up in a blue handkerchief. He looked at me and smiled. 'I wanted to wait until the war was over before I gave this to you, but then I thought if I saw you, if we were brought together somehow, then maybe it would need to be this way, instead.'

I frowned, and opened the handkerchief. Inside was a silver ring with a round stone of aquamarine.

I bit my lip. 'You remembered?'

He winked. 'I never forgot.'

CHAPTER FIFTY-SEVEN

Present day

'How's the fishing?' I asked Stan over the phone the next day.

'Excellent, if you like pike.'

'Mmm.'

'What's up, my young padawan?'

I laughed. 'I'm looking for information about the War Office during the First World War. Do we know anyone at the Ministry of Defence?'

'Let me go get my old address book,' said Stan. 'Is it more official stuff you're after?'

I pictured him scratching around in his desk.

I told him about what I'd found out concerning the diary, particularly the bit about John Asprey deserting during the Boer War.

He whistled. 'You don't hear of that every day. Apparently in the First World War it was execution by firing squad. Bastards! Most of them were kids, scared out of their minds and pressured into volunteering.'

'I know. Not that it excuses it – fear is fear – but John Asprey was much older when he was at war.'

'Yeah, true, but it was a nasty one. Some of the things they were made to do… I'm not sure I could.'

I thought about my history lessons at school, about concentration camps, the unfair treatment of women and children in the Boer War. Perhaps it just ate him alive. 'I can imagine,' I said. 'How would we confirm something like that?'

'I think your best bet would be to call them up. Use my contact – his name's Derrick Truss, he'll probably talk to you, do some digging on your behalf, get the background story. Let me call him first.'

When I got the go-ahead, Truss answered straight away. He said he'd look into it and get back to me. Though he did have some basic information he could share over the phone.

'It seems highly unlikely,' he said, 'that he would have been executed – not if he wasn't doing active duty when they found out. Generally in those circumstances there was a prison sentence of some kind.'

'But what if they wanted to set an example?'

'Well, I mean, who knows? I don't think it would have been the standard procedure is all I can say.'

All I knew was that the fear of what might happen had driven the Aspreys out of their home, never to return.

A few days later, Truss emailed through his findings. I found that, after a lengthy investigation that spanned most of the war, resulting in major financial losses, John Asprey had been cleared of all charges. When I saw the signature at the bottom I had to wonder though: it was signed by none other than the Earl of Monthesay, Lord Arnold Hammond, Charles's father.

CHAPTER FIFTY-EIGHT

Calais 1917

Tilly

Fen's letters stopped coming.

A week turned into three, and then a month. I was beside myself with worry and fear. I grew thin and haggard. It felt like time stretched forever in an agony of waiting. At night I twisted the ring he'd given me, over and over, and took no comfort in thinking and dreaming of how we'd make a home out of that little cottage by the sea.

I wrote letters to everyone I knew.

Some of the soldiers that I'd helped gave me the names of the right people to ask.

In October, I finally got a response: Fen was missing, presumed dead.

It was Celine who told me to prepare for the worst when she found me howling in the supply cupboard, unable to stand. I think, in her own way, she was trying to be kind.

'It won't be some fairy tale,' she told me. 'You must see that now. I have seen many people think this way. He is gone.'

'He's gone?' I started to shake, to sob.

'Yes.'

She seemed sure. But even as I raged, a part of me wouldn't believe, would never believe.

CHAPTER FIFTY-NINE

Present day

I threw the diary against the wall and descended into a flood of tears.

How could it end that way?

A mess of tears and snot, I searched in vain for an extra page, a hidden compartment. Something, anything, besides this.

What had happened to him? I felt cheated. But I knew I had no right. This wasn't some made-up story, this was Tilly's life, and I knew, perhaps as well as anyone, that real life hardly ever unfolds the way we'd like it to, not like in a story. Yet, it had felt at times like a novel, larger than life. It couldn't end this way could it? Couldn't she have said something else? Even if the worst had happened to Fen, what happened to her?

I picked the diary back up and paged through it again. I re-read each and every letter, hoping I'd missed one. But I found nothing except this cold, impenetrable silence.

The marina was quiet; all I could hear was the gentle slosh of the water as it lapped against the boat. I made myself a cup of tea, but couldn't stop the tears from falling into it.

I sat in the egg chair, thinking.

Finally, I switched on the light and got dressed. In the cool summer's night, I walked silently across the gangway to my car.

There was only one place I could go now, and that was the cottage. As I drove along the coastal road, I had one last hope, and I held onto it as tightly as I could in the pre-dawn light.

CHAPTER SIXTY

Present day

The garden was so beautiful it took my breath away. The early sunshine was warm on my shoulders as I stood, barefoot, in the garden. Everything was in bloom. There were globe thistles and irises, delphiniums and forget-me-nots, lobelia and larkspurs. Each flower was unusual, so different to the last, except that each and every one of them was blue.

I stood and held my chest. I think perhaps that's when I knew.

I turned, slowly, and saw him standing in the garden.

'Did you do this?'

He nodded. His eyes were so very blue. He was still wearing that same tweed jacket, the one with the patches on the elbows.

The old man stepped forward, and I saw that he had some trouble with his left foot.

'Was an accident,' he said in explanation, when he saw me looking.

I swallowed. Felt the tears begin to prickle again. 'So you kept it then, I see,' he said, looking at the diary in my hands.

'I did. Though there are a few things it left out.'

'Did it?'

'Yes. Like what happened to her. Did she come back?'

He nodded. 'She did. After the war she lived here for many years.'

'And Fen?' I asked, holding my breath.

He looked at me. He was old and grey and part of me thought I was losing my mind, but right then I'd never been more sure of anything in my life.

'You're him, aren't you?' I asked.

He didn't answer, and for a second I wondered if he wouldn't, or if I was wrong.

Then he looked at me and smiled. 'I promised her I'd come back.'

I gasped and closed my eyes, overcome, feeling the tears rush down my face. When I looked up, he was gone.

A LETTER FROM LILY

Thank you so much for reading *Summer at Seafall Cottage*! If you enjoyed it, please would you leave a review? It really helps to spread the word.

If you're wondering what's next – there's loads! I'm currently working on a new novel featuring magic, food and family in a gorgeous cottage in the Yorkshire countryside. To find out more, please join my newsletter www.bookouture.com/lily-graham, follow me on Facebook and Twitter, or pop on over to my website www.lilygraham.net, where I chat about my dream writing shed, beautiful escapes and what makes the perfect cottage, as well as my latest competitions and much more.

 @Lilywritesbooks

 LilyRoseGrahamAuthor

www.lilygraham.net

AUTHOR'S NOTE

The idea for Tilly's code in the diary was inspired by the book *The Journal of Beatrix Potter 1881–1897*, transcribed from her code writings by Leslie Linder. I have Victoria break the code in a similar fashion. It's a really interesting read.

With regards to education in Edwardian times I looked at www.edwardianpromenade.com/women/the-education-of-girls-and-women/. It must be noted that, as aristocrats, it was highly unlikely that Tilly or her sister, Rose, would have received the education they did, as most young women from noble families would have been stuck with a governess. Of course, there were exceptions, and in this work of fiction, such is the case with Tilly and Rose.

The history of nursing in the First World War is fascinating, including how some volunteer nurses were regarded. Yet despite their lack of knowledge, they served such an important role and were incredibly brave, particularly when we think how protected some of these young women were likely to have been. My research was based on 'World War One: The many battles faced by WW1's nurses', which can be found at www.bbc.co.uk/news/magazine-26838077/.

The camp in the oatfield is a true story, as is the case of 'Meddlesome Millie', the Duchess of Sutherland, who was disdained by her peers, for her involvement in the war. It was one of those instances where a woman was told to mind her place but thankfully did not. She helped so many soldiers and was remembered so fondly for all that she did, being one of the first people to take action and provide much-needed facilities and care to the wounded. You can read more about her and the hospital here: www.florence-nightingale.co.uk/resources/the-hospital-in-the-oatfield/?v=79cba1185463. And here: www.westernfrontassociation.com/the-great-war/great-war-on-land/casualties-medcal/2383-millicent-duchess-of-sutherland-ambulance.html#sthash.mtV0GEKq.dpbs

For the description of the trenches I looked at www.firstworldwar.com/features/trenchlife.htm.

Some liberties were taken with war records, which may not have been accessed in the way Victoria did in the novel.

The language of flowers was particularly fascinating. For further information, please see www.thelanguageofflowers.com.

ACKNOWLEDGMENTS

Thank you so much to my wonderful husband, Rui, for all your encouragement and support during the writing of this book, and for dragging me away at times to make sure that I was fed and saw something besides the inside of my writing room.

The fact that there is a book at all is thanks to my lovely editor, Lydia Vassar-Smith. Thank you so much for your belief in this novel and for all your advice and encouragement.

Thank you to Dad for being so sweet and reading all my books and helping spark the idea of the mysterious gardener. You'll recall it happened in the summer while we were chatting last June!

Thank you to my wonderful family. Mom, you first inspired my love of storytelling and made childhood magical. My wonderful Granny Monica, you first encouraged my love of reading by bringing round a ginormous box of books that was just for me – a rare treat when you have so many siblings!

Thank you as ever to the BFF, Catherine. You are always there when I need you. Thank you so much for always patiently listening to all my stories!

A lot of work goes into bringing a book into the world and the Bookouture team are exceptional at doing so while being just so lovely to boot. Thank you to the lovely Natalie Butlin, Kim Nash and the whole talented team.

Thank you to my bulldog, Fudge, who found out that she could climb stairs after all, and so began visiting me every day in my little snug and lying on my feet, giving me a daily dose of vitamin D (dog), which surely is the best kind.

And last, but most importantly of all, thank you to all my readers. You all make this writing lark worthwhile, from taking the time to leave a review to some of the emails and comments I have received from around the world, telling me that *A Cornish Christmas* helped them to cope with the loss of a loved one or that *The Summer Escape* has inspired them to go after their own dreams or book a holiday to Crete. These are messages I never expected to receive in my wildest dreams, and it truly touches me more than I can say – so thank you!